At
Seventeen

I0974224

by
Gerri Hill

Bella
BOOKS

Copyright © 2013 by Gerri Hill

Bella Books, Inc.
P.O. Box 10543
Tallahassee, FL 32302

Printed in the United States of America on acid-free paper.

First Bella Books Edition 2013

Editor: Medora MacDougall
Cover Designer: Judith Fellows

ISBN: 978-1-59493-358-5

Other Bella Books by Gerri Hill

About the Author

Gerri Hill has twenty-two published works, including the 2011 and 2012 GCLS winners, *Devil's Rock* and *Hell's Highway*, and the 2009 GCLS winner *Partners*, the last book in the popular *Hunter Series*, as well as the 2012 Lambda finalist *Storms*. She began writing lesbian romance as a way to pass the time while snowed in one winter in the mountains of Colorado and hasn't looked back. Her first published work came in 2000 with *One Summer Night*. Hill's love of nature and of being outdoors usually makes its way into her stories as her characters often find themselves in beautiful natural settings. When she isn't writing, Hill and her longtime partner, Diane, can be found at their log cabin in East Texas, where their vegetable garden, orchard and five acres of piney woods keep them busy. They share their lives with two Australian Shepherds and an assortment of furry felines. For more, see her website: www.gerrihill.com.

PART ONE

LOVE IS AGELESS

CHAPTER ONE

"You want to open up a store in your hometown? In Brook Hill? I think that's great," Charlotte said as she handed Shannon a glass of red wine.

Shannon nodded her thanks. "The location is all Jarod's idea. But it'll give us a chance to be with our mother while we're getting it up and running. And then allow us to check in on her more often if we've got a store located there."

"So you're not going to move her into the assisted living facility after all?" Tracy asked as she joined them on the patio.

"That was the original plan, but if we've got a store there, we'll be around more than we are now. She certainly wasn't thrilled with that option," Shannon said. "Jarod's been going down there once a week as it is. The cancer is still in remission, but it really took its toll on her the second time. She's fatigued. There's so much she can't do anymore." She took a sip of wine and put the glass on the table. "While we're getting the store up and going, I'll stay with her. That'll give me a chance to see how she's really doing. I keep telling myself that seventy isn't old."

But they needed to make some kind of decision. Her brother had taken on the role of caregiver for the last couple of years. Not that Shannon had refused to. It's just that she didn't dare spend more than one day there at a time for fear she'd run into Madison.

Charlotte stared at her for a moment, and Shannon wondered if she was slipping into her role as psychologist.

"You've been very vague as to why you rarely go to take care of her," Charlotte said.

Shannon smiled at her. "Are you intending to put me on your couch, Dr. Rimes?"

Charlotte shook her head. "No. I promised I would never do that to you." She grinned. "Although you would make an excellent study. But I was simply curious if it was something keeping you here or if there was a particular reason you avoided going *there*."

"What is it you're fishing for, *Doctor*?"

Charlotte laughed. "Tracy and I have known you for six years now, Shannon. Yet you remain a mystery."

"I'm not a mystery," she insisted. Not intentionally, at least.

"Why didn't you bring Ally?" Tracy asked. "You are still dating, aren't you?"

Shannon reached for the wine bottle, adding a bit more to her glass before answering. She hadn't seen Ally in two weeks and hadn't spoken to her in at least six or seven days. Were they still dating?

"I've been busy," she said evasively.

Charlotte gave her slow smile that said she knew she was lying. "And yet another one slips away."

Shannon shrugged. "It wasn't serious, as you know."

"They never are, are they?"

"We like her," Tracy said.

"Only because she and Charlotte can talk *doctor* stuff." Shannon raised an eyebrow. "Have I really known you guys for six years?"

"Six years and countless dinners, yes," Charlotte said. "But we still know so very little about you."

Shannon paused, her glance going between her two closest friends. "What more do you want to know?"

"Why do you avoid going home? Why is it your brother insisting you open a store there and not you?"

Shannon leaned back, wondering why she'd never told them about Madison. Truth was, she hadn't told *anyone* about Madison.

"I avoid going back home for fear I'll run into Madison. Madison Lansford." Saying the name out loud brought back a rush of memories.

"An old lover?" Tracy guessed.

"Yes."

Charlotte relaxed in her chair too, a slight smile on her face. "Tell us your story."

Shannon didn't know where to begin. Five years ago when she'd last seen Madison? Ten years ago? College? High school? Their first kiss? The first time they met?

"The Lansfords were the richest family in town," she said. "They lived in a huge mansion on the outskirts. Well, outskirts back then. The city has grown around them now and it's quite an estate. Anyway, my mother worked for them. She started out as a maid then became a cook and ended up supervising the rest of the staff by the time she retired."

"So Madison was someone you knew as a child?" Tracy asked.

"Yes. After my dad died, we were struggling. My mother couldn't pay the rent. Jarod's ten years older than me and he had already joined the army, so he wasn't around to help. It was just me and my mother. The Lansfords were kind enough to allow us to move there. There were servants' quarters downstairs off of the main kitchen," she said, remembering the four small rooms she shared with her mother. "I was ten."

* * *

"It's so big," she whispered, looking up at the mansion as she stood beside her mother.

"It's just a house."

Shannon grabbed her mother's hand and followed her around to the back, all the while looking over her shoulder at the massive building.

"Mrs. Fletcher, I see you made it finally."

"Hello, George. Yes. My car is stuffed to the brim. I'll need to make one more trip, I'm afraid."

"I'll help you unload it." He stood back. "And who is this pretty lady?"

Shannon looked up at him. "I'm not a lady," she said. "I'm ten."

He laughed and bent down to her level. "Well, then what should I call you?"

Shannon shifted nervously and gripped her mother's hand a little tighter. "Shannon," she said.

"Well, Shannon, that's a pretty name. I'll never call you lady again."

"Thank you, mister."

"You can call me George."

Shannon glanced at her mother for permission and was rewarded with a nod and a smile.

They walked into the biggest kitchen she had ever seen. She stopped and looked around with wide eyes.

"Shannon, don't touch anything," her mother warned.

She turned, hurrying after her mother. Down a short hallway, George held open a door for them. Her mother went inside, but Shannon stood at the doorway.

"Is this where we're going to live?"

"Yes. You'll have your very own room," her mother said.

She bit her lip. "I already had my own room."

"Did you have a TV in your room?" George asked.

Shannon shook her head.

"Well, then. I bet I can rig one up for you here," he said.

"You can?"

"Now, George, don't go promising things," her mother said. "I can't afford another TV and Mrs. Lansford might not want—"

"Alice, Mrs. Lansford said to make you feel at home. If adding a TV cable in your daughter's room will help, then it's no problem. And I happen to know where I can get my hands on a spare TV."

Shannon looked from him to her mother, waiting with hopeful eyes. Other kids at school had TVs in their rooms. Now she could be cool like them.

"Well, I suppose if it's not too much trouble," her mother conceded.

Shannon smiled brightly up at George. "I can help too. My daddy taught me how to do all kinds of things. I even know all the different types of screwdrivers," she said proudly.

"Is that right? Well, then maybe you can be my assistant."

"Shannon, George is going to help me carry boxes in, then you can start unpacking. Okay?"

"Okay, Momma," she said.

Before they left, her mother turned back to her. "Don't wander upstairs. The Lansfords are nice enough to let us move here, but up there is their home. You won't be allowed up there. Understand?"

"Yes, ma'am," she said, not really understanding.

As soon as her mother was out of sight, Shannon went back into the kitchen, still amazed at the size. Who needed two stoves and two refrigerators? Beyond the kitchen was another hallway, this one much wider than the one that led to their new rooms. She went toward it, noticing a staircase in the back. Her eyes followed its length, and she gasped as her curious gaze was met by one equally as curious.

A girl about her age stood at the top, watching her. Her blond hair was long and silky looking and Shannon stared at her. The girl finally moved, coming down toward her.

"Where's Alice?"

Shannon stood at the foot of the stairs. "Who are you?"

The girl put her hands on her hips. "Who are *you*?"

"Shannon Fletcher," she said.

"I'm Madison Lansford. I live here."

Shannon smirked. "So do I."

The girl frowned. "No, you don't."

"Do too."

"Shannon?" her mother called and Shannon grinned.

"See? That's my momma."

"Alice is your mother?"

"Yep."

"But Alice doesn't live here."

"We do now," Shannon said and hurried back to their new rooms. She was surprised to find the girl following her.

"Why, Miss Madison, what brings you down here?" George asked.

Madison looked around George to where her mother was already unpacking a box. "I was hungry and wanted a snack," she said. "What are you doing?"

Her mother smiled at her. "We're going to be living down here. Didn't your mother tell you?"

Madison shook her head.

"Well, this way, I'll be here all the time, not only during the day," her mother said. "In case you need something late at night, then I'll be here for you."

Madison looked at Shannon. "And she'll be here too?"

"Yes. Shannon will have a room here too."

Madison smiled. "Good. Then we're going to be friends." She took Shannon's hand and tugged her back out. "Let me show you my playground."

Shannon looked back at her mother for confirmation.

"Yes, it's okay. It's outside."

Shannon nodded and followed Madison, only to turn back around at her mother's voice.

"Don't get into any trouble."

"She always says that," Shannon mumbled.

"Why?"

"I don't know." Then she smiled. "Sometimes things break."

"You can't hurt anything out here," Madison said, breaking into a run when they rounded the corner of the back garage.

Shannon stopped in her tracks. The playground was as big as the one at her school. And all for one person. Wow.

"You want to swing?"

Shannon nodded, joining Madison. She pushed off with her feet, noticing how dirty her shoes looked compared to Madison's.

"We have the same hair," Madison said.

Shannon looked at her pretty blond hair but shook her head. "Mine gets darker every year," she said.

"Why?"

"I don't know. My momma said I'm going to have brown hair like her."

"Oh. How old are you?"

"How old are *you*?"

"Nine."

Shannon smirked. "I'm already ten. *Much* older than you."

Madison laughed. "That's not much older."

"Is too."

Madison stopped swinging and stared at her. Shannon stared back, her young mind marveling at the color of Madison's eyes.

"Okay. If you want to say you're *much* older, you can. We're still going to be friends."

"I'm smarter too," Shannon said confidently. This time, Madison smirked.

"But I'm prettier."

Shannon blinked at her. "My momma says I'm pretty."

"You are. Just not as pretty as me," she said with a sweet smile.

Shannon nodded and pushed off with her feet, starting the swing again. "Okay, you're prettier."

CHAPTER TWO

"So you lived in a mansion?"

Shannon laughed. "God, no. We lived in the servants' quarters. The house was on a slope so from the front, it appeared to only be three stories. It was actually four. We lived on the first floor. So did George. At the time, I didn't understand the perception of *servants' quarters*. But I was not allowed upstairs. Well, not at will. If they weren't having company and no guests were around, then Madison was allowed to have me up to her room. Provided, of course, that none of Madison's real friends were there. It wouldn't do to see the maid's daughter up there."

"My, what snobs," Charlotte said. "Are there people still like that?"

"What? People wedded to the separation of the classes?" Shannon asked. "The Lansfords were old money," she said. "Candice Lansford followed every social rule. She was quite serious about their status in the community."

"I know you said Brook Hill had grown, but is it large enough to support one of your stores?"

"Brook Hill and the surrounding area has over a hundred thousand people. My fresh market concept should go over well there. The closest Whole Foods or other organic grocery is two hours away, in Dallas."

"This will be your fourth store?" Tracy asked.

Shannon nodded. "Yes. I still can't believe how successful we've been. But the big superstores, they only go into major cities. Even though our stores are much smaller, we can still offer organic produce, vegetarian and vegan options, bulk grains and beans." She had to stop herself, knowing she could talk forever about their business. "It's been a huge success in the smaller cities where we're their only option."

"You'll only be gone during the inception then? You're not planning on leaving the Austin area, are you?"

"No. I can't see myself ever living in Brook Hill again."

"So tell us more about Madison," Charlotte prompted. "You became fast friends, I imagine."

Shannon nodded. "At first, her mother was horrified that she was slumming with the hired help. Of course, they had been so supportive when my dad was ill; they basically took my mother under their wings. I'm convinced that's the only reason I was allowed into Madison's life."

"I'm assuming you didn't go to school together?"

"Oh, no. We were in the same grade, but she went to the private school in town. We had no mutual friends at all. At first, we only played outside, or in the kitchen, or in my room. It was a while before she took me upstairs," she said. "I was twelve."

* * *

"Are you sure it's okay?"

Madison took her hand and tugged her up the stairs. "I want to show you my homework. You said you were good at math," she reminded her. "I promise I won't force you to play with my Barbie collection."

"Your mother might get mad," Shannon said. Actually, she had no idea if that was true or not. Mrs. Lansford rarely made an appearance down in the kitchen, so Shannon had only seen her a few times since they'd been living there.

"It's my room," Madison said, as if that made all the difference.

Once she pushed the door open to the main floor, Shannon stood still, looking around in awe. Antique furniture, sculptures, huge paintings—all things she'd never seen before except on field trips.

"It's like a museum," she said quietly so as not to disturb the silence.

"Yes. A museum," Madison agreed.

Shannon didn't understand the sad look on her face. "You don't like it?"

Madison shook her head. "I can't touch anything. I can't sit on the furniture. I don't really live down here."

She started walking again, and Shannon followed her to another staircase, this one wide and curving along the wall as it rose to the third floor.

"That's some big stairs," she said.

"There is an elevator too. My parents usually take it. I like to walk on the stairs, though." At the top, Madison led her down a short hallway that opened up into a small sitting area. "I live here," she said as she spread out her arms. "My parents' rooms are on the top floor."

"You have all this," she said, turning and looking around, "to yourself?"

"Yes."

She opened a door, letting Shannon look inside. It was a bathroom, larger than her own bedroom.

"This is for my guests," Madison said. "But you can use mine if you want. It's in my bedroom."

"So you have different rooms?"

Madison nodded. "Playroom. Study room. Bedroom. Bathroom. TV room."

Shannon's mouth dropped open. "Wow."

Madison shrugged. "You want to look at my homework now?"

"Okay."

Double doors opened up into what was a small living room—the TV room, Shannon guessed. Madison crossed the carpet silently, going to another room. Shannon followed, her eyes darting around in awe. It was bigger than what she and her mother shared now.

Madison opened the door to her study room. It contained a desk and chair, two bookshelves…and a phone. Shannon pointed at it.

"Why?"

Madison shrugged again. "Mother says one day I'll have boys calling me." Shannon made a face and Madison laughed. "I know. They're so…gross." She shuffled through some papers on her desk and handed Shannon a page. "Algebra."

There was only one chair so Shannon sat down on the floor and leaned against the wall. She was surprised when Madison joined her.

"These are pretty easy," she said. "What don't you understand?"

"None of it. It makes no sense to me."

"We learned this last year. You mean that fancy private school is just now going over this?"

Madison bumped her knee with her own and smiled. "We have more important things to learn there than algebra."

"I'm sure."

They spent the next thirty minutes going over Madison's homework until she somewhat understood. There were ten problems. Madison only got one right.

"So you won't be a mathematician when you grow up," Shannon teased her.

"You really are smart, aren't you?"

Shannon shrugged. "Yes."

Madison was quiet for a moment. "My birthday is coming up."

"I know. I remember from last year."

"I'll be twelve, just like you."

"I'll always be older."

"Five months is not *older*," Madison said as she playfully punched her arm. But the smile left her face. "I'm having a party." She looked at Shannon with sad eyes. "My mother said you can't come."

Not that Shannon expected to attend, but the hurt look in Madison's eyes made her own heart ache.

"That's because I'm not one of your real friends," she reminded her.

"You're my best friend," Madison said. "My mother says you can't be, though. She says I should pick someone else."

Shannon was old enough to know what that meant. Madison couldn't possibly be friends with their maid's daughter. She needed to stay within her social class. When no one was looking, when no one was around, then Madison could stoop down to her level. That hurt Shannon, but she knew it wasn't Madison's fault. She couldn't be mad at her.

"How about I ask my mom to make you a small cake and we'll have our own party?"

Madison's eyes lit up. "Just me and you?"

Shannon nodded. "Yeah. Just us."

And two weeks later, one day after Madison's real birthday party, they sat outside, not far from the playground they had outgrown. The gazebo was rarely used as it was too far from the main house for guests. When her parents entertained, they used the more formal patio area that faced the backyard. Of course, Shannon knew all that because she helped her mother in the kitchen preparing appetizers and sometimes she helped the other cooks with the meal itself. The gazebo had become *their* place.

"You have to make a wish," Shannon instructed.

When she asked her mother to make a small cake, she'd done just that. It was barely bigger than a saucer. Her mother had produced a single candle and had given Shannon some matches to light it with.

Madison stared into her eyes and Shannon felt an odd sensation in her stomach. Madison nodded slowly.

"Okay. I made my wish."

Shannon tilted her head. "What was it?"

Madison leaned down and blew out the candle, laughing. "I can't tell you. Then it won't come true."

Shannon handed Madison a fork and they dug into the cake. It was chocolate with a thick layer of creamy icing—her favorite. She didn't know what Madison's favorite was.

"Do you like it? I didn't know what kind to ask for," she said.

Madison licked chocolate from her lips. "This one."

"Good." She swallowed her bite, then wiped her mouth with the back of her hand. "So how was your party yesterday?"

"It was okay, I guess. My parents rented the pavilion at the country club. They had an ice cream machine. We went swimming too."

"Did you have a big cake?"

"Yes. But it wasn't nearly as good as this."

That pleased her and she smiled. "Fancy dinner too?"

Madison nodded. "I would have rather been here with you though." She put her fork down. "Stephen Cole was there."

"The boy your mother likes for you?"

"Yes. He kept tickling me in the pool. He says we're going to be dating soon."

Shannon rolled her eyes. "You're twelve. You're not going to start dating."

"When will you start dating?"

Shannon swung her foot back and forth, searching for an answer. "I hadn't really thought about it. I don't really like any of the boys at school."

"Me either. But that's all Tamara talks about now. Stephanie too."

Shannon knew Tamara and Stephanie were two of Madison's friends, but of course she had never met them. She wondered if they even knew she existed.

"I guess maybe we'll start liking them too," she offered, wondering if that was true.

"I guess."

CHAPTER THREE

"You knew you were gay when you were twelve?"

Shannon laughed. "I didn't know what gay meant, I just knew I didn't like boys."

"You already had a crush on her then?"

Shannon nodded. "I'm not sure I knew it, though. I was just the friend she had to hide from everybody. I know it drove her mother crazy. She tried her best to keep us apart."

"She didn't like you?"

"Not so much that. She was always cordial to me. But the friendship that Madison and I had, she wanted that for her with one of the country club group. She made sure Madison spent plenty of time with them. Tennis lessons, swimming lessons, riding lessons. Dance. All activities that didn't involve me."

"Yet at the end of the day, Madison came home to you," Charlotte said with a smile. "I'm sure that did worry her mother."

"Madison never got any better with math so I tried to tutor her. But we couldn't let her mother know. The first time she caught us, I was thirteen."

* * *

"Shannon, it just doesn't make sense to me. Why does it have to be so hard?"

"It's not hard. You're just not understanding it. You're going to be in high school pretty soon. It's going to get a lot harder."

They were sitting cross-legged on the floor of Madison's study room. Madison flopped down dramatically, one arm covering her eyes.

"High school? I can't do basic math and you're bringing up high school?"

Shannon's eyes followed the length of her body, landing on her exposed armpit. She grinned devilishly, then attacked, tickling Madison mercilessly.

Madison squirmed, laughing as she slapped at Shannon's hands. "Stop! I'll get you back, Shannon Fletcher."

"Promises, promises," she said, finally relenting.

Madison grinned. "I hate it when you do that."

"Yeah? Then why are you smiling?"

Madison sat back up, still smiling as she stared at her. "I don't know. You make me happy."

Shannon got a funny feeling in her stomach when Madison looked at her like that. She nodded. "You make me happy too."

The silence lingered as they stared at each other. Shannon finally looked away and reached for Madison's homework. She was about to go over another problem when Madison's bedroom door opened. A few seconds later, Mrs. Lansford stood at the threshold to the study room.

"Girls? What are you doing?"

Shannon stared at the floor, speechless. Mrs. Lansford scared her. But Madison's words made her raise her head.

"I'm helping Shannon with some homework," Madison said. "That's okay, isn't it?"

Mrs. Lansford slid her gaze to Shannon, prompting her into action.

"I needed some help in…math," she said quietly. "Since Madison is so good at it and all…"

Mrs. Lansford nodded. "Yes, well our public school system is sorely lacking in that regard. Of course Madison can assist you, Shannon. She has a more formal education than you, it only stands to reason." She smiled quickly, then it was gone. "I came to tell you that your father will have a business guest for dinner. You'll take your evening meal up here, dear. I'll have Stella bring it up."

"Yes, Mother."

"Well, carry on."

As soon as the door closed they broke into a fit of giggles. "'It only stands to reason,'" Shannon mimicked.

"'Carry on,'" Madison said in a clipped British accent, causing more laughter.

"So, Miss Smarty-pants, what are you going to teach me?"

Madison's smile faded. "I'm sorry. But if she knew you were helping me, well...she would send me to a real tutor, one they would pay a lot of money to. It wouldn't do for you to be smarter than me."

"Because I'm the maid's daughter?" Shannon didn't want to be angry, but she was.

"Shannon, you know how it is."

Shannon stood, intending to leave. "Yeah, I know. I'll never be as good as you, no matter what."

Madison got up too, grabbing her arm as she turned to leave. "You're my best friend. Please don't leave."

Shannon stared at the hand that was holding her arm. Again, she got a funny feeling in her stomach and she didn't know what it was. She did know, however, that she liked it.

"You only want to keep me around so that you don't fail your test tomorrow," she said, her anger fading as teasing took over.

"Yes. That's the only reason I tolerate you," Madison agreed with a smile.

She then surprised Shannon—and possibly herself—by pulling Shannon to her and hugging her tightly. Shannon was trembling as her arms slipped around Madison's small waist. The cartwheels in her stomach increased, and she closed her eyes, wondering what was happening to her.

Madison had a funny look on her face when she pulled away. They stared at each other for the longest time, then Madison nodded as if she'd found an answer to an unspoken question.

Shannon nodded too, pretending she not only knew the question but the answer as well.

"You want to watch TV?"

Shannon looked at the papers on the floor. "What about your test?"

"It's a lost cause," Madison said.

"But—"

Her protest was cut off as Madison took her hand and led her into the small living room that was adjacent to her bedroom.

"Just for a little while. Stella will bring my dinner up at seven. Your momma will be expecting you back down."

Shannon plopped down beside Madison on the sofa, math forgotten. "Will your mother be mad?"

Madison shook her head. "She won't come back in here. She's getting ready for their dinner guest."

Shannon tried to relax, but she couldn't even begin to focus on the TV. Madison had scooted closer to her and they sat there, their thighs pressed together, both glancing from the TV to each other. When Stella knocked on the door, Shannon and Madison moved away from each other guiltily. Shannon had no idea what they should feel guilty about.

Still, with one last look into Madison's eyes, she bid her a hasty goodnight.

CHAPTER FOUR

"Let me help with that," Shannon offered as Tracy brought the salad to the table.

"I've got it. Open the other bottle of wine," she suggested instead.

Charlotte was bent over the stove, inspecting the huge pan of lasagna. "Smells great. How much longer?"

"When we finish our salads, it'll be ready to serve."

Shannon slapped her hand away as Charlotte reached out to grab a taste. "You know her rules," she said.

"If only I'd learned to cook, she wouldn't be able to hold all those rules over me," Charlotte said with laugh. She linked arms with Shannon as they made their way back outside to the patio. Tracy had already served generous portions of salad onto their plates.

"I want to hear more about you and Madison," Tracy said as she took the wine bottle from Shannon. "Were you falling in love with her at thirteen and you didn't even know it?"

"It was around that time that I started to get a clue," she said with a smile. "The butterflies in my stomach thing only happened around Madison. Never around guys. The thought that I might be gay terrified me."

"You've said you've always had a close relationship with your mother," Charlotte said. "You talked to her about it, right?"

"Are you kidding me? I couldn't talk to her about *that*," Shannon said with a grin. "At least not when I was that young." She took a bite of salad and glanced at Tracy. "This is great."

"Thank you." Tracy raised her eyebrows. "So did you talk to Madison about it?"

"No. And she didn't talk to me about it either."

"Ah. So you were *both* feeling that way," Charlotte stated.

"Yes. We simply didn't talk about it. We never talked about it."

Tracy leaned forward and smiled wickedly. "Did you kiss her?"

Shannon nodded. "I was fourteen."

* * *

"I don't want to go out with Stephen," Madison complained as they sorted through her clothes. "Why is she making me?"

"You said yourself when you got into high school you'd have to start dating," Shannon reminded her.

"I don't even like Stephen," she said as she tossed yet another blouse onto the bed. "Do you like this one?" she asked, holding it up to her chest.

"Yes. It makes your eyes look bluer."

Madison stared at her for a moment, her head tilted. She tossed that blouse on the bed with the others as she walked closer. "He's going to want to kiss me."

Shannon nodded. Even though she had no idea who Stephen Cole was, other than the boy Madison's mother had picked out for her years ago, she still felt a twinge of jealousy.

Madison took her hand and their fingers linked together. It was something they did often—hold hands. Sometimes, it was casual with Madison leading her this way or that. Other times, they would stare at each other, their fingers moving softly against the other's skin, touching, memorizing, tracing. Those were the times Shannon loved. Now, Madison's thumb was trailing across the back of her hand, and Shannon swallowed nervously.

"I don't know how to kiss," Madison said quietly. "I've never kissed anyone."

"I'm sure it won't be hard to learn," Shannon said, hearing her voice crackle with nervousness.

Madison took a step closer. "Maybe...we should practice."

Shannon could feel her heart pounding in her throat and she was surprised she was still able to breathe. She looked into Madison's eyes, seeing that she was completely serious. She was afraid she was going to start hyperventilating. Madison gave her the sweetest smile Shannon had ever seen.

"Do you want to?" she whispered.

Shannon stood mutely in front of her, afraid to speak. Apparently Madison found the answer she was looking for. She leaned closer, touching her lips to Shannon's. She pulled back quickly and Shannon opened her eyes. It had been too brief for her to even register the kiss. Suddenly feeling brave, she found her voice.

"I...I don't think that's how it's done," she said as her fingers tightened around Madison's.

Madison smiled slightly. "No? How is it done, then?"

Thinking they were crazy to be doing this, Shannon nonetheless pushed down her fear of Mrs. Lansford walking in on them. Her desire to kiss Madison overrode her good sense, and she took a step closer to her friend.

She wet her lips before leaning closer. She was fascinated as Madison's eyes slipped closed as she waited for her kiss. Feeling bold—and a bit daring—Shannon lowered her head, slowly moving her lips over Madison's, praying she was doing it correctly. The only thing she had to go on was kissing scenes she'd seen in movies. She opened her mouth, fitting Madison's lower lip between her own. This caused a fire in the pit of her stomach and she moaned. Embarrassed, she tried to pull away, but Madison held her in place, her own lips opening to Shannon.

When they finally parted, she noted they were both breathing hard, nearly panting. She was afraid to look at Madison and even more surprised when Madison's mouth found hers again. Madison's hand slid up her arm and around her neck, her fingers threading through her hair. Their lips moved together again, pressing harder against each other. She gasped when her body came into contact with Madison's. She longed to put her arms around Madison and pull her tight, but she was so afraid. She was, however, satisfied to hear a quiet sound leave Madison's mouth.

Their need to breathe pulled them apart. Madison looked at her shyly, a slight smile on her lips.

"Kissing is kinda fun."

Shannon smiled. "Yeah. It is."

As they stared at each other, Shannon felt something pass between them. She knew they were communicating without words, but she had no clue as to what they were saying. When they heard the outer door open, they stepped apart, Madison quickly picking up the discarded blouse and again holding it up for her inspection.

"This one?"

Shannon grinned. "Yeah. I like that one."

Mrs. Lansford stood in the doorway, her gaze going between the girls to the pile of clothes on the bed.

"I see you're having a hard time deciding on what to wear."

"Shannon likes this one. Do you?"

Mrs. Lansford came closer, nodding. "Yes. That would look lovely on you, dear." She looked at Shannon. "You have good taste."

Shannon shrugged. "I should probably go help my mom with dinner," she said. Mrs. Lansford only nodded. Shannon glanced over at Madison. "Have fun on your date. I can't wait to hear all about it," she lied. The look in Madison's eyes told her she knew she was lying. Shannon winked at her before fleeing the room.

* * *

"Oh my God. That's so sweet," Tracy said.

"Did you practice a lot after that?" Charlotte teased.

Shannon blushed at the memory. Yeah, they practiced a lot after that. And they got good at it. Did she really want to share all of that with her friends?

"We did," she admitted.

"The lasagna can wait a few more minutes," Tracy said. "I want to know how her date went."

* * *

"What's wrong? You seem restless."

Shannon paused, realizing she'd been pacing. She stared at her mother, not sure what to say.

"Madison went on her first date last night," she said.

Her mother nodded. "Yes. With Stephen Cole."

"Do you know him?"

"He's been over with his parents before," she said. "Has Madison not introduced you?"

Shannon rolled her eyes. "Come on, Mom. You know I'm not allowed up in the big house when they have company."

"Oh, that's right. I had forgotten. You're over there so much as it is."

Shannon shrugged. "We're friends."

"I know, honey." Her mother picked up the remote and muted the TV program she'd been watching. "I'm so sorry Mrs. Lansford treats you the way she does. It's only because I work—"

"I don't care about that, Mom. I wouldn't want to hang out with those kids anyway." She sat down on her usual corner of the couch, not knowing why she was so restless. Madison and Stephen had gone to the movies, driven there by George in Mr. Lansford's Rolls Royce. She was surprised Mrs. Lansford hadn't rented out the whole movie theater for them. Today, Madison had tennis lessons. Shannon was waiting for her to get home so they could talk. While she didn't necessarily want to know about her date, she was curious as to whether Stephen had tried to kiss her or not.

"Well, speaking of dating, I wonder when you're going to want to start. I think fourteen is a little young, though." Her mother looked at her thoughtfully. "Do you have anyone in mind?"

Shannon snorted. "No. I'm not ever going to date."

Her mother smiled, then put her TV program back on. Shannon got up and went into her room and continued her pacing in private. Soon, she heard the TV shut off and knew her mother was out in the big kitchen, starting dinner for the Lansfords. That was one of the perks of living there; whatever decadent meal the Lansfords would eat, Shannon and her mother would enjoy as well.

When the clock clicked past six, Shannon left her room, hoping Madison would be home soon. She went into the kitchen to offer to help, knowing her mother would shoo her away. Only when Stella had the day off would her mother allow her in the kitchen. She sat on the bottom step, waiting, hoping Madison wouldn't be late. She didn't have to wait long before the door opened at the top.

Madison stood there, still in her tennis outfit. She smiled at her and Shannon returned it.

"Want to come up to my room?"

Shannon jumped up, taking the stairs two at a time.

"Dinner's at seven, Shannon," her mother called to her.

"I know," she called back.

She and Madison hurried up the stairs to Madison's rooms. When the door closed behind them, they stood staring at each other, neither speaking.

"My mother is playing bridge," Madison finally said. "She's not home yet."

Shannon nodded, knowing Madison shared that with her to let her know they would not be interrupted.

"How was…how was your date?"

Madison went into her bedroom and Shannon followed. "It was awful. He spilled his Coke on me."

"That's terrible," Shannon said, secretly pleased. Or maybe not so secretly as Madison laughed at her.

Shannon's breath caught as Madison ripped her T-shirt off, leaving her in only her bra. She disappeared into her bathroom, and Shannon sunk down on the bed, trying to control her breathing. She heard the shower come on and assumed Madison was bathing after her tennis lesson.

"Be out in a second," Madison called. "I was so sweaty."

Shannon licked her lips. "Okay."

When Madison returned, her hair was damp and she was in clean shorts and a shirt. Shannon was still sitting on the bed. Madison sat down beside her, her eyes roaming across Shannon's face.

"I thought about you a lot today."

Shannon swallowed nervously. "Yeah?"

"Stephen didn't try to kiss me."

"Good," Shannon whispered.

Madison nodded. "Maybe we should practice some more. I mean, I want to be prepared when it does happen."

"Of course."

Madison smiled as her gaze drifted to Shannon's lips. "I liked the way you kissed me."

Shannon could feel her pulse race and she was afraid. They shouldn't be doing this, she knew. But that didn't stop her. She leaned closer, meeting Madison's mouth. The tentative, shy kisses they'd shared the day before were gone. Shannon nearly fainted when she felt Madison's tongue graze her lip. She couldn't stop the moan that slipped out when she felt Madison guide her down on the bed.

They lay facing each other, hands resting lightly on each other's waists as they kissed. Feeling bold, Shannon let her own tongue trace Madison's lower lip. She was shocked when Madison's mouth opened and their tongues met. It felt so good, and they moaned as their kiss changed from the simple exploration of lips to a full-fledged mouth and tongue exchange.

Shannon's body was on fire and she didn't know what to do. Her hand moved lower to Madison's hip, and her fingers caressed her, moving down farther to where her shorts stopped. Madison moaned again when Shannon's hand moved across the exposed skin.

They pulled apart, gasping for breath, their eyes meeting questioningly. Shannon was about to roll away when Madison's mouth returned to hers. Somewhere in her lustful haze, Shannon knew they should stop. Mrs. Lansford would be home any minute. If she caught them kissing…oh, Shannon didn't even want to think about the consequences. Her hand squeezed Madison's leg, then she eased back from the kiss, her lips leaving Madison's mouth to trail across her face, then her neck. Madison nearly purred, and Shannon had to force herself to stop.

She finally rolled to her back, away from Madison as she tried to catch her breath. Madison too lay on her back, staring at the ceiling. Shannon could hear the short, quick breaths that she took.

She squeezed her legs together, feeling a sharp throb between her thighs.

"I really, really like that," Madison whispered.

"Me too."

"We can't ever tell anyone."

"I know." Shannon sat up. "I should go. Your mother—"

"Yes." Madison sat up too and ran her hands through her hair as she took a deep breath. "She'll be home soon." She reached out and touched Shannon's face, her thumb rubbing lightly across Shannon's lower lip. "You're so pretty."

Shannon smiled but said nothing. Madison was the pretty one, not her. Madison's hand fell away and her gaze left Shannon's lips.

"I'll see you tomorrow," Shannon said as she stood.

"I won't be around much," Madison warned. "Stephanie is having a party at the country club."

Shannon's heart sank, again reminding herself that she and Madison were from two different worlds. She nodded mutely, then left, but not before seeing the sad look in Madison's eyes.

CHAPTER FIVE

"You must have been an emotional wreck," Charlotte said. "That's a lot to contend with at fourteen."

"Thanks," she said, taking the plate of lasagna from Tracy. "Looks great." She nodded at Charlotte, acknowledging her statement. "I knew what we were doing was crazy, yeah," she said. "Going through puberty and realizing your best friend was the one who turned you on was scary as hell. But if her mother would have caught us kissing…" she said with a shake of her head, "I can't even begin to imagine her reaction."

Charlotte laughed. "Oh, I think you can imagine it. That's what scared you."

"So did you and Madison talk about it?" Tracy asked. "I mean, you can call it *practice* all you want, but I'm sure you both knew what was really happening."

"Yes, we knew what was happening, but we didn't talk about it. She was doing what she was supposed to do—date Stephen Cole. Everything was separate about our lives except that. Different schools, different friends. Her mother kept her busy with tennis lessons, dance, swimming. As she got older, she spent more and more time with her friends. Not that she wanted to. But it was *expected* of her."

"Because she was a Lansford," Charlotte stated. "So Brook Hill was still a small enough city that those old separation of the class rules still applied. Amazing."

"Like I said, her mother took it very seriously."

"So did you find it difficult to see each other?"

"Sometimes. As busy as she kept Madison, her mother had as many activities of her own. Dinner was at seven and neither her mother nor father made it home much before then." She took a bite of the lasagna and nodded. "This is delicious, Tracy. Thanks for making it vegetarian."

"Thank you. And you're welcome."

"How long before kissing was no longer enough?" Charlotte asked bluntly.

"You mean, when did we start touching?"

"I'm assuming you didn't dive right in and become lovers. You were virgins," she said.

"Virgins but not clueless," she said. "I wanted to touch her but I was afraid." Shannon smiled. "The first time I dared to touch her breasts, I was fifteen."

* * *

"I made an A on my test," Madison said excitedly, holding up her test paper for Shannon to see.

"Well, look at you," she said. "See? I told you it'd be okay."

"I know. I was still shocked though."

Shannon followed Madison into her study room and plopped down on the floor where she normally sat. Madison sat cross-legged beside her, a smile on her face.

"What?" Shannon asked, smiling too.

"Stephanie is having a dance party tomorrow night."

Shannon cocked her head, grinning. "And? You want to practice dancing?"

Madison nodded, her expression serious. "Can we?"

Shannon got excited at the thought but didn't want to appear too eager. "What kind of dance?"

Madison's soft smile sent a chill down Shannon's spine. "Slow."

Shannon swallowed, wondering how her legs would support her if she and Madison were dancing. For as much practice kissing as they'd done, there'd never been much touching involved. Even when they'd dared to lay on Madison's bed, there still was no full body touching. But slow dancing? Their bodies would be close together, their hands would be free to move at will.

"Can we?" Madison asked again.

Shannon finally nodded. She knew she wouldn't refuse Madison. They stood and Shannon shifted nervously.

"Music?" she managed.

Madison shook her head. "Let's just dance," she whispered.

Again Shannon nodded, but she had no clue how to start. Truth was, she'd never been dancing before. Madison stepped closer, taking Shannon's hands and drawing them around her waist. Madison's hands ran slowly up Shannon's arms to her shoulders, finally snaking around her neck. Shannon's eyes slipped closed as she felt Madison's body brush against her own.

"You're supposed to lead," Madison said quietly, her breath warm against Shannon's ear.

Shannon shuffled her feet, moving against Madison. She tightened her hold around her waist, managing to contain a moan as their bodies bumped together. She became aware of her racing pulse, of her quick breaths, and she told herself to calm down. They were only dancing. But when Madison's fingers threaded through her hair, she heard Madison's rapid breathing as well and she realized she wasn't the only one affected by their closeness.

Feeling brave, she let her hands wander, rubbing lightly across Madison's back. She drew her nearer as she lifted her head. Their mouths were as close as they could be without kissing. Shannon's eyes fluttered open, finding Madison's still closed. She moved to her lips, intending a slow, innocent kiss. But there was nothing innocent about it when Madison moaned into her mouth, her tongue immediately finding Shannon's.

The pretense of dancing ceased, replaced by the most extensive make-out session of Shannon's young life. Their feet stopped moving entirely as they pressed as close together as possible. As much as she'd fantasized about Madison, it had not prepared her for the real thing. They were breathing heavily as their kisses turned frantic. Shannon's legs felt weak and she clung to Madison, arms wrapped tightly around her waist. They had kissed plenty in the last year, but it was never like this. This was raw and sexual, and Shannon's body responded to it, a constant throbbing between her legs making her hips arch into Madison.

And then she did something she'd only dreamed of—she let her hand travel unimpeded to Madison's breast. She wasn't sure what Madison's reaction would be, but she couldn't stop the natural progress of her hand. She groaned when she felt Madison's small nipple harden against her palm.

Madison tore her mouth from Shannon's, a loud moan escaping as she gasped for breath, her own hips straining to make contact with Shannon. Shannon squeezed the nipple between her fingers, her mouth finding Madison's again, their tongues brushing hotly against the other.

Even in the lustful state she was in, she heard it. The elevator. She groaned in frustration as she pulled away from Madison. They stood staring at each other, breathing as if they'd run a race.

"I…I should go," she managed.

Madison's blue eyes were still boring into hers. Shannon had to force herself to take another step away from her. Her movement seemed to snap Madison out of her trance, and she wrapped her arms around herself before nodding.

Shannon fled then, knowing it would not do for Mrs. Lansford to catch her there, not in the state she was in. She'd just made it down the flight of stairs to the main floor when she heard the elevator door open. She paused at the door that would take her downstairs to the kitchen, taking deep breaths, trying to calm her aroused body. It scared her to death knowing that it was sexual. They weren't pretending to kiss, pretending to dance. She knew what it meant. She wondered if Madison knew or if she was still pretending they were just practicing.

She finally pushed open the door, walking slowly down the steps. She could hear her mother and Stella in the kitchen. She hoped to sneak by to her room, but her mother spotted her.

"Come give me a hand loading the tray, Shannon."

"Okay," she said, but she avoided making eye contact with her mother. She picked up the dish her mother pointed to and carefully carried it over to the serving tray. She knew the routine. Stella would have already been up to the dining room and set the table. Stella would also serve the Lansfords at seven o'clock, as soon as Mrs. Lansford rang the bell indicating they were ready. The serving tray would be loaded with three, sometimes four courses. A soup or light appetizer to start, sometimes a salad, followed by the main course and ending with dessert. Shannon got out the crystal drinking glasses and filled them with ice and water. She also added two coffee cups and saucers for Mr. and Mrs. Lansford's after-dinner coffee. She went to the oven without asking, pulling out the bread that was warming there. Her mother always put a rose on the serving tray, which Shannon found funny as Stella would be the only one to see it.

"Are you okay?"

Shannon looked up. "Yes. Why?"

"You look flushed. Are you hot?"

Shannon nearly broke into a fit of giggles, but she refrained. "I feel fine."

Her mother studied her, and Shannon grew uncomfortable under her gaze. "When you came down, you were short of breath," her mother stated.

Shannon swallowed nervously. "I ran down," she said. That, at least, wasn't a lie. "Mrs. Lansford came home." She shrugged. "I didn't want her to catch me up there. She thinks we spend too much time together as it is."

But her mother shook her head. "I don't think so."

"You don't?"

"No. I remember when I was your age. Jane Sizemore and I were best friends. You rarely saw one of us without the other. You and Madison don't have that luxury since you don't go to the same school."

"And don't have the same friends," Shannon added.

"Right. And Mrs. Lansford keeps her plenty busy, doesn't she? So I don't think you spend too much time together."

Shannon gave her mother a quick smile. "Thanks, Mom."

By Saturday afternoon, though, Shannon still hadn't seen or talked to Madison. She sat in the gazebo, her legs stretched out, an unopened biology book on her lap. She was a little afraid that maybe Madison was angry with her, maybe she'd taken it too far and now Madison was avoiding her. But really, Madison was the one who had started it. She was the one who had suggested *dancing*.

Footsteps approached and she turned, hoping to find Madison. She was shocked to see Mr. Lansford instead.

"Hello, Shannon."

Shannon swung her legs to the ground, suddenly feeling nervous in his presence. "Hello, Mr. Lansford."

"It's not often I find you out here without your shadow," he said with a smile.

"I hope you don't mind. I can go back inside and—"

"No, of course not. We rarely use this anymore. I know you and Madison have claimed it now. I actually was hoping to catch you alone. I wanted to thank you," he said.

Shannon stared at him. "For what?"

He smiled again. "Despite my wife thinking Madison has suddenly turned into a mathematician, I know we have you to thank for her good grades."

Shannon blushed. "I…I only helped her a little," she admitted.

"I know from Alice that you are a straight-A student," he said. "I also know my wife thinks Madison is tutoring *you*."

"I'm sorry. We—"

He held his hand up, stopping her. "Not to worry. I only wanted to thank you." He turned to leave, then stopped. "And I think it's best if Mrs. Lansford is none the wiser, don't you?"

Shannon smiled. "Yes, sir."

"Good."

Shannon relaxed, again stretching her legs out. Over the last five years she'd only had a few conversations with him and never alone. She had always been afraid of him. He was a tall and imposing figure, and she tended to avoid him as much as possible. She was afraid of Mrs. Lansford too but for many different reasons.

She finally opened up her biology book, intending to read the next two chapters when she again heard movement. This time it *was* Madison. She smiled at her, her stomach doing flip-flops just from the sight of her.

"What are you doing?"

Shannon held up her book and Madison made a face. "Is that all you do is study?"

"That's why I make all As," she said.

Madison sat down opposite her, a slight smile on her face. They stared at each other, and Shannon felt her heart start to speed up. She tried to think of something to say, anything to break the spell Madison had on her.

"I…I saw your father," she said.

"Oh yeah?"

"He came out here. He wanted to thank me," she said.

"What for?"

Shannon grinned. "Your math grades."

Madison laughed, then sobered up. "Was he angry?"

"Not at all. He also promised he wouldn't tell your mother."

Madison nodded. "Yes, that's the difference between them. He's more concerned with my grades rather than the perception that I might not be smart enough and need a tutor."

"You're smart enough," Shannon said.

"Not smart like you."

Shannon shrugged. School came easy to her, sure, but she did study more than Madison did. Of course, she didn't have all of the extra activities that Madison had. She had more time to study.

They were quiet, just staring at each other, smiling. Shannon could feel the electricity between them. She wondered if Madison had put a name to it yet.

"You…you dance a lot better than Stephen does," Madison finally said.

"Oh yeah? How was the dance party?"

Madison looked away. "It was okay, I guess." She paused, then looked back at Shannon. "He wanted to do what you did."

Shannon unconsciously licked her lips. "What's that?"

Madison was wringing her hands together nervously. "He…he wanted to touch my breasts."

Shannon felt her heart lurch in her chest at her words. Her gaze dropped to Madison's breasts for long seconds before looking back up. Their eyes held, and again Shannon felt her heart hammering in her chest.

"Did you let him?" she asked quietly.

Madison shook her head. "No. I didn't want him to."

Shannon felt a sense of relief at her words. "I'm glad."

Madison looked down, again wringing her hands together. "My parents are going out tonight," she said. "They're going to a dinner party. They won't be home until late."

Shannon raised her eyebrows. It was Saturday. Madison usually did something with her friends—or Stephen—on Saturday nights.

Madison met her eyes again. "Maybe…maybe you could come up to my room?"

"You're not going out?"

Madison gave a quick smile. "I'll cancel."

Shannon nodded. "Okay."

Madison stood. "Good. I'll see you later then."

Shannon watched her walk away, her eyes glued to her backside, following the easy sway of her hips. She let her breath out with a heavy sigh, wondering what the night would hold.

CHAPTER SIX

"Oh my God, that is so sweet. I think you have the best first-time story ever," Tracy said.

"Sweet? I was a nervous wreck," Shannon said. She picked up the last of her garlic bread and took a bite. "I'm stuffed," she said.

"I hope you saved room for dessert."

Shannon eyed her carefully. "What did you make?"

"Tiramisu."

Shannon nearly moaned at the thought of the decadent dessert. "I suppose I'll have to force it down."

"I know it's your favorite, so don't try to sound put out," Tracy said with a laugh.

Shannon looked at Charlotte. "How do you stay so thin?"

"I hope you don't think she cooks like this all the time. The only time I get dessert is when you're over for dinner."

Shannon grinned. "Damn my sweet tooth."

Charlotte leaned her elbows on the table and rested her chin on her hands. It was a pose Shannon knew well. Charlotte was now Dr. Rimes and she wasn't trying to hide it.

"Did you think you were gay or did you think you were experimenting?"

"I had the hots for my best friend. I had no interest whatsoever in boys. Yeah, I was pretty sure I was gay."

"And what about Madison?"

"Honestly, at that age, I think she was just experimenting. Being gay wasn't acceptable for her. It wasn't a possibility," she said. "It was never a possibility."

"Even though you became lovers?"

"Even then. Whatever excuse Madison needed to make for it, she did. But being gay was never it."

"That must have been difficult for you."

"Yes, Dr. Rimes, it was very difficult." She met her gaze head-on. "It still is."

"Which is why you avoid going home at any cost. Even to see your mother."

"Stop trying to make her feel guilty," Tracy said. "I'm loving the story. Tell us more. Tell us what happened when you went to her room that night."

Shannon smiled. "What do you think happened? My hormones were raging and I was fifteen."

* * *

"We're going to watch TV," Shannon said.

"Don't stay too late," her mother warned.

"I won't," she said as she headed up the stairs and into the mansion. Once on the second floor, she paused, listening, but all was quiet. She jogged up the next flight to Madison's rooms, stopping to catch her breath before knocking lightly on the door.

"Come on in," Madison called.

Shannon pushed the door open, finding Madison on the sofa, the remnants of her hamburger dinner spread out. Whenever the Lansfords had dinner plans elsewhere, her mother would prepare something for her that they rarely had—hamburgers.

"I was hoping you'd come up and have dinner with me," Madison said.

Shannon stood there, her palms sweating slightly. She wiped them on her jeans. "I was going to, but my mother had everything set up for us down there." She walked deeper into the room, standing beside the sofa. "How did you get out of going out with Stephen?"

Madison smiled and gave a fake cough. "I'm sick. Very, very sick."

"He was okay with that?"

"Doesn't matter," she said dismissively. "One of his friends was having a *guy* party. He was just as happy to go there." Madison patted the seat beside her. "Come sit."

Shannon did as instructed, her heart hammering nervously in her chest as she felt Madison's thigh brush against hers. The TV was on, but Shannon had no clue what program they were supposed to be watching. Her thoughts were solely on Madison.

"Are you nervous?" Madison whispered.

Shannon nodded.

"Do you like kissing me?"

"Yes."

"I like kissing you too," Madison said. "Is it wrong that we do?"

"Your mother would kill me," Shannon blurted out. Madison laughed.

"That is true." She reached over and took Shannon's hand. "But I'd much rather kiss you than Stephen."

"Why?"

Madison tilted her head as if thinking. "It doesn't...feel the same when he kisses me." She made a face. "And he's all slobbering and stuff."

Shannon grimaced, trying to imagine kissing a boy. She was fairly certain she would *never* kiss a boy. But right now, she wanted to kiss Madison. She looked into her eyes, trying to find a hint that Madison wanted her to kiss her. She found more than a hint.

She leaned closer, their breaths mingling as their mouths drew together. It was almost like that first time, just the barest of touches. She heard Madison sigh and felt her fingers tighten around her hand. Shannon deepened the kiss, her mouth fitting perfectly against Madison's. Her pulse sprang to life and she moaned against her lips. They drew apart slightly, breathing fast. Their eyes met and Shannon thought there was a touch of fear in Madison's gaze. Fear of what, she had no clue. She was about to pull away, thinking Madison was having second thoughts, but Madison stopped her.

"Kiss me again," she whispered.

Shannon complied, taking her mouth again. Her intent to go slow faded when she felt Madison's tongue trace her lower lip. She opened her mouth, her tongue touching Madison's. They moaned and Shannon felt Madison's free hand clutching at her shirt. Madison shifted and lay back, pulling Shannon with her. For the first time, their bodies touched completely as Shannon rested her weight on top of Madison. Their kisses became scorching, and Shannon's brain couldn't keep up with her body. She wanted to touch Madison. Oh, she wanted to do so many things. She felt weak thinking of them. They finally broke apart, their need to breathe superseding their need to kiss.

Shannon leaned up, again searching Madison's eyes for a sign of what she wanted. She didn't have to ask. Madison took her hand and moved it under her shirt.

"Touch my breast," she murmured.

Shannon was afraid she would faint when her fingers traveled across Madison's smooth, warm skin to touch the silky fabric of her bra. Feeling more confident than she should be, she lowered her mouth again, kissing Madison as her fingers traced the hard peak of her nipple. Madison moaned and arched her hips into Shannon. Shannon felt lightheaded at the contact, and her tongue darted into Madison's mouth. Her hand seemed to have a mind of its own as her fingers impatiently shoved the bra away, seeking the taut nipple. When she found it, she rubbed her index finger across it, again hearing Madison moan.

"Feels so good," Madison whispered.

"Do you want me to…kiss it?" Shannon asked, praying she would say yes.

Madison's thighs parted, and Shannon's lower body slipped between them, their hips moving together instinctively.

"Yes," Madison breathed. "Kiss it."

Shannon sat up enough to shove Madison's shirt higher. She licked her lips at the sight of Madison's breast. Not having a clue as to what to do, she tentatively kissed the area around her nipple, loving the sounds Madison was making. When her lips bumped her nipple, her tongue came out, flicking across it. This caused Madison's hips to jerk. Shannon whimpered as her hips pressed hard into Madison.

"Suck on it," Madison murmured. "*Please.*"

Surprised she didn't pass out right then and there, Shannon closed her lips over the hard pebble and sucked the tip into her mouth. Madison groaned loudly, and her hand threaded its way through Shannon's hair, holding her tight against her breast.

"Oh God, Shannon…that feels so good."

Yes, it felt too good. The dampness between her legs told her how good it felt. It also told her they needed to stop before things went too far. She eased back, trailing kisses across Madison's stomach before lifting her head.

"Don't stop," Madison begged.

"We have to," Shannon said as she bent to kiss her again. "Your parents will be home soon."

Madison pulled Shannon into a tight hug. Shannon lay on top of her, trying to catch her breath. Madison finally loosened her grip, letting Shannon sit up.

"Did you like that?"

Shannon nodded.

"Next time…I want to do that to you."

Shannon felt her heart jump into her throat at the prospect of Madison's mouth on her breast. She couldn't find her voice and simply nodded.

Madison smiled at her and leaned closer, placing a light kiss on her lips. "Thank you."

Shannon wasn't quite sure what she was thanking her for, but again, she nodded. They sat back, pretending to watch the TV when all they were doing was looking at each other. Before long, their hands were clasped again and their thighs were pressed against each other. And one look into each other's eyes was all it took. Their kisses were frantic now, tongues battling wetly and both moaning into the kiss. Shannon felt Madison's tentative touch at her waist, felt the hand slide higher. Before Madison could touch her breast, Shannon pulled back, gasping for air.

"I should go," she said between breaths.

Without waiting for Madison's reply, she hurried to the door, not daring to look back at her.

CHAPTER SEVEN

"What a tease she was," Tracy said. "How did you stand it?"

Shannon pushed her dessert plate aside and literally rubbed her stomach. "That was so good, but I am stuffed," she said.

"We don't see you often enough," Tracy said as she brought the coffee carafe over to the table. "Were you in love with her?"

Shannon smiled. "I think I fell in love with her when I was ten."

"Do you feel like she manipulated you?" Charlotte asked.

"No. Believe me, I was a willing partner in everything."

"Yet she controlled it," she said.

"I assure you, dear Dr. Rimes, that the fact that I was making out with my best friend—at her bidding—since I was fourteen did not scar me. I never once thought she was manipulating me. Madison was as emotionally invested as I was. The difference was, I could accept that I was gay. She could not. She was predestined to not only date Stephen Cole, but to marry him as well."

"And was that something *you* accepted?"

Shannon stirred a little sugar into her coffee, thinking back to those times. "Yes, I accepted it. There were no options as far as Madison was concerned. Her mother had her life all neatly arranged to suit her. Madison had very little say in anything she did. I think that's why her time with me was so precious to her," she said. "It was the only thing she ever did that was her choice, the only thing that didn't have her mother's fingerprints all over it."

"But you didn't see each other that much, did you?" Tracy asked.

"No. Especially when we were in high school. Madison had so much going on, we were lucky to see each other once a week. Even then, we weren't always alone. My mother was always there, and if her mother was home, we didn't dare go to her room." Shannon smiled. "It was becoming very dangerous for us to be alone," she said. "We were like an inferno ready to explode."

"What about you?" Charlotte asked. "Did you have any friends? Did you have any after-school activities?"

"I had a few friends," she said. "I mean, I wasn't totally blind as to what was going on. I knew Madison and I had no future. I knew what my role was in her life. So I made some friends in high school. I did some of the normal things you do. I'd go to movies with them and hang out at the pizza place."

"But no one knew about Madison?"

"No. They knew where I lived, knew my mother worked for the Lansfords, that's it." Shannon shrugged. "I never told anyone I was gay."

"So when did you take things to the next level?" Tracy asked. "Since you didn't have much time together anymore, I mean."

Shannon sipped from her coffee, smiling slightly as she remembered the first time she'd touched Madison, the first time she held Madison as she climaxed.

"It was a Sunday. Her parents were at an estate auction and we had the afternoon. I was sixteen."

* * *

Shannon stood outside of Madison's door, trying to calm herself down. She was as nervous as she'd ever been. Two weeks had passed since she and Madison had been alone together and, even then, it was only for a few minutes. Not long, but long enough for them to kiss, to touch each other's breasts. There was nothing shy anymore about either of their touches. And today they would have hours together. Shannon actually trembled at the thought.

She took one more deep breath, then knocked on the door. It was opened immediately. Their eyes flew together, and she realized that Madison was as nervous as she was.

"I came as soon as I heard them drive off," she explained.

Madison took her hand and tugged her inside, closing the door behind her. And then she did something she'd never done before. She locked it.

When she turned back around, there was a look in her eyes that Shannon hadn't seen before. It didn't frighten her in the least.

"I want to lay down with you," Madison said.

Shannon nodded and let Madison lead her by the hand, following her into the bedroom. Shannon had no time to think as Madison's hands quickly pulled her shirt over her head. Warm hands shoved her bra aside, unclasping it and letting it fall to the floor. Shannon was trembling as she stood there, her eyes closed, and Madison's hot mouth closed over a nipple.

"God, Madison," she murmured.

Madison pulled away, then quickly removed her own blouse. She was not wearing a bra, and Shannon's knees felt weak.

"Lay down with me," Madison said. "I want you on top of me."

"Yes."

They had done this on the sofa before—many times—but never on the bed. The look in Madison's eyes told her today would be different. She kicked her shoes off before sitting on the edge of the bed. Madison scooted over, giving her room. Shannon's eyes traveled over her body, clad only in shorts. Her gaze settled on her breasts—breasts she now knew very well. Her mouth watered at the sight.

"Come here," Madison said quietly.

Shannon moved to her, supporting herself on her hands as she lowered her body to Madison's. Madison's legs parted, and Shannon sank between them, causing them both to moan softly as their breasts touched and then their mouths, their kisses long and slow. There was no need to hurry today. They had the afternoon to be together.

"I love the way you kiss me," Madison murmured as Shannon's lips moved across her face to her neck. She found the spot below Madison's ear that she loved to nuzzle, and Madison's hands traveled across her back to her hips, cupping her and pulling her tightly against her.

Shannon could feel the dampness in her shorts as she arched against Madison. She groaned, imagining Madison as wet as she was. She raised up on her arms, exposing Madison's breasts to her. She lowered her head, capturing a nipple firmly in her mouth. She loved the feel—the taste—of her breasts. She loved how Madison moaned when she suckled her, like she was doing now.

"You drive me crazy when you do that," Madison breathed.

"I love your breasts. They're perfect," Shannon whispered as she moved to her mouth again, her tongue moving past her lips with ease. When she pulled back, Madison was staring at her, her eyes as dark as she'd ever seen them.

"I want…I want you to touch me."

Shannon leaned on her elbow as she blinked stupidly at her. "Touch you?"

"Yes. Touch me." She took Shannon's hand and moved it between their bodies. "Touch me there."

Shannon groaned at the thought of touching Madison. She'd be lying if she said she hadn't fantasized about doing that very thing. In fact, she often touched herself, imagining that it was Madison she was stroking. But now…

"Don't you want to touch me?"

"God, yes," Shannon said. She shifted to her side, giving herself room. She could see her hand trembling as she moved it between Madison's legs. Before she even touched her, she could feel the heat between her thighs. "I want…I want to be inside your shorts… inside your panties too."

Madison's answer was to unbutton her shorts and slip the zipper down. Shannon didn't hesitate as her hand slid past the waistband of her panties, sliding across smooth skin. Madison's wetness coated her fingers and she moaned quietly, letting Madison draw her down for a kiss. She had touched herself before, she knew what felt good to her, but would Madison want that?

She pulled back from the kiss, staring into Madison's eyes. "You're really wet," she said.

Madison only nodded. Her lips were parted, and she was breathing as fast as Shannon was.

"Can I…do this?" she whispered as her fingers rubbed lightly across her swollen clit.

Madison jerked her hips in response. "Yes," she whispered. "That feels really good."

Shannon bent her head and, finding Madison's breast again, sucked her nipple into her mouth. The wet silkiness of Madison's arousal filled her hand, and she slid her fingers back and forth across her clit, stroking it fast like she did to herself. Madison was moaning loudly and Shannon left her breast to kiss her, trying to silence her. Even though she knew they were alone, she was still terrified of being caught.

Madison seemed to have no fear of that as she tore her mouth from Shannon's, gasping for breath as her hips moved wildly against Shannon's hand. Shannon shifted her weight, trying to hold Madison still as her fingers glided across her clit.

"Oh *God*, Shannon…please don't stop."

"Never," Shannon promised as she increased her tempo. All too soon Madison's hips lifted off the bed, and Shannon watched in awe as her body convulsed. She covered her mouth again, catching Madison's scream just in time. She pressed her fingers hard against her, causing Madison to whimper as her legs clamped tightly together.

Madison went limp on the bed, and Shannon slowly pulled her hand out from her shorts. She brushed Madison's nipples with her damp fingers, watching as they hardened immediately. Madison's eyes were closed, and her chest rose and fell quickly with each breath. Without thinking of what she was doing, Shannon lowered her head to her breasts, her tongue swirling around each nipple. The musky taste of Madison's passion that she'd painted there almost caused her to climax right then as she cleaned both nipples. She felt Madison's hands pushing at her, and she stopped, pulling away guiltily.

"I want to touch you like that."

Shannon groaned as Madison's words sunk in. She nodded mutely and rolled to her back. The hungry look in Madison's eyes thrilled her, and she unbuttoned her shorts, giving Madison room.

"I've never had an orgasm before," Madison admitted as her mouth trailed across Shannon's breasts. "Have you?"

"Yes."

Madison paused, and Shannon recognized the hurt look in her eyes. "When? With who?"

Shannon smiled. "With myself."

"You touch yourself?"

"Sometimes. I think about you and I touch myself," she said.

"And...and that makes you have an orgasm?"

Shannon nodded. "I've wanted to touch you for so long now."

"Why didn't you?"

"I didn't know if you wanted me to."

"I did." Madison stared into her eyes as her hand drifted lower. "And I want to touch you."

Shannon's eyes slammed shut as she felt Madison's fingers brush through her damp curls for the first time. Like she'd done, Madison found her clit. She touched it lightly, enough to make Shannon's hips jerk in response.

"Like that?" Madison asked as she stroked her.

"Yes, like that," Shannon managed through her ragged breath. She wanted to make it last, but she was about to explode. She felt it deep in her belly, building like a giant wave. As soon as Madison's tongue touched her nipple, the wave crashed down on her. She grabbed Madison's hand and held it tightly against her as her hips arched into it. She bit down on her lip to keep from screaming out in pleasure.

She released Madison's hand, but Madison didn't remove it. Instead, she lay down beside her, resting her head on Shannon's shoulder as they tried to catch their breaths.

"That was so much better than when I do it myself," she admitted with a smile.

"I'm glad."

Shannon closed her eyes, daring to ask the one question that haunted her. "Do you let Stephen touch you like that?"

Madison shook her head. "No. I don't let him do much of anything. He wants to, though." Madison turned to look at her. "I don't want him to. It doesn't feel the same with him. It doesn't feel like much of anything with him."

"What does it feel like with me?"

Madison smiled. "Fire. A hot, wonderful fire."

CHAPTER EIGHT

"Oh, my," Tracy said as she fanned herself. "Is it hot in here?"

Shannon laughed. "You wanted to know."

"As I said earlier, this is the *best* first-time story I've ever heard."

"What would have happened had you gotten caught?" Charlotte asked.

Shannon's smile faded. "Her mother would have killed me."

"What about your mother?"

Shannon's smile returned. "My mother would have killed me." She nodded at Tracy who silently asked if she wanted more coffee.

"I think it's romantic," Tracy said.

"Romantic? Raging hormones at sixteen? I don't know how romantic it was," Shannon said. "Neither of us knew what we were doing."

"You apparently learned quickly," Charlotte said with a laugh. "I suppose this was before you could just Google anything you wanted to know."

"Twenty years ago? Yeah. We were on our own."

"But Stephen was still in the picture. How did you reconcile that?"

"It was what it was. Stephen was always in the picture. I knew my place. Despite what I may have wanted for us, I knew it could never be."

"What do you think she wanted for the two of you?"

Shannon looked at Charlotte thoughtfully. "I thought you said you weren't going to put me on your couch, Dr. Rimes."

Charlotte smiled. "Sorry. I just find your story very intriguing. I'm surprised you were able to handle it as well as you did at that age."

"Like I said, I knew what my role was in her life. Yes, I was in love with her. Madly. She was in love with me too. But that was as far as it could go. We had no future. Hers was already planned out. We had stolen moments, that's all."

"That's so sad," Tracy said.

"Yes. It was difficult. I tried not to think about her dates with Stephen and what she was doing. I no longer asked. I didn't want to know."

"So who did she lose her virginity to? You or Stephen?"

Shannon remembered that night well. It was one of those special memories she would carry with her always. "Me. It was a Saturday. I was seventeen."

* * *

It was a rare occasion that they had the mansion to themselves. Well, except for George, but he would never come up to Madison's room. Her mother was at a baby shower, and the Lansfords had left early that morning for an overnight trip to Chicago. She and Madison hadn't had much alone time in the last two weeks, and she missed their closeness. She was looking forward to spending the day with her. When she knocked on her door all she heard was a mumbled "come in" from the other side.

"Madison?"

"In here."

She headed to the bedroom, surprised to find her curled on the bed, a tissue clutched in her hand. Shannon stopped in her tracks, seeing tears in Madison's eyes.

"What's wrong?"

Madison rolled onto her back and patted the space beside her. Shannon sat down, her eyes searching Madison's for a clue to explain the tears.

"I went out with Stephen last night."

Shannon nodded. "I know."

"He wants to have sex."

Shannon looked away, knowing this day would come. She had a difficult time swallowing as her throat was choked with jealousy. "I'm surprised he's waited this long," she said honestly.

"He hasn't exactly been waiting patiently. I know I'm going to have to, but God, I don't want to," she said, tears again forming in her eyes.

"Then don't," Shannon said. "Break up with him."

"Oh, Shannon, you know I can't do that. After all these years, you know how it is."

"It's your life, Madison, not your mother's. Why do you allow her to control everything? It's like college? Why there?"

Madison smiled sadly. "Ivy League. There was never a doubt— or a choice—as to where I would go."

Shannon stood and paced, running her hands through her hair. "So Stephen wants to sleep with you."

Madison got out of bed and went to her, stopping her pacing. She wrapped her arms around her and Shannon sunk into her embrace.

"I can't stand the thought of him touching you," she murmured. "I know."

They held tightly to each other, their bodies as close as possible, every inch pressed together. Shannon closed her eyes, breathing in Madison's familiar scent. Her lips traveled slowly across Madison's neck, stopping below her ear. She was rewarded with a quiet sigh.

Madison pulled back, meeting her gaze with one equally intense. "I want...I want you to be my...first. I want you to be... inside me, not him."

Shannon couldn't look away. For all they'd done in the past two years—the kissing, the touching, the exploring—she'd never been inside Madison. She knew every inch of her body, but she'd never been inside her. Just as Madison had not touched her that way. It was something they never talked about. But so many times—when Shannon's fingers were coated with her wetness—she wanted to slip those fingers inside her, to make love to her that way. Many times she'd come close to asking but had always pulled back, taking what Madison had offered and nothing more.

Now, Madison was offering more.

"Are you sure?"

"You've been my first for everything, Shannon. Besides, we've done everything to each other *but* that."

Shannon nodded. It was true. Her hands—and even her mouth—had been everywhere on Madison's body, everywhere but buried inside her. The thought of making love to Madison like that made her legs tremble. She drew Madison to her again, kissing her slowly, thoroughly, drawing a moan from her as her hand cupped her breast, her thumb raking across her nipple. Feeling in control again, she led Madison to the bed. She could see a hint of nervousness in her eyes and smiled reassuringly at her.

"I'm as nervous as you are."

Madison smiled too. "Good."

They undressed each other, hands fumbling with buttons and zippers, eliciting quiet laughs from them both. Madison drew the covers back on the bed and pulled Shannon with her. This was what Shannon loved—being completely naked and touching—something they rarely had the opportunity for. Quick, stolen moments were all they usually could afford.

Not today. Today they had to themselves. Today they would hold nothing back.

"I love the way this feels," Madison murmured against her lips as their kiss ended. "I love being with you like this."

Shannon bent lower, capturing a nipple with her mouth. Madison's breasts were very sensitive and she knew just how to please her as her tongue flicked across the tip. Madison held her tighter as her hips began a slow, familiar roll. As always, the fire between them sprang to life. Shannon held her weight on her hands, letting their lower bodies move together. Madison's hands roamed across her back, settling on her hips and guiding Shannon more firmly between her legs.

"Kiss me."

Shannon did as she was asked, taking Madison's mouth in a wet, hot kiss, her tongue circling Madison's as they dueled. She broke off the kiss, going back to Madison's breast instead. She was hungry for her—all of her—and she moved down her body, her lips trailing a path to the spot she loved most. Madison loved it too. She was already moaning, her thighs spread invitingly for her.

Shannon parted her, her tongue slicing through the wetness she knew she'd find. She hummed with pleasure at her first taste, her eyes slipping shut as her mouth closed over her swollen clit. As she'd done with her nipple, she sucked it into her mouth, causing Madison's hips to jerk against her face. She held her down, feasting on her, feeling Madison's hands in her hair, holding her in place.

"Oh *God...Shannon.*"

When she felt Madison's thighs trembling around her face, she pulled back. Madison whimpered, her hands urging Shannon back between her legs. But Shannon sat up, entering her with two fingers, feeling the tightness of Madison's walls closing around her.

Their eyes met, each holding the other captive. Shannon paused, then plunged deep inside her. She felt only a little resistance as she entered her, then Madison opened fully, reaching for Shannon.

Shannon went into her arms, using her hips to guide her hand now, pulling out slowly then entering again. Madison was panting in her ear, holding her tight as her hips matched the rhythm Shannon set.

In and out, her fingers glided with ease, each stroke going deeper inside of her as Madison met each thrust.

"Yes...*yes.* God, *Shannon—*"

Shannon turned her head, finding Madison's ear. With her tongue, she mimicked her fingers, in and out, loving the sounds of pleasure Madison freely voiced. Her hips rocked against her hand, shoving her fingers deeper inside of her, faster now, trying to keep up with Madison's frantic movements. Madison's hips arched high, and Shannon felt her muscles contract, felt her fingers sucked tightly inside of her. Madison screamed out, her hips jerking once, then again and again, before sinking limply down.

Shannon was breathing heavily from her exertion, and she kissed Madison's face, her neck, their bodies damp with perspiration. She shifted, intending to pull her fingers from Madison, but Madison stopped her, her hand resting on top of Shannon's.

"Not yet. I want to feel you inside me."

"Did I hurt you?" Shannon whispered.

"No." Madison turned her head, her gaze settling on Shannon's. "I love you."

Shannon felt tears sting her eyes. Those were three words they had never said to one another. Shannon's heart nearly burst as Madison said them to her now.

"I love you too."

CHAPTER NINE

"Oh my God. I'm in love with you guys," Tracy said.

Shannon settled back on the sofa, balancing her coffee cup on her thigh. "It was a special day," Shannon admitted.

"And did she reciprocate?" Charlotte asked.

Shannon smiled. "We spent three uninterrupted hours in bed that day. I'm amazed either of us could walk the next day."

"How in the world did you keep your affair from her mother? And your mother, for that matter?" Tracy asked.

"I guess they were simply blind to it. I'm sure when we looked at each other it was written all over our faces."

"What about Stephen?" Charlotte asked. "I'm assuming she eventually slept with him."

Shannon felt the familiar stab of jealousy, even after all of these years. She nodded, almost afraid to speak. She cleared her throat first, swallowing down her jealousy.

"She had sex with him, yes. Not often," she said. "Enough."

"How do you know not often?"

"Because she told me."

"And you believed her?" Charlotte asked.

"Madison never lied to me about anything. Like I said earlier, I knew what my role was."

"You were in love with each other," Tracy said. "How could she let Stephen touch her?"

"I know it's hard for you to understand," she said. "And now that I'm older—wiser—I realize how dangerous it was for us. Emotionally dangerous, I mean. Madison was someone I couldn't resist—ever. And as I knew my role, she knew hers. And her role was playing the part that Candice Lansford had made for her. That included dating—and sleeping with—Stephen Cole. But Madison had the same problem I did," she said.

"Which was?"

"She couldn't resist me either."

"So you were what? Seniors in high school then?"

"Yes. That was in the fall. We didn't have another chance to be alone like that until the holidays. She was busy with Stephen and her friends, with parties, with events at the country club. Her mother switched her from tennis lessons to golf so a lot of Saturdays when we used to find time to be together were spent on the golf course." She shrugged. "I had a couple of good friends from school that I hung out with. It helped keep my mind occupied, if nothing else."

"It must have been terribly lonely for you," Charlotte said.

Shannon glanced at her. "I could have surrounded myself with a hundred people and it wouldn't have mattered."

"Oh, sweetie, how did you cope?"

"I'm not sure," she said to Tracy. "Our senior year, it just crawled by, yet it passed so quickly. College was looming and I knew our separation was near. She was headed off to her fancy Ivy League school and I was destined to start my career at the community college. It was all we could afford."

"But you said you went to—"

"Yeah. The university." She smiled at the memory. "Because of my tutoring Madison, Mr. Lansford set up an account for me. He didn't tell my mother. He certainly never told his wife. He took care of everything. Got me admitted, got me a scholarship, everything. When he signed over the account to my mother, it was the first time I'd seen her cry since my father died."

"Oh, wow. That's awesome."

"I never told Madison. He asked me not to, and even though there were no other secrets between us, I did keep that from her. I think she would have been proud of him for doing that, but I honored his wish."

"Did you get any more time together?" Charlotte asked.

"Not much. We had this graduation party. It was the weekend before our last day. Madison's class had a party that same night too. Both parties kinda ended up at this one guy's house. My friends were going so I went over there too." She looked at them. "It was the first time I met Stephen. I was eighteen."

* * *

The spiked punch was sweet and Shannon took a big swallow, enjoying the taste. Loud music blared from the living room, and she followed Angie back outside to the patio where it was a little quieter. There, she felt eyes on her and she turned. She was stunned to find Madison watching her. She pulled her gaze from Madison, looking at the handsome boy beside her who had his arm around her waist. She clenched her jaw, then turned away, not wanting to see them together.

"Listen, I'm going back inside," she told Angie.

"I thought you hated the music?"

"Gotta pee," she lied. She turned to go, then stopped when she heard her name called. She turned slowly around, facing Madison again.

"I didn't know you would be here," Madison said. Shannon could tell the smile she offered was forced.

"Me either. Our other party broke up, and my friends drug me to this one."

"Hey, how do you know her?" Stephen leaned closer. "I don't think I've seen you before."

"This is Shannon Fletcher," Madison said. "She...she lives... she—"

Shannon took pity on Madison's attempt not to embarrass her. She squared her shoulders and looked at Stephen. "My mother Alice works for the Lansfords. I live there."

"Oh. The hired help," he said dismissively. "Will that be your profession as well?"

"Stephen!" Madison said loudly. "That's so rude. Shannon is valedictorian of her class. She can do anything she wants to do."

"Whatever. Let's go inside where our friends are. I didn't realize the *public* school was invited."

Madison jerked her arm away from him. "Go on. I'll be there in a minute."

Shannon turned away from the kiss he gave her, feeling sick to her stomach. Then a warm hand touched her arm, guiding her off the patio and into the yard.

"I'm sorry, Shannon. He's a jerk."

"Doesn't matter."

"It does matter. I don't like him talking about you like that, and I don't like him talking about your mother."

"It is what it is, Madison. My mom works for your family. She's a servant," she said. "To people like Stephen, servants have their place and it's not socializing at a party with people like him."

"Stop it, Shannon. Don't ever belittle your mother or yourself." Madison moved closer to her, her voice quiet. "You're the best person I know. I love you."

As always, those words made her heart swell. She looked into Madison's eyes, seeing the truth there. "I love you too," she whispered.

Madison squeezed her hand. "Let's go home."

"What? But he'll—"

"I don't care. Let's go home. I haven't…touched you in so long." Her voice lowered to barely a whisper. "I want to make love to you."

Chills spread across Shannon's body at the fiery look in Madison's eyes. She tossed her cup of punch down on the grass and took Madison's hand, leading her around the side of the house and out onto the street. Her mother's car was parked a block down, and they ran for it. Once inside, Madison reached for her, finding her mouth, kissing her hard and fast.

"Hurry."

Shannon fumbled with the keys, finally starting the car and darting out into the street. It was the first time they'd ridden together, and she slowed, wanting to enjoy this time alone. Madison seemed to understand. She moved closer, her hand rubbing lightly on Shannon's thigh.

"Your parents are home, aren't they?"

"I think so."

They looked at each other, and Shannon raised an eyebrow. Did Madison expect her to sneak into her room with her parents there?

"Let's go parking," Madison said.

Shannon laughed. "Love's Lookout?"

"There shouldn't be many there. Everyone's at graduation parties tonight." Madison's hand moved between her legs and Shannon parted them. "I want to make love to you," Madison said again.

"I'm going to have a wreck if you keep doing that," she warned, hoping Madison wouldn't stop.

"I can feel how wet you are," Madison said as her fingers traced the seam of her jeans. "I can't wait to touch you."

Shannon gripped the steering wheel tighter as Madison pressed against her clit. "Madison...please."

"Please what?"

Shannon raised her hips. "Touch me now."

Madison's fingers made quick work of her button and zipper, easily slipping her hand inside her jeans and panties. Shannon spread her legs, moaning when Madison touched her.

"God, you're so wet," Madison said as she unbuckled her seat belt, scooting closer. Her mouth assaulted Shannon's ear and Shannon moaned again, finding it hard to focus on driving. "Are we there yet?" Madison murmured in her ear. "I want to be inside you."

"The hell with it," Shannon said, pulling over to the side of the street and killing the lights. She pushed the seat back as far as it would go, then slid her jeans down, giving Madison room. Her hips jerked as two fingers entered her. She turned her head, their tongues entwining as they kissed. Madison knew just how to touch her. Her thumb bumped her clit each time she entered her, faster and faster now, and Shannon panted into each stroke, feeling her orgasm build with rapid speed.

Madison's mouth went back to her ear, her breathing fast. "Come for me," she whispered. Her tongue bathed her ear. "I wish my mouth was on you. I wish I was licking you like this."

Shannon exploded in a sea of color, blinding her as she pressed Madison's hand hard against her.

"Good *God*," she groaned hoarsely.

"I love you, Shannon. Don't ever forget that."

CHAPTER TEN

"God, woman," Tracy said with a laugh. "In a car parked on the street?"

"Stolen moments wherever we could find them."

"And Stephen was none the wiser?" Charlotte asked.

"Stephen was pissed as hell," she said with a smile. She set her empty coffee cup on the side table, wondering why she was traveling down memory lane this evening, sharing intimate details of her life, details she'd not told another living soul.

"Do you really think you'll run into her if you go back to Brook Hill?" Tracy asked.

Shannon shrugged. "It's not so much that I might run into her, it's the fact that she's there. Each time I go there, I vow I won't see her. Each time, I do. After the last time, I told her I couldn't do it anymore. Each time I left her, I was an emotional wreck."

"So your answer is to stay away?" Charlotte asked.

"That seems to be my only means of resistance to her."

"The fact that she would be with you while supposedly being committed to Stephen disturbs me," Charlotte said. "She was obviously in love with you, yet her commitment was to him, not you."

"Dr. Rimes, the commitment she made was to marry him, not to love him."

"And you were in too deep to put an end to the affair?"

"I tried. The summer before college was a whirlwind and we rarely saw each other. Stolen moments here and there, but we never had enough time alone to really be together. She was gone a lot that summer and when she moved away, I barely got to say goodbye to her. We weren't alone and it was awkward for us. I cried that night after she left," she admitted. "That's when I decided I needed a change. I stayed in the dorm that first year. I made friends. I even had a girlfriend," she said with a smile. "And I stayed away. When Madison would be home, for whatever reason, I'd make up an excuse as to why I couldn't go home. Thanksgiving. Christmas. I stayed away if Madison was home."

"You were so young. That must have been hard," Tracy said.

"Oh, yeah. It was hard. And I was lonely. But I knew if I was ever going to get on with my life, I had to do it. Madison was obviously getting on with hers."

"So you didn't call or write? Nothing?"

Shannon shook her head. "No. Our *affair*, as you called it, Charlotte, was simply that. A secret affair."

"So when did you see her again?"

"It was the holidays. I had asked my mother if she knew when Madison was going to be there. I was fully prepared to spend my third Christmas alone. I had a job at Whole Foods that was flexible, but I could always use that as an excuse." She glanced at Charlotte. "My mother was smarter than I thought and apparently she figured out I was avoiding Madison."

"So she lied to you?"

"Yes. I went home a couple of days before Christmas, thinking I would spend time with her. I was even intending on staying a little longer because Jarod was on leave. We only saw him once a year or so as it was. So I had it all planned out." She smiled, remembering seeing Madison standing at the top of the stairs. "I was twenty."

* * *

"Hey, Mom, I'm home," she called, looking around the large kitchen and seeing no one. She would have thought her mother would have been preparing dinner already. She turned, heading down the familiar short hallway to their rooms when she heard the door open at the top of the stairs. She stopped and glanced up, shocked to see Madison staring back at her. How many times had that happened? Madison standing at the top of the stairs like a goddess, beckoning her?

"Shannon…"

Shannon nodded. "Hi."

Madison came down and Shannon's heart started hammering in her chest as she let her backpack fall to the floor. It had been over two and a half years since she'd seen her. The girl she'd fallen in love with had grown into a beautiful woman. Her long blond hair was a little shorter, just reaching her shoulders, but her blue eyes were as intense as ever.

Shannon was rooted to the spot as Madison came closer, unable to pull her gaze from Madison's. Then Madison was there, hands sliding up her arms and around her neck. Shannon's hands slipped around her waist and settled into her hug. She breathed in her familiar scent and, just like that, two years were forgotten as their bodies reunited.

"I missed you so much," Madison whispered into her ear.

"I missed you too."

"We need to talk."

Shannon pulled back, out of her arms. "There's not really anything to talk about, is there?" She was shocked to see tears in Madison's eyes.

"I'm getting married."

It was like a blow to the chest. Shannon took a step away. "*Married?*"

"They're announcing it at the Christmas dinner party tomorrow."

It wasn't like she didn't know this day was coming, but still, it was a knife to her heart. She finally nodded. "I hope…I hope you'll be very happy," she said as she picked up her backpack.

"Shannon, please…"

"Please what? You're getting married."

"I need to talk. I need…you."

Shannon shook her head. "I can't do this. I can't be your friend. I can't…listen while you talk about Stephen and getting married. I can't do it." She met Madison's teary stare with one of her own. "It hurts me."

"I know, Shannon. I know it hurts. It hurts me too." She took a step toward her. "Please, I need to talk."

Before Shannon could reply, the door opened to their rooms and her mother came out. They each took a step back, separating themselves.

"Shannon! You're home." Her mother smiled broadly, then glanced at Madison. "And Madison, you too. So good to see you again." She hugged them both. "You look more beautiful every time I see you."

"Thank you, Alice."

If her mother noticed the tension between them—or the tears—she made no acknowledgment of it. For that, Shannon was thankful.

"I'm sure you girls have a lot of catching up to do. Why don't you go out to the gazebo? I don't think a single soul has used it since you girls left for college."

Madison looked at her with raised eyebrows, and Shannon reluctantly agreed. They were silent as they walked out, the only sound the crunching of the winter-dead grass. The gazebo's boards creaked with their weight. Shannon took her normal spot facing away from the house. Madison continued to stand, looking out across the lawn.

"Are you dating anyone?"

Shannon was surprised by the question. "I go out. I date," she said.

Madison turned around to face her. "Girls?"

Shannon gave a short laugh. "Yes, Madison. Girls. I'm gay. That's what you do. You date girls. You don't go out and get married to a guy."

Madison held her gaze. "I don't want to marry him. I don't love him, you know that."

"Then why are you doing this?"

"Oh, Shannon, come on, you know how it is. You know how it's always been. There's no choice. There's never been a choice."

"You always have a choice. It's your life."

"Is it? The only part of my life that's *my* life is when I'm with you," she said, her voice hoarse with unshed tears.

Shannon felt tears in her own eyes and blinked them away. Madison again turned her back to Shannon and wrapped her arms around herself as if warding off the winter chill.

"I can't do this. I don't want to marry him. I'm dreading it." Madison wiped at her face, her tears falling now. "They want to do it in the summer. I'll be twenty-one, just out of school."

"They?"

Madison turned around, her eyes damp. "My mother. Stephen's mother. They have it all planned."

"What does Stephen say about it?"

Madison's quick laugh was bitter. "He thinks if we get married I'll want to have sex with him more often." Madison looked her straight in the eyes, whispering, "I can't stand his touch." She looked away, staring out toward the mansion. "I just go through the motions. I know he can tell. I just can't do it." She looked back at Shannon. "I want it to be you. I always want it to be you."

Shannon brushed her own tears away. "Then put a stop to it. End it. You and me, we can go somewhere, we can—"

"What? Run away?" Madison shook her head. "We're a little old for that, aren't we?"

"We'll be out of school soon. We can start a life together," she pleaded.

"You don't think they'd find us? They would drag me back here. They would never allow it."

"Allow? Madison, you'll be twenty-one. What are they going to do?"

"That's not how it works. You know that. Do you really think my mother and father would let it rest if I left home? If I went somewhere that they didn't plan? Did something on my own? With another woman? Do you think they would really allow that?" She shook her head. "That's not how it works."

She finally sat down, close to Shannon. "The others, Stephanie and Tamara, they don't mind the control. They're happy planning weddings, planning when they're going to have children, planning their children's lives, like our parents did with us. It's just one big cycle." She tried to smile. "They can't understand why I'm not excited about it. I can't talk to them. I can't even relate to them." She paused, her hands twisting together nervously. She finally looked up with pleading eyes. "Please, Shannon, I've got to be with you," she whispered. "Shannon, please?"

Shannon felt the familiar tug at her heart. She couldn't resist Madison. She never could. She didn't know why she was even attempting to. Two years of trying to get Madison out of her mind, out of her heart, vanished in a heartbeat. She nodded.

Madison nodded too, relief showing in her eyes. "My parents are going to a Christmas party tonight. I'm supposed to meet Stephanie for dinner. I'll cancel." She cleared her throat. "I've got to be with you."

"I'll…I'll come up to your room after they leave."

The walk back to the house was also made in silence, but it was a different silence than before. Their arms brushed as they walked, shoulders bumped, glances coming together then away. The fire between them spread with each step. They parted in the kitchen, silently acknowledging the flames that surrounded them. After more than two years without Madison's touch, Shannon was starved for her.

She tried to make dinner as normal as possible, chatting with her mother about school and her job at Whole Foods. She took that opportunity to mention to her mother about her change in diet.

"I love your cooking," she said, "but after the holidays, I'm going vegetarian."

Her mother raised her eyebrows. "You're what?"

"Vegetarian. You know, no meat."

"I know what it means, Shannon. I'm wondering why."

"Well, because I'm exposed to it. Most of the people who work there are vegetarians or vegans," she said. "It's healthier and better for the environment. And for the animals, of course."

Her mother smiled at her but said nothing.

"What?"

"Nothing. It's just, well, you're all grown up now."

"I wouldn't say *all* grown up," Shannon said with a laugh. She wiped her mouth with a napkin before drinking from her glass of tea. She looked at her mother thoughtfully. "I thought you said Madison wasn't going to be here until after Christmas."

"I must have been mistaken," she said innocently.

"Uh-huh," Shannon said.

"I know it's none of my business, Shannon, but I couldn't help but notice that you seem to avoid coming home if Madison is going to be here. You two were so close growing up. Did you have a falling out?"

Shannon couldn't meet her mother's questioning gaze. "Not really," she said. "We just have different friends, different schools." She shrugged. "You know," she said evasively.

"You grew apart?"

"Something like that."

Her mother looked like she wanted to ask another question but apparently thought better of it. Shannon was relieved.

"Well, maybe you two can reconnect over the holidays then," she said.

Shannon nodded. "Yeah. I'm going to go up later. We're going to…watch a movie."

"It'll be just like old times then."

Shannon offered to help her mother clean up, but she shooed her away. "The Lansfords have already left. Why don't you go spend time with Madison?"

"Okay. Thanks, Mom. I won't stay up there too late," she said as she headed for the stairs. She had to stop herself from jogging up. Once inside the main house, she took the stairs two at a time up to Madison's floor. She paused to catch her breath before using her childhood knock—two quick taps, then three slower ones. The door was opened immediately.

There was no preamble, no conversation. As soon as the door closed, Shannon pulled Madison to her. They moaned when their lips met, mouths opening to each other after all this time. She spun Madison around, pinning her against the wall. Her hands slid under her shirt, pleasantly surprised to find no bra.

"Oh, Shannon…"

"You feel so good," Shannon murmured as she cupped her breasts. They were fuller than she remembered; they fit perfectly in her hands. Madison's nipples turned rock hard as her thumbs rubbed across them.

"Please take me to bed. I need to be with you," Madison whispered as she pulled her mouth from Shannon's.

But Shannon wouldn't be rushed—it had been too long. She tugged Madison's shirt over her head, her gaze fixed on her breasts. She bent lower, capturing a nipple with her lips, sighing in pleasure as Madison's fingers threaded through her hair, holding her tight against her.

"God, I've missed you," Madison said, releasing her enough so that Shannon could move to her other breast.

Shannon slowly kissed her way up, pausing to nibble below her ear, knowing what it did to Madison. Her lips found their way to her mouth again, and Madison opened to her, her tongue drawing Shannon's inside. Impatient hands fumbled with her jeans and Shannon stepped back, helping Madison unbutton them.

"Bed," Madison said again.

This time Shannon heeded her request, leading her into the bedroom. They undressed quickly, then Madison pulled Shannon with her to the bed. Shannon paused, her eyes taking in every glorious detail of Madison's body, a body she used to know so well.

"You're even more beautiful than I remembered," she said quietly. She looked up, falling into the blue eyes she'd missed so much. "So beautiful," she murmured again.

"Make love to me," Madison whispered. "I need you to make love to me."

"Yes…anything you want," Shannon said as she parted Madison's legs with her thigh and settled between them. "Anything."

She moved down her body, feeling Madison's wetness coat her stomach. Madison's hands urged her downward, her hips rising up, telling Shannon where she needed her. Shannon kissed her breasts, moving lower, her tongue tracing a pattern across her skin, lower still until she met the intoxicating scent of Madison's arousal. She parted her with her hand, exposing her to her greedy eyes. She was moaning before she even tasted her, her tongue slicing through her boldly before twirling around her swollen clit.

"God...*yes*," Madison hissed as her hips rose up to meet Shannon.

Shannon took her quickly, feasting as if she'd been starving without her, her tongue moving with lightning quickness across her clit, pausing when she sensed Madison's impending orgasm. She slipped her tongue deep inside her, feeling Madison's thighs tighten against her head.

"Shannon...*please*," Madison begged.

Shannon went back to her clit, teasing her, back and forth, Madison writhing beneath her. She finally relented, sucking Madison's clit hard inside her mouth, holding it tightly, knowing just how much pressure to use. Madison's hips jerked off the bed and Shannon pressed her back down, holding her as she climaxed.

"Dear *God*," Madison murmured as her body relaxed, her legs going limp. "Come up here," she whispered, pulling Shannon into her arms.

Shannon lay beside her, letting Madison hold her. She closed her eyes, absorbing all that was Madison.

"I love you," Madison whispered.

Shannon squeezed her eyes tighter. The words were bittersweet, but she couldn't help but return them. It was the truth.

"I love you too."

Madison rolled them over, resting her weight on top of Shannon. Shannon's eyes remained closed as Madison kissed her, her mouth traveling lower to her breasts. Shannon hadn't had many lovers. She tried. But as Madison had said earlier, it was like going through the motions. No one touched her—body and soul— the way Madison did. She reveled in it now as Madison's tongue bathed her nipple.

"You're so soft," Madison said, her lips trailing back up to Shannon's mouth. "I've missed you so much, Shannon. I think about you all the time."

"Me too," Shannon admitted.

Madison pulled back, staring into her eyes. "How many lovers have you had?"

"A few. Not many," Shannon said.

"Is it like this with them?"

"No. It's never like this with anyone else."

"Do you think of me when you're making love to them?"

"Yes."

Madison's hand moved between their bodies, pausing only a second before slipping between Shannon's thighs.

"And do they make you this wet?" she whispered.

Shannon shuddered as Madison's finger rubbed lightly across her clit. "No," she gasped, spreading her legs, giving Madison more room.

"Do you want me inside you?"

"Yes."

Madison slipped two fingers inside her and Shannon moaned at the contact, her hips rising up to meet her. Madison kissed her again, her tongue tracing her lower lip before sneaking inside her mouth. Shannon's tongue curled around it.

"Do you want my tongue inside you?"

"God, *yes*," Shannon murmured.

After two more quick strokes, Madison's fingers left her, replaced with her tongue. Shannon moaned when she felt it slip inside her, and she grabbed Madison's head, pressing her tightly against her.

"Feels so good. So good," she whispered.

Madison's hands cupped her hips as she settled between her legs, her tongue moving now over her clit, stroking it quickly, knowingly. Shannon's head fell back, mouth open as she gasped for breath, her hips rolling against Madison's tongue. She jerked up sharply when Madison sucked her clit into her mouth.

"Madison...*God*," she breathed. "*Yes*. Harder..."

Shannon's hands thrashed as Madison's lips and tongue seemed to be everywhere at once. She nearly lifted off the bed when her orgasm hit, ripping through her, and she swore she saw stars. Before she could recover, Madison's fingers filled her again, plunging deep inside.

"I need to be inside you," Madison said as she claimed her mouth again.

Shannon gave in to her demands, their tongues battling as Madison's fingers pumped inside of her. Shannon reached between them. "Let me touch you too," she said, finding Madison wet and ready.

Madison parted her thighs as Shannon slipped inside her. Madison lowered herself, burying Shannon's fingers deeper. Their eyes held as they moved against each other, slowly at first, enjoying the contact, then faster, both of them panting as they pleasured the other.

"God...*Shannon*," Madison gasped. "So good...so good."

Shannon couldn't speak as she climaxed. She turned her head into the pillow, trying not to cry out. Two, three more thrusts and Madison climaxed as well, her mouth covering Shannon's to muffle her scream.

"I love you," Shannon whispered, her arms circling Madison and holding her tightly. "I love you."

She felt Madison shaking, felt wetness at her neck from Madison's tears. Shannon closed her eyes, tears falling from her eyes too.

"I love you, Shannon," Madison murmured against her neck. "I'll always love you."

CHAPTER ELEVEN

"Oh my God," Tracy said. "My heart is breaking for you."

Shannon nodded. "It was hard. And my heart broke that night. She was getting married."

"I assume you weren't invited to the wedding," Charlotte said.

"No. My social standing didn't merit an invitation by Mrs. Lansford. Do you really think I would have gone if I had been invited?"

"Did you try to talk her out of it?" Tracy asked. "You two were so in love. It's tragic."

"The wheels were in motion. Madison had no say in it. She went back to school after the break, and I took the opportunity to visit my mother quite often. As soon as I graduated though, I knew Madison would be coming back home. Her mother had spent the whole spring planning and preparing for the big event," she said.

"That's when you started avoiding Brook Hill?" Charlotte asked.

"Yes. Once Madison returned, I never went back. I talked to my mother about a week before the wedding, and she said Madison had 'pre-marital jitters,' I think is the term she used. Her moods went from unresponsive to hysterical bouts of crying."

"Oh God. Why didn't she just tell them no," Tracy said. "It's such a waste."

"I almost broke down, I almost went to her. I knew she was suffering. I knew I could calm her. But in the end I couldn't bring myself to go. The emotional scar was going to be too much."

"Were you still working at Whole Foods?"

"Yeah. After I graduated, I stayed on. I loved it. Loved the atmosphere. And at that point, I still didn't have a clue as to what I wanted with my life. It would be another six or seven years before Jarod retired from the military and we opened our first store. Back then, I was just trying to get over Madison and get on with my life. My career took a backseat to all of that."

"Did you ever have a steady girlfriend?" Charlotte asked. "One that you could commit to?"

"Are you morphing into Dr. Rimes again?"

"Have you ever had therapy for this situation?"

Shannon shook her head. "Are you suggesting I need it?"

"You're nearly thirty-eight years old and you've never been in a serious relationship. Your mother is a cancer patient, yet you avoid going to her aid because you still fear a woman you fell in love with when you were a teenager." She smiled quickly. "You think?"

"Once my mother retired and moved to her own place, I went to see her. I do go there still. I just don't stay for days at a time like Jarod does."

"For fear of running into Madison."

"Yes. I don't think that means I need therapy," she said.

"Are you still in love with her?" Tracy asked.

"No," she said quickly, but one look into their eyes told her they knew she was lying. "I've convinced myself that I'm not," she amended. "That has nothing to do with me never being in a serious relationship. I've just never met anyone who…well, who I've fallen in love with."

"How long was it before you saw her again?"

"Nearly two years. It was October. My mother's birthday. I wanted to surprise her. Madison obviously didn't live there with her parents, so I thought I could make a quick trip down, take my mother out for a birthday dinner and leave early the next day. I was twenty-two."

* * *

"It's so good to see you," her mother said, squeezing her tightly in a hug. "I was beginning to think you would never return to Brook Hill."

"It's hard to get away," she said. "Besides, we talk on the phone several times a week."

"That's not the same." Her mother stood back, inspecting her. "Your hair looks good short like that," she said, brushing her fingers through it. "You're so attractive. You look just like your father."

Shannon blushed, pleased her mother thought so.

"Well, do you want to stay here and visit or get an early dinner?"

"Let's go out," she said. "You don't have to be around here for dinner, right?"

"No, no. Stella does all the cooking now." Her mother grinned. "I coordinate."

Shannon smiled back at her, knowing her mother loved her new role. "We'll go someplace nice," she said. "You want to change?"

"Yes. I was wondering why you were so dressed up. I don't think I've seen you in anything but jeans since you were twelve." Her mother guided her to the door. "Why don't you go visit with George? You haven't seen him in years, have you?"

"No, I haven't."

"He was working the flower beds around the gazebo. I'm sure you can find him there."

"Okay, I'll go say hello. Give you what? About fifteen minutes?"

"Sure. I'll meet you outside."

Shannon closed the door to her mother's rooms, smiling at Stella who was already busy in the kitchen. Shannon didn't know the other young woman who was helping. She turned to go when the upstairs door opened.

"Alice? Are you down here?"

Shannon's pulse raced, Madison's voice still able to give her chills. She turned slowly, cursing her luck that Madison was at the mansion. The world simply stopped when her eyes met Madison's.

"Shannon," Madison whispered. "Oh my God."

"Hi."

Madison hurried down the steps and was in her arms before Shannon could take another breath. They held each other tightly and that's when she felt it. Madison was pregnant. She stepped back, her eyes going to Madison's belly.

"When did you get here?" Madison asked.

"Just now. It's my mom's birthday. I'm taking her out." She looked up at her. "You're pregnant," she stated bluntly. Madison was married. She obviously had sex with her husband. And she was pregnant. Shannon's heart shattered at the thought.

"Yes." Madison held her gaze. "I'm so sorry," she whispered.

"I need to go," she said abruptly, turning to leave.

"Shannon, wait," Madison said, grabbing her arm. "Don't."

Shannon was aware they had an audience, and she didn't want to cause a scene. "I was going to go say hello to George."

"I'll walk with you."

They were silent as they walked outside. Shannon took the familiar path down toward the gazebo, fully intending to find George, then leave.

"I...I like your hair that way," Madison said, the first to speak.

"Thanks" was all she said.

"Were you going to call me?"

"No."

"Alice says you rarely come home."

"I stay away, yes."

"Because of me?"

Shannon stopped and faced her. She was stunned by the sadness in her eyes. "Yes. Because of you," she admitted.

"I miss you being in my life."

Shannon squared her shoulders, refusing to let her off easy. "It's your choice that I'm not in your life, Madison. I miss you. I miss *us*," she said. "But you're married. You're pregnant with his child."

"Shannon—"

"I'm trying to get on with my life. Just like you've gotten on with yours. So I can't see you. I can't talk to you." She took a step closer. "You want to know why? Because I'm in love with you. And I can't have you. Because you're married. And you're pregnant with his child."

She ignored the tears that were streaming down Madison's face and walked past her, following the brick walkway through the perfectly manicured lawn down to their old gazebo. George was on his knees with a small trailer of bricks beside him.

"Hi, George," she said, noting her voice was thick with emotion. Madison's tears always affected her that way.

He glanced up, a smile on his face. "Shannon. What a surprise," he said as he stood. "I'd give you a hug, but you probably don't want any part of this," he said, holding out his hands to her.

"What happened?"

"Oh, had a tree fall and it knocked all these bricks out of the flower bed wall. Just trying to patch it up." He wiped his dirty hands on his jeans. "You come to celebrate your mom's birthday?"

"Yeah. Thought I'd take her out to dinner and visit. It's been awhile since I've been home," she said.

"I know. Alice misses you," he said, his tone slightly accusing. Shannon didn't mind it. She'd known him since she was ten. With her father dead, George became the sole male influence in her life. Jarod wasn't around enough for that. George had let her tag along with him while he worked on his many projects and he'd taught her a lot.

"I've got a full-time job now, George. It's harder to find time to get away."

"I suppose so. She especially misses you around the holidays. You might try to spare a few days at Christmas," he suggested.

She nodded. "Point taken."

"Good. I'll look forward to seeing you then."

She smiled and squeezed his shoulder. "Thanks. I should get going. It was good to see you again."

"Take care of yourself," he said as she turned to walk away.

She paused, watching as he went back to work. She let her gaze travel to the gazebo, remembering all the times she and Madison had raced down the hill, settling on the benches, their eyes on each other and not on the beautiful flowers George maintained around it. A profound sadness overtook her, and she turned, blinking her eyes quickly, trying to erase the gazebo and all its memories from her mind.

Madison was gone when she went back up to the driveway. Shannon was relieved and sorry. Her mother was waiting, though, and she pushed thoughts of Madison away...thoughts of Madison and Stephen making love, making a baby.

CHAPTER TWELVE

"Pregnant? They didn't waste any time, did they?"

"I'm sure it was part of the arranged schedule her mother had planned for her," Shannon said, her tone bitter. She glanced at Charlotte, waiting for her critique.

"I'm assuming Madison didn't work," Charlotte said. "Her degree was for show?"

Shannon nodded. "Lansford women don't work," she said. She cleared her throat, nearly talked out. "I should get going. It's late."

"Oh, no. Not yet," Tracy protested. "You can't leave without finishing your story."

"There's not a whole lot left to tell. I've only seen her a couple of times since then," she said.

"How about more coffee? It's decaf," Tracy said.

Shannon nodded. "Okay. I'll have one more cup."

"How did you manage to avoid her all these years?" Charlotte asked. "I mean, on the occasions that you did go to Brook Hill."

"It was five years later that my mother first got sick. Before that, when I'd go visit, I wouldn't announce it. I would just show up. Stay one night and leave the next morning. I never saw Madison," she said. "When my mother got sick, Jarod was already retired from the military and we'd opened our first store about six months earlier. We took turns then, being with her, taking her to doctor's appointments and whatnot."

Tracy handed her another cup of coffee. "And you hadn't spoken to Madison that whole time?"

"No. I was able to put her out of my mind. I dated. I had friends. It was only when I went to Brook Hill that she was front and center in my mind."

"But you did see her again?"

"Yes. I was twenty-eight."

* * *

"Are you comfortable?" Shannon asked as she fluffed the pillows under her mother's legs.

"Quit fussing," her mother said. "I'm fine."

Shannon sat in the chair beside her mother's bed, worry etched on her face. She tried to hide it, but her mother smiled reassuringly at her.

"I'm not going to die on you just yet, Shannon. Quit looking so scared."

"You've never been sick before," she said.

"Cancer is a scary thing, isn't it? But the doctors seem to think we have a handle on it. I have to believe in them."

Shannon blew out a breath. "Have you thought any more about it?"

"Retiring? Yes."

"And?"

"And you and Jarod are right. It's time. But where would I go? You were ten when we moved here. I know it's not much, but it's been home these last eighteen years."

"I know, Mom. We'll find you a house. Something bright and airy, with a small yard." She looked around. "I always kinda felt like we were in a dungeon down here."

"Yes, I know. That's why you spent most of your time outside, down in the gazebo," she said with a smile. "Or up in Madison's room."

Shannon looked away, not wanting to think about that. Madison wasn't a part of her life anymore. That was over with. It had been more than five years since she'd seen her. Eight since they'd…slept together. Amazing how here, in the mansion, that memory was still so fresh.

"You haven't seen her son, have you?" her mother stated. "He's such a cute little boy. And so smart."

Shannon didn't reply. Her mother knew very well that she'd never seen him.

"Whatever has happened between you and Madison, you were such good friends at one time. I don't understand why you avoid her."

"I don't avoid her," Shannon said. "She doesn't live here anymore."

"You could make an effort to go see her. She's been so good to me. Whenever she's here, she always comes down to visit," her mother said. "She always asks about you. I know she misses you."

Shannon stood. "Mom, don't," she said, turning her back to her mother. She felt a lump in her throat and she tried to swallow it down. "Madison and I don't need to see each other."

"Why?"

She shook her head. "It's complicated." She turned when she heard a knock on the outer door. She glanced at her mother with raised eyebrows.

"It's probably Stella with lunch," she said.

Shannon walked into the other room and opened the door, her breath leaving her as she found Madison standing on the other side. Madison seemed as surprised as she was.

"Shannon," she whispered.

Shannon couldn't speak, her gaze drawn to the little boy standing beside Madison. She looked back up. "Hey."

"You…I wasn't expecting you. I had mentioned to your mother that we might stop by."

Shannon had to smile at this, wondering why her mother failed to mention that. "We just got back. She's lying down." She glanced again at the boy. "This must be your son."

"Yes. Ashton, say hello to an old friend of mine. This is Shannon, Miss Alice's daughter."

He held his hand out. "Pleased to meet you. May I call you Shannon?"

Shannon's eyes widened. She knew he was all of five, but there was no childlike awkwardness to his speech at all. She couldn't help but smile at him.

"Yes, you may call me Shannon."

"Madison? Ashton? Is that you?"

Madison's gaze was fixed on Shannon as she answered. "Yes, Alice." Ashton went toward the bedroom, proof that he and Madison were frequent visitors. Shannon and Madison followed.

"There's my handsome boy," her mother said.

"Hi, Miss Alice," he said, accepting her one-armed hug. "How was your chemotherapy today?"

"Not so bad this time, honey."

Shannon glanced at Madison. "How old is he again?" she whispered.

"A very intelligent five," Madison whispered back.

"Madison, Shannon and I were just talking about you. I'm so glad you came over," her mother said.

"Ashton remembered your appointment today. He wanted to check on you."

"Well, why don't you girls go catch up? Ashton can keep me company," she said.

Shannon was about to protest, but Madison had a desperate look in her eyes that she couldn't ignore. They walked back out in silence, their path taking them—perhaps unconsciously—toward the gazebo.

"He's a cute kid," Shannon said, breaking the silence. "He looks like you."

"Yes, thanks. But it's a little disconcerting when your five-year-old is smarter than you are."

"Really? How gifted is he?"

"Very. He was reading by age two. This next year, he should finish up his coursework through eighth-grade level."

"Wow."

"I know." Madison met her gaze. "How have you been?"

"Okay," she said with a shrug.

"Your mother says you've opened up a health food store. That's wonderful, Shannon."

"Jarod and I did. It's small but so far, profitable. We've been more than pleased."

"I'm proud of you," Madison said as they walked into the gazebo, still painted a pristine white.

Shannon watched her, her gaze roaming over her face, her body. When Madison turned to her and their eyes held, Shannon gave voice to her thoughts.

"You're so lovely, Madison." Madison pulled her gaze away but not before Shannon saw tears there.

"I don't know how you can see that. I'm so terribly, terribly… miserable," she said, her voice cracking with unshed tears.

"Madison—"

Madison looked back at her, this time unable to hide her tears as they streamed down her cheeks. "I miss you. I miss you so much," she said, nearly sobbing.

"Madison, don't," Shannon said, taking a step toward her. "Please don't cry."

"I hate my life," she said. "The only good in my life is Ashton. He's the only thing that has kept me sane." She wiped impatiently at her tears. "I'm so…miserable. And I'm so very lonely without you."

Shannon went to her then, pulling her into her arms. Madison clung to her, her tears turning to sobs. Shannon's tears fell too. She buried her face against Madison's hair, breathing in her familiar scent.

"Please don't cry," she murmured. "Please don't."

Their arms tightened and Shannon's body reacted, pulling Madison closer against her. She recognized the change in their hug. So did Madison as she pressed even closer to her. Shannon wanted so badly to kiss her; she knew she was getting close to crossing the line. She stepped back, away from her.

"We can't do this," she whispered.

"Please, Shannon. I need you so much," Madison said, her eyes pleading.

But Shannon shook her head. "I can't do this. It hurts me too much. I want to be with you. I want to make love to you. But I can't. It hurts me to leave here, to leave you. I can't do it anymore, Madison. Not if I want to keep my sanity. I just can't."

"Shannon—"

"No. What we had, it was special. It will always be special. You will always have a place in my heart. But I can't see you. Why do you think I avoid you? Because it hurts," she said, now her turn to wipe at her tears. "It hurts me right now, wanting to be with you so badly, but knowing I can't have you. Not all of you. Not even a little part of you."

"I love you, Shannon."

"I love you too. Why else do you think it hurts so damn much?" She shook her head. "I don't want to see you again, Madison. I can't." Her gaze locked with Madison's, both their eyes still shrouded by tears. "I don't want to see you ever again."

Madison turned away, her arms folding around herself. "I'm so sorry. I'm so sorry about everything."

Shannon cleared her throat, getting her emotions under control again. "I should get back to my mother. I'll be leaving in the morning."

Madison nodded. "I'll be in to get Ashton in a minute. I just need some time," she said.

Shannon clenched her fists together, wanting so badly to go to her, to hold her again. Before she could do just that, she spun on her heels, heading back to the house. She had to get Madison out of her life, out of her head…and most importantly, out of her heart. The only way to do that was by leaving.

CHAPTER THIRTEEN

"Oh, Shannon," Tracy said. "You both must have been heartbroken."

"Yes. But that was a bit of a breaking point. I think Madison finally understood how much I was hurting. After that, I didn't fear going to see my mother as much. I knew Madison wouldn't come around," she said. "And she didn't."

"I wonder why you two could never talk about it," Charlotte said.

"There wasn't anything to talk about," she said. "We knew the score. What good would it have done to talk about it?"

"Well, I think you did the wise thing by not giving in. She obviously wanted to be with you. Sexually, at least."

"It may seem to you that Madison only wanted the sexual part of our relationship, but that's not true. She was honest when she told me she was miserable in her life. That tortured look in her eyes was there from the first time she told me she was getting married," Shannon said. "Like I said earlier, she was as emotionally invested as I was. But one of us had to be strong and end our affair."

"So her son? When you say gifted, is he a genius?" Tracy asked.

"Oh yeah. My mother keeps me updated," she said with a smile. "You would think he was her grandson. He's about to turn fourteen and he's already graduated college with a dual degree."

"Child prodigies usually finish college as early as eleven or twelve," Charlotte said.

"Don't know about that," she said. "My mother said his IQ tested at 152."

Charlotte's eyes widened. "That's exceptional. Maybe emotionally he wasn't ready for college," she said.

Shannon took that as a dig at Madison, but she said nothing. She'd been around the kid a couple of times. He seemed very mature to her.

"It sounds as if Madison and your mother became close," Charlotte said.

"Yes, they did. I think Ashton had something to do with it. My mother talked freely about Madison whenever I did visit her. But Madison never came around. It was almost as if she was avoiding me now."

"Did your mother retire then?"

"Not right then, no. Her cancer went into remission," she said. "Four years later, it flared up again. This time breast cancer. It was after that that we convinced her to retire. Even then, she wasn't ready."

"I imagine not having you or Jarod living in Brook Hill, the Lansfords were her family. Retiring from there must have been hard," Charlotte said.

"Yes, but my mother had maintained friendships outside of the Lansford household. There were a few ladies who she saw frequently," she said.

"You saw Madison again?" Tracy asked.

"Yes. I went down to help my mother move. That was actually the last time I saw Madison. I was thirty-two."

* * *

"It's going to be so hard," her mother said. "This has been home for so long." She turned, taking Shannon's hand. "You were just ten when we moved here. Do you remember that day?"

Shannon nodded. "Yes. I remember thinking how big everything was. The house, the kitchen." And she remembered a young Madison standing at the top of the stairs, watching her—a memory etched in her memory forever. "You're going to love your new place, Mom."

"Oh, I suppose I will. I'm looking forward to sitting on the patio, to tending to a flower garden again instead of admiring George's handiwork," she said with a laugh. Her smile faded quickly. "What'll be hard getting used to is being alone. Here, there were always people around."

It was something Shannon and Jarod hadn't considered. Her mother had friends, that was their main concern. They didn't think about whether she'd be lonely or not.

"Are you having second thoughts?" she asked.

"It's too late for that. Besides, I'm sixty-five years old. It's time." Her mother took a deep breath, then smiled. "Let's get to it. Madison and Ashton are coming over to help too," she said.

Shannon stared at her. "Mom, that's not really necessary. You and Jarod got everything pretty much packed up. He and George already have most of your furniture moved," she said. "They don't—"

"I'm sure it was Ashton's idea. He's going to miss me being here." Her mother paused. "And it'll give you and Madison a chance to catch up. She says it's been five years since you've seen each other."

"Yeah. Something like that."

It was her mother's turn to stare. "I don't understand you two. You were inseparable for so many years. What happened to your friendship, Shannon?"

"We just...things are different now," she said. "Our lives are very different."

"Maybe—"

Her words were cut off as Ashton burst into the room. Shannon hadn't seen him since he was about five and he'd grown considerably. The cute kid she'd first met was a handsome young boy, his face breaking out in a smile as he accepted her mother's hug.

"We're all ready to help, Miss Alice."

"And I'm glad you volunteered." She and Shannon looked to the doorway, but it was empty. "Where's your mother?"

"Grandmother had some papers for her to sign. She said she'd be right down." He turned to Shannon. "You're Shannon," he said. "Is it okay if I still call you Shannon? Or do you prefer Miss Shannon?"

Shannon smiled, amused by his formality. "Just Shannon," she said.

He grinned too. "Okay, Just Shannon."

Shannon laughed, then it faded as she felt Madison's presence. She turned to the doorway, finding the empty space now filled with the most beautiful woman she'd ever seen. Madison's hair still reached her shoulders, the blond strands silky and inviting.

"Hello, Shannon," she said. "Good to see you again."

She seemed a bit aloof in her stance; Shannon didn't quite know what to make of it. No hug? No embrace? No "I missed you"? Of course, Shannon couldn't really blame her. The last time they'd seen each other—the last time they'd spoken—Shannon had all but said she never wanted to see her again. So with her mother and Ashton watching, she mimicked Madison's cool greeting.

"Madison. Hello."

"I hope we're not intruding, but Ashton insisted we help." Madison smiled as she glanced at her son. "He's dreading her moving."

"I certainly don't mind the help," she said. "Although Jarod took care of the heavy stuff earlier in the week."

Madison nodded. "Yes, we had a chance to visit with him too."

Shannon hid her surprise. Jarod had not mentioned that to her. Of course, like everyone else, Jarod had no idea of her and Madison's history. She didn't reply, instead, glancing at her mother with raised eyebrows.

"Shall we get started?"

"Let's start with the living room boxes and get them out of the way first," her mother suggested.

The four of them got to work, albeit silently, she and Madison taking pains to avoid each other. Shannon was torn between being happy for that and being offended that Madison was blatantly ignoring her. Which, of course, was ridiculous. She was ignoring Madison as well.

If not for the chatter between Ashton and her mother, the silence would have been terribly uncomfortable. As it was, she and Madison sidestepped each other almost to the point of exaggeration.

The moving van she'd rented filled quickly. Less than two hours later, they loaded the last box, leaving their old rooms empty. They stood there, looking at the blank walls and bare floors. Shannon could see the sadness in her mother's eyes. It was the nearly ten-year-old Ashton who broke the silence.

"I'm sure you'll like your new place better, Miss Alice."

"You think so? Will you come visit me?"

"Of course. That is—" Ashton glanced at his mother for confirmation.

"Of course we'll come visit, Alice. I don't think I could keep this one away."

Shannon wondered how often Madison and Ashton visited her mother as it was. She had assumed they only stopped in to chat with her when they were over visiting Madison's parents. The familiarity—and affection—between the three of them said otherwise. It almost seemed as if Madison and Ashton had taken her place in her mother's life. That stung a little. It was because of Madison that she kept her distance from Brook Hill in the first place.

She watched with a bit of jealousy as Ashton took her mother's hand and led her out. She glanced at Madison, who had an amused expression on her face.

"In case you hadn't noticed, Ashton is quite fond of your mother," Madison said. As if being privy to her earlier thoughts, she added, "I hope you don't mind. He thinks of her more as a grandmother than my mother."

"I don't mind. She looks to be attached to him as well."

"We haven't finalized college though. He wants to stay close, but he has endless opportunities."

"College? Don't you have a few years yet?" she said. The kid was ten after all.

Madison smiled. "Next year. But given his age, I would go with him. Well, not to classes, but to live. He couldn't live in a dorm."

"Damn. He really is that smart?"

"Yes. Mensa member."

"If you move with him, I guess that'll put a kink in your marriage, won't it?" she said, the words out before she could stop them.

Madison's smile faded. "Whether I live here or not, it won't change the state of my marriage, Shannon."

She watched Madison leave, wishing she hadn't mentioned her marriage. And no matter how much she wanted to pretend otherwise, the fact remained that Madison was married to Stephen. Married to him. Living with him, sleeping with him…having sex with him.

She closed her eyes for a second, chasing that last thought from her mind. When she opened her eyes, she saw nothing but the empty room of where she'd called home since she was ten. That seemed a lifetime ago now.

She left, closing the door behind her, knowing she would never return to the Lansford mansion again. The main kitchen was empty, but she heard Stella's voice down the hall. She should go bid her goodbye but thought otherwise. She'd only seen her a handful of times in the last ten years.

The others were outside waiting for her, but Madison refused to make eye contact with her. Her mother was watching them intently and Shannon forced a smile to her face.

"All ready?"

"I suppose so."

The trip was made quickly across town. Ashton rode with her mother in her car, and Madison followed behind the rented van in a sleek, black Mercedes. Madison looked right at home behind the wheel of the luxury car. As before, she and Madison avoided each other as they unloaded the van and piled boxes in the living room and kitchen. The furniture was already in place, some pieces that had been in storage and some new. While it wasn't an abnormally large house, it was certainly bigger than the four rooms her mother had been living in. While her mother seemed disappointed to be leaving the mansion, Shannon also recognized the look of excitement on her face.

"I'm not sure what I'm going to do with all this space," her mother said.

"I'm sure you'll enjoy it," Madison said. "Especially the windows. I always thought it was so dark in your place. Shannon's old room was practically a dungeon," she said with a glance at Shannon.

Shannon smiled, acknowledging the name she and Madison had dubbed the room with back when they were kids.

"Yes, it'll be nice to sit and see outside. That will be a welcome change."

"And you said you were going to put in flower beds," Ashton reminded her.

"Yes, I did." Her mother turned in a circle, looking at all her belongings piled around them in boxes. "I can't thank you enough for helping with all this."

"It was no trouble," Madison assured her.

"How about an early dinner?" Shannon suggested.

"Pizza!" Ashton said excitedly, his expression that of a ten-year-old boy and not the Mensa member that he was.

"It's not something we get often," Madison explained.

No, probably not. While Madison and Stephen didn't live in a home quite as elaborate as the mansion, Shannon knew they had a household staff, complete with a cook. She wouldn't be surprised if Mrs. Lansford coordinated the meals for them as well.

Shannon nodded. "Pizza it is. Mom? Is that okay with you?"

"Oh sure. Have it delivered here and we can break in the dining room table."

"If I may," Ashton said, "the best pizza in town is at Bruno's. They don't deliver, though."

He looked at Shannon expectantly, and she noticed for the first time that his blue eyes were identical to his mother's. She never could say no to those eyes.

"Okay, Bruno's. I guess I could be persuaded to pick up our dinner."

"You and Mom can pick it up. You haven't had a chance to visit yet. I'll help Miss Alice with unpacking."

Shannon looked at Madison with raised eyebrows, wondering what the little imp was up to. Genius level IQ, sure, but still, he was ten. A bit young to be this manipulative, she thought. Madison apparently thought the same thing as she stared at her son silently. He had the good grace to shift uncomfortably under her stare as he moved closer to the protection of Shannon's mother. She couldn't help but smile. So he *was* ten, after all. Of course, it gave her mother an opening as well.

"That's a good idea, Ashton. When they were young, those two were inseparable. Now, they rarely see each other."

It was Madison's turn to glance at Shannon. She shrugged. Madison did the same.

And twenty minutes later, they were backing out of her mother's driveway, Shannon riding shotgun in Madison's Mercedes.

"Nice car," she said.

"Thanks."

"Did your mother pick it out?" she asked, unable to resist the dig. Surprisingly, Madison laughed.

"How did you guess?"

Shannon smiled too. "I picture you in a hybrid or something, not this."

"Ashton and I wanted a Prius," she said. "He's very practical."

"And he's more than book-smart too," she said.

"Yes. I think Alice must have told him stories about when we were younger. He asks about you frequently." Madison glanced at her. "I don't really have any friends," she said. "Not close ones. He's commented on that several times. It makes him curious, I think."

"Why don't you have friends? What about Stephanie? And who was the other one? Tamara?"

Madison nodded. "Oh, we see each other. But the relationship I have with them now is as superficial as it was back in high school and college. We only have one thing in common."

"Your social status?"

"Yes."

"Something we never had in common," she reminded her.

Madison glanced at her quickly. "But we had everything else in common."

Shannon stared at her profile, thinking she was as lovely as ever. She was also surprised that Madison would allude to their affair. After all, it had been well over ten years since they'd been intimate. It struck her like a blow to the chest to realize the last time she'd touched Madison, the last time she'd made love to her, was when Madison had announced she was getting married. It was a night she still remembered in great detail—when she allowed herself to remember it, that is.

"What are you thinking about?"

Shannon realized she was still staring at her. She blinked several times and cleared her throat. "I was…I was thinking about the last time…we made love."

Their eyes held for a quick moment, then Madison turned her attention back to the road. "It was Christmas. My parents were announcing my engagement," she said quietly. "It was the last time I ever made love with someone."

Shannon's heart broke at that moment. While she knew Madison's marriage was a farce, she still blamed her for going through with it. And even though Madison had told her many times how miserable she was in her marriage, this was the first time it really hit home. Madison's life had been as loveless as her own.

"It was the last time for me too," Shannon admitted.

"I'm so sorry."

Even though dusk was upon them and the shadows were heavy in the car, Shannon could still make out the misting of tears in Madison's eyes.

"No need to be sorry. It's not like I haven't tried," she said. "I just haven't met anyone yet who…who made me feel the way that you did."

Madison gripped the steering wheel tightly, her glance going from Shannon to the road and back to Shannon.

"There are two things I want to do right now," Madison said. "One is to cry, but I've found that does little good."

"The other one?"

Madison suddenly turned off the main road and onto a side street. She drove a couple of blocks and turned into the parking lot of a closed dry cleaners. Her hands still gripped the wheel with enough strength to turn her knuckles white.

"The other one is to kiss you." Madison turned to look at her. "And to be held by you."

Shannon's pulse quickened, even though there was more sadness in Madison's eyes than desire. She told herself she could have resisted the desire. But the sadness? No. It was too much to see those beautiful blue eyes shrouded in sadness.

"I think that's two things, not one," she said with a slight smile.

Madison didn't return her smile as their eyes held. "Please, Shannon. I need you so much."

Shannon reached over and released Madison's seat belt before doing the same to her own. Her hand was trembling as she touched Madison's face. She was shocked by the transformation in Madison's eyes. The sadness faded almost immediately, replaced with relief, contentment and yes, desire. But she no longer had thoughts of resisting her. She was drawn to Madison's lips as the proverbial moth was to a flame. Just one touch and the years washed away in an instant. Madison's fingers gripped tightly to her forearms as her mouth opened to her. Then, as if they were teenagers again, they fumbled to touch—the console getting in the way as it had back then.

Madison moaned into her mouth when Shannon brushed Madison's breast, her nipple hard and taut against the thin material of her blouse. Shannon deepened the kiss, her tongue slipping inside Madison's mouth, stroking her own.

But it was all they could afford. The console—and the fact they were parked in a public parking lot—drew them apart.

Their breathing was ragged, hands still touched one another, foreheads rested together. Shannon finally pulled back, meeting Madison's eyes in the near darkness. Everything she wanted, she saw reflected back at her. Unfortunately, it was something they couldn't have.

"We should get going before they send a search party," she said, her voice husky with desire.

Madison nodded but didn't release her. "I miss you so much, Shannon. I miss you being in my life."

"I miss you too," she said. "But I need more than an affair with you, Madison."

"I know. I need more than an affair too."

They silently put their seat belts back on, but before Madison backed away, she reached over and squeezed Shannon's hand. Shannon squeezed back, knowing it was all they would have.

CHAPTER FOURTEEN

"Would you have turned her down if she'd offered an affair?" Charlotte asked.

"Yes."

"But would you have slept with her that night if you'd had the chance?" Tracy asked.

Shannon grinned. "Probably."

"So that's the last time you saw each other?" Charlotte asked. "Five years ago?"

"Yes. But the avoidance was mutual this time. She saw my mother often, but she never came around if I was there. And as you know, that's not often."

"You're going back now, though," Tracy said. "What's going to happen?"

Shannon shrugged. "If I'm staying with my mother, then the chances of seeing Madison are good. What'll happen, I don't know."

And she didn't. It would be awkward. It always was. But to be there, for months, was going to be challenging. Keeping memories away was one thing. Being back in Brook Hill, where all the memories were *real*, where Madison was *real*, would no doubt be a test of her resolve. Because, for her own sanity, she had to stay away from Madison.

"Well, I don't envy you," Charlotte said. "I'm sure it will be stressful for you."

"Stressful or not," Tracy said, "the romantic in me hopes you do get to see each other." She smiled at Shannon affectionately. "I know you're still in love with her. You deserve a happy ending."

Shannon sighed heavily. Was she still in love with Madison? Probably. But she shook her head slowly.

"This isn't a fairytale. I'm afraid there will be no happy ending for us."

PART TWO

LOVE IS TIMELESS

CHAPTER FIFTEEN

Madison hugged Ashton tightly, embarrassed by how much she was going to miss him.

"Mom, it's not like you're sending me to another country," he reminded her.

"I'm just going to miss you," she said. "You're…well, you're all I have."

His intelligent blue eyes studied her for a moment, then he took her hand and led her to the sofa.

"We should talk."

She rolled her eyes. "I'm the mother," she reminded him. "You're fifteen."

"Yes, but I'm the smart, mature one," he said. "I don't have to go, you know."

"Ashton, it's the best medical school in the country. Of course you have to go."

He tilted his head at her, his watchful eyes carefully studying her expression. "Have you stayed married to Dad all these years just for me?"

The question caught her off guard. She had played the game so long, she thought she was quite good at it. Had he seen through her façade?

"Why would you ask me that? Your father and I—"

"—are not happy. At least you're not."

She stood, keeping her back to him. She wasn't prepared to answer his questions, wasn't prepared to see the truth in his eyes.

"Ashton, you have a car waiting to take you to the airport. This is not the time—"

"Mom, it's Grandfather's private jet. I think I can be a little late." He came to her and turned her around. "This is important. I'm leaving. I'm not going to be here to take care of you."

She smiled at his statement. He was so grown up, yet he was still a boy. She sometimes wished he had been just a normal kid, but that was selfish of her. He had a gift and he never shied away from it. She brushed the blond hair on his forehead, pausing to cup his cheek.

"I love you, you know."

He nodded. "I love you too. That's why I want you to be happy."

"Oh, Ashton, it's not that simple. When I was your age, there were no choices for me. Your grandmother had everything arranged." She looked him in the eye, hoping he would understand. "That included who I would date, where I would go to college... and ultimately who I would marry. Being happy wasn't part of the equation. I don't want that for you. I want you to make your own choices and do what makes you happy."

"You mean if medical school is not for me?"

She nodded. "I know your father, your grandparents, all pushed you down this path. I know firsthand how good they are at pushing in the direction they want. But it needs to be your decision. I don't want you to have any regrets."

"Like you do?"

She smiled sadly. "Yes. I have regrets. Lots of them. But it's too late for me. You have the world in front of you. Don't let them influence you too much."

"Mom, you're only thirty-eight. You could still—"

"I'm only thirty-*seven*," she corrected with a smile. "I still have a few months to go, thank you very much."

"Sorry," he said with a grin. "What I mean is, it's not too late. If you want to make changes, well, you have my blessing," he said, his young face sporting a blush now. "With Dad, I mean."

She pulled him into a hug, then released him. "Thank you. But it's not that simple."

He cleared his throat slightly. "Miss Alice said the happiest she's ever seen you was when you were young and you and Shannon were always together. She said your eyes always had a spark in them. Then you left for college and…well." He looked at her sadly. "I don't ever see that spark, Mom."

"Oh, honey," she whispered, hugging him yet again. "It's…it's so complicated."

Yes, everything with Shannon was complicated. She hadn't seen her in five years. She knew from Alice that Shannon would be back in town in the next month or so. They were going to open up another store. She knew Alice was proud of the success Shannon and Jarod had, rightfully so, but she sensed Alice was happier with the fact that they would be around more. She knew a big part of that was her fault. Shannon stayed away because of her. Maybe that's one reason she'd always felt the need to check in on Alice. Alice was the person she wished her own mother had been. And she knew for a fact that Ashton was much closer to Alice than he was to his own grandmother. Alice was warm and caring, two things glaringly missing from her mother's personality.

Yet Shannon was coming back to Brook Hill. They would surely run into each other at some point. Would it be awkward, like it usually was? Would they warm up to each other eventually? Would they dare be alone together? Would the spark still be there after another five years had passed?

A part of her hoped it still burned as brightly, but another part feared that it did.

With Ashton leaving, her life was at a crossroads. Dare she make a change? Was she strong enough to stand up to her mother? To Stephen?

Was she brave enough?

CHAPTER SIXTEEN

"So what do you think, sis?"

Shannon followed Jarod through the dusty parking lot. The new shopping center was being built on the southwest side of town, where most of the new subdivisions were going up. Brook Hill was expanding yet again and this seemed a perfect location for their store.

"How much leeway would we have on the design?" she asked.

"This whole section on the north side is not rented yet. We could take as much as we like." He grinned at her. "This could be our largest store. We could take four or five units, really expand our inventory."

Their first three stores, while not exactly tiny, were not big enough to be compared to the large grocery stores found in most subdivisions. If they rented five sections of this shopping center, it would be huge compared to their others.

"That's a big investment," she said cautiously. "If it bombs, then—"

"It's not going to bomb. We've done our research, like always. And if it's a success, then we've set a new standard."

She trusted his business sense, she always had. But he was usually the practical one, the conservative one. She'd wanted to make a big splash with their first store, and he'd talked her down, keeping it in a range they could afford. It was a model that had worked three times so far. This, this would be huge for them. Not only the inventory, but finishing the construction on the inside as well.

"And the bank? This would be a larger loan than before."

"I've already got it approved, sis."

She stared at him, then glanced to the construction going on around them, knowing she would go with his instincts. "Okay." She nodded. "Then let's do it. Another Fletcher's Natural Foods Market."

He stuck his hand out and they shook, as if sealing a business deal. Which, in a sense, it was. Jarod managed the business side of things and the day-to-day running of the stores. Shannon designed the layout of the stores and managed their inventories. Both were involved in the hiring as they each had standards they wanted. They paid more than other grocery stores, but they demanded more. That was something she'd learned from her early days of working at Whole Foods.

As they walked back to Jarod's truck, she bumped his arm. "What about Joan and the kids? Has she decided yet?"

"After school is out, they're going to move here for the summer, see how the kids like it. If it goes well, then we'll enroll them in school here."

"Wow. You'd really move back to Brook Hill permanently?"

"Mom needs us," he reminded her. "I feel like I missed out on so much, spending twenty years in the military. You were left to take care of things for so long."

"It's not like she needed taking care of back then," she said. She felt a stab of guilt. She, too, had been away, but for very different reasons.

"What about you? Have you decided what you're going to do while this project is going on? You want to go in together and rent a house?"

"I think I'll move in with Mom. When Joan and the kids come on weekends, well, you need your time with them. And it'll be good to be around to help Mom. I know she'll love the company."

CHAPTER SEVENTEEN

Madison stopped in her tracks when she saw her. Shannon was as tall and lean as ever, her hair still cut stylishly short. But the tank she was wearing left little to the imagination. Madison's hungry eyes roamed over her, the muscles in her arms and back straining with the weight of the desk she and Jarod were unloading. As if sensing her presence, Shannon paused, her head turning slightly, eyebrows raised. Madison smiled tentatively. She hadn't known Shannon would be there. Alice had not mentioned when they would be arriving. She was about to offer an apology and make a quick escape when Shannon grinned at her.

"A little help here, if you don't mind."

She hurried over, her eyes meeting Shannon's briefly before she grabbed onto a corner. She smiled at Jarod and nodded.

"Good to see you again."

"You too," he said. "This one," he said, motioning to Shannon, "thought we could move this monster without help. Glad you came by."

"I was dropping by to see Alice. I didn't know you two would be here," she said.

"Officially moving in next week," Shannon said. "But I had to have a desk," she said, glancing at the heavy piece of furniture they all had a hand on. "If you could help us turn it to get it up the steps, that would be great."

"Where's your mother?"

"Doing what she does best," Jarod said. "Cooking."

Madison wasn't certain she was helping at all, but she did manage to keep a grip on one edge of the desk. Jarod took the brunt of the weigh as he maneuvered them through the front door.

"Don't scratch the wall!" Alice called from the kitchen.

"I'll fix it if we do," Shannon said as she squeezed by the door.

"Madison! What a surprise," Alice said as she came to inspect the damage. "And they've got you helping."

"I'm not sure I'm really doing anything though," she said with a smile as she kept a hand on the desk.

"In here," Shannon said, moving them into the spare bedroom.

It had already been transformed, Madison noted. The standard double bed and old dresser had been replaced by a king bed and matching chest of drawers. She couldn't imagine how the desk was going to fit.

"Tight squeeze, sis," Jarod said skeptically.

"I know. But I measured. It'll fit."

"Am I in the way?" Madison asked as she and Shannon were pressed against the wall, the desk leaning heavily against them.

"We've been in tighter spots," Shannon murmured with a smile.

Madison grinned in return. It had been so long since she and Shannon had been playful with each other, she hardly knew how to react.

"You're not going to have any room to even walk around in here," Jarod said as he set the desk down in the corner.

"I don't care. I need my desk," Shannon said, running a hand across its polished surface. "Scoot it back a little," she said as she picked up one corner and shoved it back against the wall.

"It looks good in here," Madison said. "It's a special desk, I assume?"

"Well, it's not a fancy antique piece or anything," Shannon said. "When I got my own place, it was the first piece of furniture I bought. Back when computers were computers and not laptops," she said with a grin. "But it's comfortable and I need two laptops so this way I can spread out and not infringe on Mom's space."

"More like clutter Mom's space," her mother corrected. She glanced at Madison. "You'll stay for lunch?"

"Oh, I don't want to intrude," she said. "I just came by to check on you. I didn't know Shannon and Jarod would be here already."

"You're not intruding. I baked a small roast this morning. We're going to have roast beef sandwiches." She looked at Shannon. "Well, we are. Shannon has some tofu slices marinating. I have no idea what she plans to do with them."

"I'm going to pan-fry them and serve them in a gluten free wrap with lettuce, peppers and sprouts and topped with my secret sauce," Shannon said. "And it'll be crunchy and fresh and you'll all wish you had some."

"I'll stick with the roast beef, sis."

"You own health food stores," Shannon said. "How can you continue to eat that way?"

He shook his head. "Joan cooks meatless meals quite often," he said. "But I draw the line at tofu," he said, making a face.

Shannon looked at Madison. "You?"

"Well, since your mother went to all the trouble, I should probably have the roast beef sandwich too," she said with a smile.

"Chicken," Shannon muttered.

Madison laughed. "I have never had tofu that I've liked. Sorry."

"Then you and Jarod will have to sample it."

Even though she and Shannon had not had a second alone together, the conversation was not strained in the least. It was pleasant, actually. For the first time in the last eighteen years, there was no underlying tension between them. That was a bit puzzling. Perhaps Shannon had put it behind her? It had been five years since they'd seen each other. The last time, well, they had had a few stolen moments in the car, that was all. The fire had still been there. Now? Now Shannon seemed to be past it. Maybe she had moved on. Maybe she was dating someone. Maybe she was in love with someone. That thought brought a sharp pain to her heart. She was being selfish, she knew. Shannon deserved a life, deserved to be happy. Which she seemed to be as she chatted with her mother and brother, always including Madison in the conversation as well.

"So Mom says the Whiz Kid is off to medical school?"

Madison nodded and smiled. "Yes. He's been gone three weeks." She turned to Alice. "He said to tell you that he misses your brownies, and if you should happen to make up a batch, I promised to send him a care package."

"Oh, of course I will."

"Fifteen and in med school," Jarod said with a shake of his head. "Amazing."

"I know. I've had years to get used to it, but it still amazes me sometimes." She glanced at Shannon. "Especially considering my math skills," she said with a laugh.

Shannon laughed too. "Of course, your mother thought you were tutoring *me*," she reminded her. "How many times did she catch us?"

Their glance held and Madison smiled at the mischievous look in Shannon's eyes. "She only caught us...tutoring a couple of times."

The look that passed between them brought back plenty of memories of them doing other things that they feared her mother would catch them at. The playfulness left Shannon's eyes and was replaced with something Madison had dearly missed.

Desire.

CHAPTER EIGHTEEN

"It was so good to see you and Madison together again," her mother said as they cleaned up the kitchen.

"Yeah?"

"You used to be so close."

"Mom, please," Shannon said. "I told you, it's complicated."

Her mother nodded. "Yes. Because she's married. I know."

Shannon stopped. "What do you mean?"

"Oh, Shannon, I'm not stupid."

Shannon feigned ignorance. "I don't know what you're talking about."

"You've been in love with her since you were kids," her mother stated bluntly.

Shannon had a moment of panic. After all these years, were they about to have "The Talk"? Jesus, she was thirty-eight years old. Was that really necessary? Well, she wanted no part of it. She turned to walk out of the kitchen, but her mother called her back.

"Shannon?"

She stopped, her back to her mother. "What?"

"Don't you think it's time you told me?"

Shannon swallowed nervously. "Told you what?"

"That you're gay."

Shannon dropped her chin to her chest with a silent groan. *Oh my God.* She slowly shook her head. "We've gone this long without talking about it," she said. "I don't know why you want to bring it up now."

"Why haven't you talked to me about it?"

Shannon turned around. "How long have you known?"

Her mother smiled. "Always. The fact that you never dated, never talked about boys, that was a clue. You were always such a private person. But you and Madison—"

"Madison isn't gay," she said quickly.

Her mother tilted her head and smiled. "I've watched the two of you since you were ten years old, Shannon."

"Look, I don't want to talk about it."

"Honey, don't you think a mother knows when her child is falling in love?"

"Oh my God," she muttered, feeling her face turn red. "I *really* don't want to talk about this," she said again.

"This part of your life…why didn't you want to share it with me?"

Shannon shrugged. "Why didn't you ever ask me?"

"I figured you would tell me when you were ready. Of course, I kept getting older, you kept getting older. We avoided the subject of your personal life. That was what we did, I guess."

"Then maybe we should stick to that," she suggested.

"I won't be around forever," her mother said. "I want to know you're happy."

"I'm happy," she said.

"No, you're not. And neither is Madison."

"Mom, Madison is married. That's not going to change."

"Mrs. Lansford was so…so demanding of her. You were so young, you probably didn't realize how much her mother expected of her. She always had her going, going…never allowed her to just be a kid."

"I know. By the time Madison was in high school, our time together dwindled. I know how busy she kept her."

Her mother nodded. "Madison was in love with you too," she stated.

A fresh blush covered Shannon's face. "Mom...*please*," she said quietly.

"No, Shannon. We're finally talking about it after all these years. I want to know. I want to understand."

Oh dear God, I can't believe this is happening. Shannon pulled out a chair from the breakfast table and sat down, resolved to meet her fate.

"What do you want to know?"

"Why did Madison get married?" her mother asked as she sat down across from her.

Shannon laughed bitterly. "Did she have a choice?"

"I know how Mrs. Lansford is, of course, but surely even she wouldn't force that on Madison."

"Everything Madison ever did in her life was dictated by her mother, as you well know," she said. "Her marriage was a foregone conclusion."

Her mother shook her head slowly. "Madison always has this sad look in her eyes, still to this day. On the outside, she appears to be fine. But when you look inside, all you see is unhappiness," she said. "Shannon, the night before her wedding, she was simply distraught. I tried to calm her. Nothing I said helped. That's when I knew," she said.

"Knew what?"

"I knew that the person she was in love with was not the one she was about to marry."

Shannon closed her eyes and squeezed the bridge of her nose with her fingers, wishing she was anywhere other than here having this discussion with her mother, of all people. She opened her eyes, finding her mother watching her.

"What do you want me to say?"

"I want you to tell me about your relationship."

"Oh, for God's sake, mom, what kind of *relationship* can you have when you're in high school? We were kids."

"Kids or not, you snuck up to her room often enough."

Shannon felt her face turn red for at least the third time, and she leaned her head on the table. "Seriously? We're having *that* discussion?"

"Oh, we're both adults, what's the big deal?"

"You're my *mother*," Shannon said as she raised her head. "I'm thirty-eight years old," she said again. "Isn't it a little late to be discussing my love life?"

"Oh, Shannon, life's so short. I just want you to be happy, that's all."

Shannon met her eyes and smiled. "I'm happy enough, Mom. I have a successful business, I'm super close with my brother and his family, I have a handful of good friends," she said. "And now I get to spend some quality time with you." She nodded. "I'm happy enough."

"Honey, all of that is great. It really is. But having someone in your heart," she said, clutching her chest, "is the only important thing."

"Hopefully someday I'll find someone," Shannon said. "And I can't believe you're being so…so *normal* about it," she said.

"You mean because Madison is a woman? Oh, I admit, it was upsetting at the time. It wasn't anything I understood. Two girls? I didn't know what to do or say, so I said nothing. But watching you, the way you looked at her, the way she looked at you, there was no doubting the love between you."

"No doubting it? She got married. There was plenty of doubt."

"I would venture to guess that she was as frightened by her love for you as she was the prospect of marrying a man she had no interest in."

Shannon only shrugged.

Her mother smiled sadly at her. "Madison and I have grown close these last ten years. Ashton, of course, was part of it. The only time Madison has any life in her eyes is when Ashton is around. I worry now, what with him gone." She reached across the table and grasped Shannon's hand. "Madison has changed. The last four or five years, she's come out of her shell a little. At least with me. I fear her mother still has a heavy hand on her." She pulled her hand away, staring off into space. "You were probably too young at the time to see it, to understand it, but Madison's mother was far more controlling than even you—or Madison—realized."

"What do you mean?"

"It was like a script. Every little detail. Everything had a purpose. What lessons she took and when. Music lessons, dance, tennis. It was all prearranged. Madison had no say. Her wardrobe, from the day she was born until well after her marriage, her mother chose everything. As you said, she had Stephen Cole picked out for her, just like she had her college picked out, her wedding date, her child's name."

"'Ashton'?"

"Yes. Everything in her life, every detail, was planned by her mother. Madison, although she hides it well, has no self-esteem, no confidence. She was never allowed the chance to grow into her own person, she was never allowed to make decisions, good or bad." She took Shannon's hand again. "I used to think that Mrs. Lansford thought of Madison as a doll, a play toy. She simply moved her from scene to scene, everything already set up and waiting for her, like a dollhouse. Madison just had to be there and play the part. So very sad for a young girl."

"Yes. But Madison allowed it. When she was older, she could have stopped it," Shannon said, remembering the day Madison had told her she was getting married. Shannon had begged her not to do it, but she doubted it ever crossed Madison's mind to say "no."

"Well, like I said, she had no confidence. But she's changed. I can see her growing, little by little. Ashton has helped. But I worry, now that he's gone. That's why, Shannon, if nothing else, maybe you two can at least salvage your friendship. Her old friends from school, well, they're so different from Madison. They are who Mrs. Lansford wanted to turn Madison into. I'd like to think that you had a part in keeping her grounded."

"Madison never quite fit the mold. She hated it. Do you remember how they would always throw a big birthday party for her?"

"Yes, to which you were never invited."

"Right. And she hated it, but she played the game. But the next day, we would have our own birthday party. Just us."

"You always asked me to make a small cake for you."

Shannon smiled at the memories. "Yeah. That was all she wanted."

Her mother squeezed her hand again. "Shannon, what she wanted was to be with you. That's all."

Shannon nodded. It wasn't the cake. It was never that simple. She sighed and pulled her hand away from her mother. "It's too late to go back, Mom. She's married, she's got a whiz kid, has her own life now. And I've got mine. We're so far apart. I don't know if we can ever get our friendship back."

Her mother stood, signaling—thankfully—an end to their conversation. "Give it a chance, Shannon. Madison needs you in her life. And I think you need her."

"Mom—"

"Please? For me?"

"Really? You're going to play that card?"

Her mother smiled. "Of course. When you're my age and battling cancer, you can play that card a lot."

Shannon laughed. "Okay. For you. I'll give it a chance."

CHAPTER NINETEEN

Madison opened her eyes, giving up hope that sleep would come quickly for once. Stephen lay beside her, facing the opposite wall, his even breathing doing little to lull her to sleep. She wondered why they still bothered to share a bed. Ashton was gone. He was the only reason they continued to pretend their marriage was…normal.

She bit her lip. Of course Ashton knew the truth. She suspected long ago he knew his parents weren't happy. But she, like Stephen, pretended that he didn't know. It was easier that way, easier than facing reality.

She rolled her head slightly, staring at Stephen's back. She couldn't remember the last time they'd had sex. Too many years to recall. She'd always been able to go through the motions, to disconnect her mind from her body. For some reason, that last time, she couldn't. She couldn't do it anymore. She'd cried, almost hysterically. She hadn't been able to stop and it had scared him, she knew. But like most things in their life—in their marriage—they never discussed it. She assumed Stephen had a mistress now as that was the last time he attempted to touch her. In public, they went through the motions, both pretending that they had a wonderful marriage. To the outside world, she was the perfect daughter, the perfect wife, the perfect mother.

She and Stephen still shared a bed. She was still his wife. She was still as unhappy as she'd been sixteen years ago when they'd married. And even though Ashton had given her his "blessing," as he'd called it, she was terrified to make a change.

Terrified to make a decision.

Because decisions were never hers to make. That was left to her mother, even years after she had married. More recently, decisions were left to Stephen. Never her. It was her own fault for never standing up to her mother, for allowing her to have so much control. She had never learned how to say no to her. Growing up, she was so conditioned to follow her mother's every wish, she didn't realize how manipulated she really was. The only part of her life that her mother never controlled was her time with Shannon. The moments with Shannon were precious and few, but nonetheless they were also the happiest moments in her life.

In the last fifteen years, they'd hardly seen each other, much less talked, but on the few occasions they had, it reminded her again how empty her life was. Even when they quarreled, even when Shannon had told her she couldn't see her anymore, those were precious moments because they were *real*. Whether they were stealing kisses or Shannon was telling her goodbye, her heart broke equally as much. Because Shannon—as much as she wanted her—was someone she could never have.

Now here they'd come full circle. Shannon was back. They'd actually been able to interact with each other in a normal way. It had felt so good to be with her, near her, again. Alice and Jarod had welcomed her into their family and she enjoyed sharing a meal with them all. But it was Shannon who drew her, like always.

Shannon was back.

How were they going to handle it? Would they try to build a friendship again? Could they? Could they be alone together and not—*God*—want to rip each other's clothes off? She took a quick breath, remembering how it had been with Shannon. Always so intense, their attraction greater than either of them could control.

She glanced again at Stephen's sleeping form, wondering if he was as unhappy as she was. Or even questioning if he cared. A separation and divorce probably never entered his mind. With his political aspirations about to kick off—he was going to run for the Senate—he couldn't afford anything to mar his reputation.

She closed her eyes. Did she dare broach the subject with him? She could picture his reaction—and her mother's—if she announced she was leaving him, leaving the marriage. Shocked? Not shocked that she was unhappy and wanted out—he knew that already. But shocked that she would actually utter the words out loud, that she would actually contemplate leaving him.

Was she strong enough? Could she fight him *and* her mother? Their assault would be relentless, she imagined. She would be treading on sacred ground should she tarnish the Lansford and Cole names by getting a divorce.

She knew the only person she trusted to talk this out with was Shannon but would it be fair to put her through that? She had caused her so much pain already. If she was going to make a change and leave Stephen, then she needed to be able to do it on her own.

Oh, but it would be nice to have a friend to lean on.

Would Shannon do that for her? Would she be her friend? Could she be?

CHAPTER TWENTY

Shannon's eyes were glued to the screen, her right hand moving the mouse slowly as she added a round table near the deli bar. Would that go over in Brook Hill? Would people actually come to the store to have breakfast? Lunch?

"Gotta do something with all this space," she murmured as she changed the low round table to a taller, square table. Three tables, two chairs at each.

"Busy?"

She glanced up, finding Madison watching her from the doorway. She smiled quickly, surprised to see her. Sitting back, she motioned her inside her bedroom-office. The desk had taken up what little room was left after she'd moved in her bed from home. There wasn't room for an extra chair.

"I'm sorry. It's a little cramped."

"I don't want to interrupt," Madison said. "I came to visit Alice."

"Oh." Shannon reminded herself that Madison was friends with her mother, not her. Madison smiled at her, albeit a little nervously.

"Are you working on the design?"

"Yeah." Shannon paused, then turned her laptop toward Madison. "Here, take a look," she said. She saved what she'd been working on, then pulled up a smaller scale schematic of the inside. "Our stores are on the small side, the largest being ten thousand square feet and the smallest—the first one—only seven thousand. So this one will be huge for us. It's over twenty thousand square feet. Twice what we're used to," she said. "I'm not sure I can double our inventory, so I've got to fill the space somehow." She pulled up the deli area again. "I want to make an eating area. Like a food court, with different options. It wouldn't be entirely vegan or vegetarian," she said. "Nothing commercial or factory farmed. That's off limits. But we try to buy locally when we can. Has to be organic. A salad bar, a taco bar, a—" She stopped. "Sorry. I'm sure you don't want to hear about all that."

"No. It's exciting."

Shannon leaned back. "I don't know if I would call it exciting, but I enjoy the planning stages."

Madison nodded. "And it shows." She hesitated, her eyes darting around the room before coming back to Shannon. "I was wondering if…if you'd like to come over for…dinner. Tonight."

"Oh, I don't know," Shannon said. "No offense, but the last thing I want to do is have dinner with you and Stephen," she said.

Madison shook her head. "Stephen is…well, it doesn't matter. He's away. He won't be there."

Their eyes met, and Shannon tried to read Madison, wondering what she was planning. She finally looked away, glancing to her screen instead. "Do you think that's a good idea?"

"What do you mean?"

"I mean, we'd be alone."

Madison's eyes widened. "Are you worried about…"

"Well…"

Madison smiled. "I have no ulterior motives, if that's what you're worried about. The last time we saw each other, we agreed there would be no…no affair," she said, her voice quiet. "Seeing as how it's been five years since we've seen each other and I'm still married…"

Shannon chewed her lower lip, then finally shrugged. "Okay. You're right. We should be past that by now anyway."

Madison met her eyes again. "I miss you in my life. I miss a lot of things," she added with a quick smile. "But I miss talking to you. I miss you being my friend. I don't have anybody I'm close with, anyone I can talk to." She took a deep breath. "I just really need to talk, Shannon."

Shannon nodded, wondering if she wanted to be that person Madison leaned on. Could she be? But as always, she had a hard time saying "no" to Madison.

"Okay. Where and when?"

She slid over a notepad to Madison, who quickly jotted down her address. After only a slight pause, she added more, then flashed Shannon a grin.

"Thank you."

Shannon nodded again, only picking up the pad when Madison had left, closing the door behind her. Shannon glanced at the address, not recognizing the street name. She smiled at what Madison had scribbled below it.

7:00. Please come early. You can help me cook!

"Since when does she know how to cook?" she murmured.

* * *

"It's a beautiful day, isn't it?"

Madison sat down beside Alice on her small patio, accepting the glass of tea with a smile. "Yes. I can't believe it's May already."

Alice studied her a moment. "Did you get to visit with Shannon?"

"Just for a bit. She was busy. Besides, I came to see you," Madison reminded her.

Alice smiled at her, but Madison could see the questions forming in her eyes. Over the years, Alice had made only brief mention of the fact that she and Shannon didn't see each other anymore...didn't talk. While never prying, Madison could tell Alice was curious as to the chasm between them.

"You were so close once. Inseparable."

Madison looked away. "We were kids. And I wouldn't exactly say inseparable. My mother made sure of that."

Alice laughed lightly. "Oh, your mother tried to keep you busy, didn't she? I never told you this—and certainly never Shannon—but your mother came to me once, insisting that I do something to break up your friendship. She felt Shannon was bringing you down, was keeping you from forming deeper friendships with the girls from your school."

"That doesn't surprise me," Madison said. "What did you tell her?"

"I told her that you two had a special bond and that it would be cruel to keep you apart." Alice shook her head. "She didn't want to hear that. She fired me."

"*What?*"

"Yes. She told me to get out. That she wouldn't have me and my daughter interfering in your life."

"Oh my God. I can't believe it. What did you do?"

"Well, we had no place to go. We would be out on the street. So I did the only thing I could think of. I called your father."

"Since you didn't leave, I assume he overruled her," Madison said. Growing up, she always believed that her mother was the one in control.

"Yes. And she didn't speak to me for *months* afterward," Alice said. "You were starting high school, I believe."

"Yes. That's when she doubled my activities," Madison remembered. "Shannon and I…well, we didn't have a whole lot of free time."

Alice held her eyes. "But you had enough."

Madison frowned. "What do you mean?"

"I mean your friendship didn't suffer." Alice looked away, staring out over her small backyard. "Shannon was never close like that with anyone else. Not in all these years. I suspect the same is true for you."

"True," she said with a sigh. "I missed her."

"I know. She missed you too." Alice returned her gaze to Madison. "I've known you a long time, Madison. It must be exhausting for you to pretend to be happy."

Madison arched an eyebrow but didn't say anything. Alice knew her too well, it seemed.

"The eyes can never hide the true state of your soul," Alice said quietly. "I look in your eyes and I see sadness. Even Ashton's presence couldn't totally quash that."

Madison looked away. What could she say to that? It was the truth.

"Whatever has happened between you and Shannon," Alice continued, "I only hope you can find a path back together. Life is so short. You shouldn't spend it being unhappy. And you shouldn't spend it trying to please others."

Madison felt a tear escape, and she wiped it away impatiently. She looked at Alice. "You know, don't you?"

"Know what? That you married a man you didn't love? I was with you the night before your wedding, remember?"

Madison nodded.

"I watched you grow up, I watched you fall in love. And I watched you go away to college with tears in your eyes. I watched you get married with tears in your eyes. Yes, I know."

Madison wiped at the tears that continued to fall, not knowing what to say. "Does Shannon know?"

"Does she know that I know? Yes."

Madison smiled as she accepted the tissue Alice produced. She blew her nose, blinking back her tears. "And here we thought no one knew." She cleared her throat. "I guess we weren't very good at hiding our feelings."

"As I told Shannon, a mother knows when her child is falling in love. Especially when it's right in front of you."

"I'm sorry, Alice. We were...we were kids. We—"

"You fell in love. Don't be sorry. But I'm sure that must have been a difficult time for you. Knowing you were to marry Stephen, I mean."

"Being gay was not an option for me," she said. "Can you imagine what my mother would have done?"

"Oh, yes, I can. Shannon and I would most definitely have been thrown to the curb," Alice said with a smile. "But Shannon told me you weren't gay."

Madison glanced at Alice quickly. "Shannon and I never talked much about it, really. We didn't label it. But everything I ever dreamed of having with someone, I had it with Shannon." She shook her head. "But I knew I couldn't keep it. Shannon accepted that she was gay. I could not."

"And now?"

"You mean now that Shannon is back?"

"No. I mean...your life. Now what?"

Madison looked away, the tissue squeezed tightly in her hand. "I want to leave Stephen." Saying the words out loud seemed to take some of the pressure off of her. She looked at Alice again. "I want to divorce him."

Alice nodded and took her hand, holding it lightly. "Then that's what you should do."

"My mother—"

"It's time your mother stopped running your life, Madison. It's past time."

"That's easier said than done."

"No. That's not true. The first step is always the hardest. Your mother takes it for granted, Madison. You've always allowed it. I saw it when you were a child. I saw it in high school. In college. Your wedding." She shook her head. "Did you have *any* say in the planning?"

"No. Of course, I didn't really care. I didn't want to get married."

"No. But you got married anyway. And your mother picked out your house and you let her. I had hoped that when you married and moved out from under her, that things would change. Even when Ashton was born, I kept hoping she would let you go, let you be who you really are."

"Oh, Alice...why couldn't you have been my mother?"

Alice smiled and squeezed her hand. "All things happen for a reason, I suppose. Life has so many peaks and valleys, ups and downs, you simply have to appreciate the highs and learn from the lows," she said. "I'll be here for anything you need, Madison. You've been like a daughter to me, you know. With Shannon staying away like she did—"

"I'm so sorry. She did that because of me."

"I know she did. She would never tell me, but I knew. I could see the pain in her eyes. Just like I could see it in yours."

Madison took a deep breath. "I don't have any expectations for us. It's been so long, I don't know if we could get that back. But I hope we can salvage a friendship. I really need her right now, Alice. I just don't know how much she trusts me."

"I too hope you can get your friendship back. You have to take it slowly. She'll come around."

Madison smiled. "I invited her to dinner," she said. "Stephen is gone this week. I wanted to talk to her about...well, about leaving my marriage. She's so independent and I'm quite the opposite. I hope I can learn from her."

"Did she accept?"

Madison nodded. "After a little prodding," she said with a smile. "I'm going to make that spaghetti you taught me. Vegetables instead of meatballs."

"I've also seen her make some kind of a white sauce, with tofu, that she puts over pasta." Alice smiled at her and patted her hand. "I'm glad she's going."

"I think she wanted to decline," Madison admitted.

"Yes, well, Shannon has become a little stubborn in her old age," Alice said with a laugh.

"Excuse me?"

They turned to find Shannon standing at the door, watching them. Madison wondered how much she'd heard as Shannon's eyes scanned hers.

"I'll admit to the stubborn part but *old age*?"

Alice smiled at her. "Come join us," she offered. "There's tea."

"I think I'll grab a beer, if that's okay," Shannon said. "I've done about as much damage as I can do on the design for one day." She glanced at Madison. "Tea okay or would you like something else?"

"Tea's fine," she said. "I can't stay much longer. I have a dinner to plan," she said with a grin.

CHAPTER TWENTY-ONE

Shannon closed the door on her truck, staring up at the house that Madison now called home. While not at all as elaborate—or imposing—as the mansion, it was still impressive and certainly made a statement as to their social status…and their wealth. She'd guess the lots were at least an acre each with the homes on them all four to five thousand square feet. The landscaping was immaculate and well-designed, leaving mature trees surrounding the house. Seasonal flowers were crowded into every available space, the color splashing brightly across the green lawn.

She stepped onto the sidewalk that curved perfectly through the trees, slicing the lawn in half. She took a deep breath as she stood at the front door, thinking again that this was a bad idea. Her mother wanted them to be friends. Madison wanted them to be friends. Shannon wasn't so sure. There was too much history between them. Too much left unsettled.

But no. It was settled, wasn't it? Madison was married. End of story. With that thought, she pushed the doorbell, hearing the subtle yet elegant ring tone announcing her presence. Madison opened the door a few seconds later, looking flushed.

"You came early. Good. Because I'm lost."

Shannon raised her eyebrows. "Well, it's a big house. I'd get lost too."

Madison laughed, her eyes sparkling. "Very funny. No, lost in the kitchen," she clarified.

"You're cooking?"

"I told you I would."

Shannon's eyes followed the length of her—silk blouse, black pants, black pumps—then back up, jewelry and makeup in place, all matching perfectly. She then looked at her own clothes—her nicest pair of jeans, her running shoes, her T-shirt emblazoned with "Fletcher's Natural Foods Market."

"You should have warned me," she said. "I didn't realize it was going to be such a formal dinner." She held up a bottle. "I did bring wine, though."

"Oh, Shannon, it's not formal." She motioned to her clothes. "This is just…never mind." She smiled again. "Please come in."

Shannon stepped inside, the entryway large and open. She paused. "Do I get a tour?"

Madison shook her head. "Trust me. You don't want one." She closed the door and Shannon followed her through the house—formal living room, a quick glance into a less formal sitting area, and finally into the kitchen.

Shannon stopped, staring at what she could only describe as a mess. Four pots, two pans and three bowls—all in various stages of meal prep—littered the stove and countertops. She laughed.

"What the hell are you doing?"

Madison laughed too. "Making dinner."

Shannon walked closer, inspecting the contents of the pots. One was filled with water and pasta. Another had vegetables, still uncooked. A third had some sort of tomato sauce. The fourth… some kind of white sauce. She looked at Madison with raised eyebrows.

"It looked easier when your mother made this."

"My mother?"

"She's been…well…teaching me to cook."

"I see."

"And it's not like you're normal," Madison said, pointing to her. "A steak would have been much easier. Of course, I don't know how to use the gas grill."

Shannon laughed. "Oh, the plight of the rich and pampered." She handed Madison the bottle of wine she still held as she surveyed the kitchen, trying to decide if she could salvage dinner. "Spaghetti?"

Madison nodded. "The sauce has been simmering for an hour now. Your mother said to make some vegetables since you don't eat meatballs or anything like that."

"Okay. Rule number one. Bring the water to a boil before you add the pasta," she said. "If you have more pasta, I think we can… do something with the rest of this." She picked up the small pot that had the white sauce. "What's this?"

"Tofu."

"My mother is teaching you how to cook with tofu? She doesn't even know what tofu is."

Madison nodded. "And it's nasty."

Shannon looked in the pot again. "So what did you do?"

"I put it in a blender," she said, pointing to the blender in question.

"No seasonings?"

Madison shook her head.

"Okay. Well, let's stick to the tomato sauce then." She put the pan in the sink. "I'm going to need wine." She sampled the sauce. "Lots of wine," she murmured. "For me and the sauce."

An hour later, they were sitting at the breakfast table with plates piled high of spaghetti and vegetables, topped with a rich-tasting sauce.

"So just how much time do you spend with my mother?" Shannon asked as she twisted pasta around her fork.

"This is so good," Madison said. "Your mother didn't mention adding wine to the sauce."

Shannon watched her. "So?"

Madison wiped her mouth with a cloth napkin before taking a sip of wine. "I see her, I don't know, often, I guess." She smiled at Shannon almost apologetically. "Honestly, at first, when Ashton was a baby, I turned to your mother for help. I didn't want a nanny and my mother was useless. So that's when it started. Ashton loves her to death, as you know." She paused. "And I felt guilty."

"What do you mean?"

"I knew the reason you stayed away from Brook Hill was because of me. I knew that Alice missed you." She held up her hand. "Not that I was trying to take your place or anything like that," she said quickly, "but I knew she missed having someone here, having someone to take care of. We became close."

Shannon raised an eyebrow. "How close?"

"Close enough that I can tell her anything. That's a relationship I never had with my own mother." Madison met her eyes across the table. "She knows about us, by the way."

Shannon nodded with a smile. "Yeah, I know. We had *the talk* the other night. Surprised the hell out of me."

Madison smiled too. "Me too. But I was glad she brought it up. She was so…understanding about it all."

"I was so certain she would have freaked out," she said.

"She lived with us. She had to have known. We obviously weren't that good at hiding it."

There were so many things Shannon wanted to say, wanted to ask, but she wasn't ready to go down that road. Instead, she chose another topic.

"Why don't you want to give me a tour of the house?"

Madison smiled slightly and nodded, acknowledging Shannon's attempt at changing the subject. She put her fork down and picked up her wineglass. "Because I hate this house. It's not a home. It's just a house my mother picked out."

"Your mother?"

"Yes."

Shannon shook her head. "You let your mother pick out your house?"

Madison smiled quickly. "Not only that, she decorated it as well."

Shannon stared at her. "Why on earth would you allow that?"

Madison looked away. "Because I didn't care. I didn't care about anything. I didn't want to be married and I didn't care where we lived." She shrugged. "So my mother took it and ran with it." She pointed to her clothes. "Same here."

"Oh my God. She picks out your clothes?" Shannon shook her head again. "Why have you *allowed* that? Madison, you're not a kid anymore. I know when we were young, she picked out your clothes, but you're an adult, you're married. You have a kid."

"I know all of that, Shannon. I know. It's just…" She shrugged again. "It's easier to go with it than to fight her."

Shannon stared at her. "So everything in your life…it's your mother?"

"Or Stephen."

"I can't believe you would continue to allow that, Madison. Why would you put up with that kind of…*control?*" Shannon got up from the table, her dinner forgotten. She leaned against the counter, her gaze drifting back to Madison. "All this time, I thought all of this," she said, motioning to the house, "was what you wanted."

"Oh, Shannon, you know that's not true. You remember how it was. My mother always made me feel so…*young*, so dependent. You, of all people, should know that. I never wanted to get married."

"Yet you did," Shannon countered quickly. "You got married. You went through with it." And suddenly, all the years of anger and frustration came rolling back in full force, and she could no longer stop the words that tumbled from her mouth. "How did it feel, Madison? How did it feel to live a lie? All this time, living someone else's life…how does it feel?"

"Stop, Shannon. Don't."

"Don't? You've been unhappy all these years, Madison. For what? For your mother? For your family?"

"There was no choice," she said. "My mother made sure the family name always came first."

"Bullshit. That's not how it works in the real world."

"That's how it works in my world."

"That's insane," she said. "You got married—you *stayed* married—for the sake of your name? That's just crazy."

"I know that."

"So why? Why do it? Why put yourself through that?" She paused, meeting Madison's eyes. "Why put *me* through that?"

Madison looked away. "Please stop, Shannon."

"No. I want to *know*. I want to know why you did it. Why were you content to live this lie? All these years, Madison. A lie. What was it like?"

"What do you want me to say?" She looked back at her again. "What do you want to me say?"

"I don't know. I don't know what I want you to say." She paced, going across the room, then back toward the table, hands running through her hair, trying to make sense of her thoughts. In her mind's eye, all she could see was Madison and Stephen together. She closed her eyes, hoping to shred the image but it lingered. She clenched her fists together. "All these years married to him, living with him," she said quietly. "What was it like, Madison?" She met her eyes, holding them. "What was it like when he touched you? Did you think of me?"

"Shannon…don't. *Please*."

"Did you? When he made love to you, were you wishing it was me? Were you wishing it was me touching you and not him?"

"Shannon—"

"Was it my hands on your body and not his?" She ignored the tears she saw in Madison's eyes as her words kept coming. "Did you *ever* think of me, Madison? Or did you forget about me? Forget about *us*? When you made love to Stephen, did you—"

"Stop it!" Madison said loudly, slamming her fists on the table, rattling the dinnerware. "Yes, Shannon. Yes. I thought of you. Always. Is that what you want to hear?" She wiped the tears from her cheeks, her eyes never leaving Shannon's. "I *hated* being with him. I hated when he touched me. Is that what you want to know?"

Madison's tears finally got to her, and Shannon hated herself at that moment. "God, I'm sorry. I'm sorry. I didn't mean—"

"No, don't. I don't want your pity," Madison said quietly. "I don't deserve it. Because it's all true."

Shannon shook her head. "I'm sorry. I had no right to talk to you that way."

"We should be able to talk about this." Madison wiped her eyes with her napkin, then tossed it down. "We've never talked about it. So I know you needed to say…all that. You've been so good about everything, Shannon. Always. I'm sorry I wasn't strong enough to put a stop to it all. But the wheels were in motion from the time I was born. Probably before. You know how it was."

Shannon went back to the table and sat down again. "Yes. I know. I'm sorry," she said again.

Madison took a deep breath, her eyes still damp with tears. "I need...I need a friend, Shannon. I don't have anybody." She cleared her throat. "I want to leave Stephen. I want to divorce him." Madison paused, letting her words sink in. "I can't do this anymore. I just can't."

Shannon stared in disbelief. "You're going to...divorce him?"

Madison nodded. "I always thought that Ashton was the reason I stayed. But that's not true. The reason is, I've been afraid to leave him."

"Afraid?" Shannon reached over and lightly squeezed her arm. "Please say he doesn't hit you."

Madison shook her head. "No. Never. But I'm afraid of what he'll say, what he'll do. I'm afraid of what my mother will say. She'll be devastated. And furious."

"It's your life, Madison. Not hers."

"I know. But I don't have any practice at this. I don't have any... any confidence in myself."

"What do you mean?"

"Everything in my life was based on what my mother said, what she did, what she provided for me. Everything I learned, everything I—"

Shannon stopped her. "Not *everything*, Madison," she said pointedly.

Madison smiled quickly. "I think about when we were young, all we did. It still shocks me that I was able to do that without being terrified of my mother finding us."

Shannon laughed. "That's because I was terrified enough for both of us."

They were quiet for a moment, then Madison reached for Shannon's hand. Shannon watched as their fingers entwined and the familiarity of it was so strong, it could have been only yesterday that they were lovers.

"I need you in my life, Shannon. As a friend."

Shannon nodded.

"I'm going to leave Stephen, but I need it to be about me. I don't want it to be about you. Do you understand?"

Shannon nodded again, raising her eyes to meet Madison's.

"I've been unhappy and I need a change...for me. I wanted you to know I have no expectations of anything...with you. In fact, I don't think I'm emotionally sound enough for that anyway." She gave a slight laugh and pulled her hand from Shannon's. "Of course, I have no idea how you feel anymore, it's been so many years. You...you probably have someone anyway."

Shannon bit her lip. Did she? Did Ally count? She decided she did.

"I...I date. I've been seeing someone. Ally." She shrugged. "For a while now." She was surprised by the pain she saw in Madison's eyes, and she wanted to take her words back, but Madison smiled quickly, hiding her emotions.

"Good for you. You deserve to have someone in your life."

At that, Shannon shook her head. "She's not someone in my life, Madison. She's just...she's—"

"Someone you have sex with?"

Shannon blushed and ducked her head. She'd never lied to Madison before. No need to start now. "God, who am I kidding?" She looked up, meeting her gaze. "I wouldn't really call it dating. I've been told I make a lousy date. You see, I forget to call. I forget dinner. Ally is simply the last woman I've tried to have a relationship with." She shrugged. "But it doesn't matter. Like you said, it's been a lot of years. I think we're past all that." She sat up straighter. "So, yeah, I can be your friend."

Madison's smile was genuine. "Thank you."

CHAPTER TWENTY-TWO

Madison fidgeted with the phone, rolling it around in her hands nervously. While she and Ashton spoke daily, it was usually later in the evening before either she or he made the call. But Stephen had returned from his business trip and was only scheduled to be home for two days before he headed to Austin to meet with his campaign manager and staff. She rolled her eyes at that thought, still not sure why—or when—he'd become obsessed with politics.

Regardless, she wanted to talk to him tonight. It had been three days since she and Shannon had spoken, and she finally had her thoughts organized enough to attempt a conversation with him. He would be floored, no doubt. His disbelief would morph into anger quickly, she knew. Not anger that their marriage was coming to an end; their marriage had been over for years. No, anger that it would make him appear weak, or worse, damaged. Her happiness wouldn't matter to him; his only concern would be how it affected him and his career.

She looked at her phone and without further thought pushed Ashton's number. She needed to tell him first...tell him that she was leaving his father. He answered quickly, sounding out of breath.

"Hi, Mom," he greeted.

"Hi, honey. Did I catch you at a bad time?"

"No. I'm on my way to the library."

"Oh? You mean you actually have to study now?" she teased.

"Hardly. I'm tutoring."

She shook her head and smiled. "How can you be tutoring? You just started."

"You know how it is," he said vaguely.

"Not challenging?" she guessed. She heard him take a deep breath before he spoke.

"I need to talk to you about something," he said, surprising her.

"Of course. What's up?"

There was only a slight hesitation. "I hate it here," he said quietly. "You were right. I let them push me into this. I have no desire to be the next great surgeon," he said.

"And you know this already? You haven't been there very long," she said.

"Yes, I know it already."

She paused, choosing her words carefully. "Honey, is it your age?" she asked. "I mean, do you feel…uncomfortable?"

He laughed. "I'm used to being the youngest one in my classes by now, Mom. Besides, there's a girl here, she's sixteen, so I'm not the only freak."

"Ashton!"

"Sorry."

She tried to wipe the smile from her face. "So what do you want to do?"

"Well, I've always been interested in astrophysics. More specifically, astronautical engineering," he said.

"In English that means what?"

He laughed. "I want to build a spaceship."

"I see."

"I mean, with my math skills, I really should look into something like quantum mechanics or relativity. I think I'd like to start with astrophysics. But ultimately, I'd like to be more space-focused," he said, his enthusiasm obvious in his voice, something she never heard when he was deciding on which medical school to attend.

"Honey, why didn't you tell us this? Why did you—?"

"Because that's what everyone wanted."

"Ashton, I told you, you have to do what makes *you* happy."

"I know. But I didn't want to disappoint Dad. And them," he added, referring to his grandparents.

She sighed. "Okay. So what do you want to do? You want to come home?"

"I'll stay until the term is over, then come home for a couple of weeks."

"A couple of weeks?"

"I've been accepted into MIT," he said. "Massachusetts Institute of—"

"I know what MIT stands for," she said with a laugh.

"So is that okay?" he asked hesitantly.

"Of course it's okay. It's your decision."

"Good. Because I've already been in touch with some of the professors there. Summer classes start in mid-June, and there's one I'd really like to take."

"I see this isn't something you're just now deciding, huh? Whatever makes you happy."

"Thanks, Mom," he said. "Well, I guess I should get going. Tutoring, you know."

"Yes." She paused, biting her lip, wondering if she should keep her own news to herself. "Actually, there is something I wanted to tell you. Do you have a few more minutes?"

"Yeah, Mom. What is it?"

She took a deep breath, not knowing whether to just blurt it out or…"I'm leaving your father," she said. Her words were greeted with silence. Maybe blurting it out wasn't the best choice. "I haven't told him yet."

"Wow," he said quietly. "I don't know what to say."

"I'm sorry, honey. I tried—"

"No, Mom. Don't. Like I told you before, I know you've not been happy."

"I haven't been happy," she agreed. "And with you gone, it's now very glaring," she said honestly. "So I need to make a change."

"Okay. I understand. Do you need me to come home?"

"No, honey. I'll be okay. I just...I wanted you to know. Your father will probably call you. I wanted you to hear it from me." She closed her eyes, picturing his young, handsome face. "I'm leaving here. I want to get my own house. Something much smaller. When you come back home, you can of course stay here with your father...or with me," she said. "It's your choice."

"Okay. We'll see what happens," he said. "Dad's gone so much anyway."

She nodded, feeling relieved at having told him. "Yes, he is. Well, you better get going. I'll talk to you tomorrow."

"Okay, Mom. I love you."

"I love you too."

She tossed the phone down beside her and leaned back against the cushions of the sofa, listening to the silence that now filled the room. Agnes had already left, leaving dinner in the oven. Agnes adored Stephen and no doubt had made his favorite—a roast so tender you could cut it with a fork.

She sighed when she heard the alarm beep, signaling the garage door opening. She got up, heading toward the kitchen. As she passed the formal dining room, she slowly shook her head. Agnes had it all set, including two candles that Madison assumed she was to light. The table would serve sixteen but only two lonely place settings adorned it this evening. She glanced fondly at the chair Ashton used, missing him even more.

She went through the kitchen, in search of Stephen. She found him in his study, a glass of scotch already in his hand.

He loosened the tie around his neck, raising his eyebrows at her. "Yes?"

She cleared her throat, trying to hold on to the confidence she'd felt earlier. "We need to talk," she said.

"Talk?" He smiled ruefully. "*Us?* Well, there's something new." He took a swallow from his glass, watching her. "What's on your mind?"

Suddenly, the rehearsed speech she'd been practicing for the last three days vanished from her mind, leaving her with only one thought.

"I'm leaving you."

He lowered the glass he was about to drink from, meeting her eyes. "You're what?"

"I can't do this anymore, Stephen. I want a divorce."

He stared at her in disbelief and all the emotions she'd expected flashed across his face in rapid succession.

"Divorce?"

"Yes."

He put his glass down, his eyes never leaving her. "Just like that? You come in here with no warning and drop that bomb?" He shook his head. "I don't think so."

"It's not just like that, Stephen. Neither of us are happy in this so-called marriage. With Ashton gone, it seems pointless to continue."

"Pointless?" He pounded his desk with a fist. "Do you think I'm going to run for the US Senate as a newly divorced man?" He shook his head. "Think again."

Madison's anger surfaced. She wasn't quite sure why she was shocked by his statement. Maybe because she didn't expect him to be so utterly blunt about it.

"Your political aspirations are of no concern to me," she said.

"No? Well, they are very much a concern to your parents." He smirked as he gave a condescending laugh. "You know very well they're not going to let you divorce me. Besides, there's not an attorney in this town who will go against me."

"My God, Stephen, when did you get so full of yourself?"

"I know my place, Madison. Just as you know yours. There's no escaping that." He stood. "Now, I would like to have dinner. There'll be no more discussion of this nonsense."

She stared at him in disbelief, realizing that this is how it had always been. He spoke to her much like her mother spoke to her, *telling* her how it was to be. And with her normal grace, she had complied with all her wishes without question, conceding again and again to her domination and control.

Well, no more. She had finally reached her breaking point.

"Enjoy your dinner," she said. "I'll be packing." She spun on her heels, ignoring his command for her to stop. She was surprised by a strong hand grabbing her arm.

"I said to stop," he bit out.

She jerked her arm away from him. "And I said I was leaving you."

"You're being ridiculous," he said.

"Call it what you want, it doesn't change anything." She pointed to her chest. "I'm *miserable*. Do you understand that?"

He shook his head. "I don't know anything, Madison. We don't talk. We don't touch." He ran his fingers through his hair, still shaking his head. "Hell, the last time I tried to make love to you, you cried." He held his hands out. "What am I supposed to do?"

"Doesn't that *tell* you something, Stephen? We don't talk, we don't touch, we don't have sex." She met his gaze. "We have no marriage. And every year that ticks by is another year wasted. For both of us."

"What are you saying? You don't love me?"

She stared at him, shocked by his obtuse question. "*Love* you? I'm not sure I even like you," she said honestly. "And I know you feel the same. You don't love me. You've never loved me."

"That's not true."

"It is true. Our parents did this to us. They pushed us together ever since we were kids. We dated because they told us to. We married because they told us to. We never had a real relationship." She silently implored him to see the truth. "Don't you want that with someone?"

He shook his head. "It's too late. We have this life now. We have a son." He paused, staring at her. "And my political career is about to kick off. I don't *need* this now, Madison."

"I'm sorry, but this is about me and what I need. Not everything is about you."

"Then think of Ashton. This will crush him."

"I've already told him. I think you should call him too," she said.

He took a deep breath, blowing it out with puffed cheeks. "You're really serious about this?"

"Yes."

"Let's don't rush anything, Madison. If you want to separate, I can leave. I'm gone so much anyway, I can—"

"No," she said quickly. "I'm leaving. This is your home. It's my decision to leave."

"But—"

"All this," she said, waving at the house, "has never felt like home."

"You can't leave here, Madison. It'll be all over town if you do. I can't have people—"

"And I can't live here. Right now, my sanity and well-being is more important than your *political* career."

He had no reply; he simply stared at her with shocked eyes. She turned on her heels, leaving him behind as she slowly climbed the stairs to their bedroom. She closed the door quietly and leaned against it. She would only have a short reprieve, she knew. He was most likely already on the phone to her parents.

She walked into her large closet, eyeing all the pretty suits and dresses, all elegant and expensive. Her eyes slid to the rows and rows of shoes, and she slowly shook her head. There was nothing in here she wanted.

She just wanted out.

CHAPTER TWENTY-THREE

Shannon donned the hardhat Jarod held out to her and followed him inside their soon-to-be natural foods store. Gutted as it was, it looked absolutely *huge*.

"My God, Jarod. What the hell are we going to put in here?"

He laughed and put an arm around her shoulder. "That, sis, is your job. But I like your idea of the food court."

She walked deeper inside and turned on her notebook. She pulled up the different schematics she'd been working on, trying to visualize where everything would go.

"I like all these windows," she said. "It'll give it a more airy feel."

"Are you sure? Because they said they could put up a façade if we want."

"This will be better. Besides, maybe we can put some live plants in here, make it a little more natural looking." She glanced at him. "The contractors?"

"All lined up," he said. "They're just waiting on the plans and the diagrams, so we can get our quotes and a time estimate."

"You have three?"

"Actually, four are bidding this time."

She walked toward the back wall, envisioning the coolers and frozen food section that would go there. She turned. "I planned everything with the aisles going perpendicular to the front," she said. She turned a circle. "But parallel maybe? I mean, it's certainly large enough. We could even have the center part of the store like usual but make both—or one or the other—of the ends parallel." She looked at him with raised eyebrows. "Just to break it up some."

"Look, you've always designed them. There's never been a problem. So go with what you like." He looked around, his voice echoing in the large empty space. "But the longer we wait, the longer—"

"I know, I know," she said. She studied the schematics again, wishing for another set of eyes. She chewed on her lower lip. She could always run it by Madison, see what she thought. Maybe she'd give her a call, see if she wanted to have lunch with them. "Okay, let's go. Let me do a little more tinkering. Give me another day, maybe two."

"Deal. I'll let the contractors know."

As they got back in Jarod's truck, Shannon said, "Mom says she overheard you talking to a Realtor. Are you going to buy a house and not rent?"

Jarod laughed. "She overheard, huh? I didn't want to say anything yet. But Joan thinks we should just go ahead and buy now."

"I thought you were going to see how the summer went, see how the kids liked it," she said.

"We were. But they're still young enough to make a change. Crissy won't be in high school for two more years yet. And Kenny, well, he couldn't care less."

"I think that's great. I know it'll make Mom very happy knowing you'll be here."

He glanced at her. "What about you? Ready to buy something?"

She shook her head. "Despite how cramped I am in Mom's little house, I don't think I want to buy anything."

"We could always sell Mom's house," he said. "Get something bigger for the two of you."

"You trying to keep me in Brook Hill?" she asked with a smile.

He shrugged. "It would be nice, yeah. We've never lived in the same place. The kids love it when you're around. You and Joan get along. It'd be nice to have the family all together," he said.

"Yeah?"

"Yeah. I missed out on a lot when you were a kid. I wasn't around. You and Mom were kinda on your own. I know it was hard after Dad died."

Shannon nodded. "It was. Harder for Mom, I guess, than me."

"I know we can't get those years back, but it would be nice for the three of us to have some time together. As a family." He paused, his glance going from her back to the road again. "I mean, I know you've got your house and friends in Austin, but—"

"I'll think about it," she said, surprised by her answer. A few months ago, she would have never even entertained the idea.

"Really?" He smiled broadly. "Great."

They'd worked closely together the last several years while they'd gotten their business going, but their relationship was more friendly and businesslike than brother and sister, especially at the beginning. She assumed it was a combination of their age difference and the fact that he'd left home when he was eighteen, leaving her growing up essentially an only child. She stared out the window, not really acknowledging the scenery as they whizzed past. Would she really consider moving back to Brook Hill?

"Listen, do you mind if I invite Madison to join us for lunch? I want an outsider to look at my designs."

"Oh, sure, that's fine. Mom will love it."

"Thanks." She pulled out her phone, finding Madison's number. She'd added it the other night, telling herself if they were going to attempt a friendship, she should at least include her in her list of contacts.

CHAPTER TWENTY-FOUR

"Mother, this is not a good time," she said, wondering why she'd answered the phone in the first place.

"Not a good time? Madison, your father and I wish to speak with you. Now, we'll expect you within the hour. I'll have Stella hold lunch until you're here."

Her mother disconnected before she could reply. Was that how it had always been? Was there ever a time in her life that she'd *ever* gone against her mother's wishes? Well, as she'd told Stephen last night, no more. She called her mother back immediately.

"As I said, this is not a good time. I already have a lunch date." She disconnected much as her mother had done, realizing how childish it was. But of course her mother was treating her as a child, why not act like one?

This time, when her mother called back, Madison ignored it as she hurried out to her car. Despite her brave words to Stephen last night, she wasn't really prepared to face her parents. Not yet. Perhaps having a pep talk with Shannon and Alice might give her the strength—and confidence—to talk to them later. But not at the mansion. If they wanted to confront her, they'd have to do it on her terms.

The late spring day was bordering on warm and she lowered her window, letting the breeze lift her hair, blowing it around her face. It felt good. *She* felt good. There was a tiny sense of freedom in the action, and she smiled, looking forward to lunch.

She'd been surprised by Shannon's earlier call and invitation to join them. She'd assumed, after their last meeting, that she would have to be the one to reach out to Shannon. While she enjoyed Jarod's company and certainly Alice's, it was indeed Shannon she was looking forward to seeing. As she'd told her the other night, she needed a friend. And after what had happened with Stephen last night, she wanted to share that with her.

Jarod opened the screen door to her knock. The house was cool and airy with the windows opened as well.

"Good to see you again, Madison," he said. "I don't know if Shannon warned you, but she's cooking lunch," he said with a laugh. "We may have to make a run for a burger later."

"As long as it's not tofu," she whispered with a wink.

"Madison!" Alice wrapped her up in a tight hug, which Madison returned.

"Hi, Alice, you're looking well."

"My kids are here taking care of me, how could I not?" She drew her inside, then led her out to the patio. "Jarod, bring us some tea, please."

Madison looked over her shoulder, hoping to spot Shannon, but all she heard was intermittent whistling coming from the kitchen.

"Who knows what she's planning," Alice said. "Although she did make a very tasty black bean and vegetable soup last night."

The small patio was covered and they pulled their chairs closer to the house and out of the sun. Madison relaxed with a contented sigh as her gaze traveled across the freshly mowed lawn, landing on the flower garden—Alice's pride and joy.

"It's so nice out here," she said. "I want something like this."

Alice leaned closer. "Have you said anything to Stephen?"

"Yes. Last night."

"How did he take it?"

"As expected. More concerned with how it affects him, not me."

Alice nodded. "Yes, I'm sure. Change is difficult." She smiled and added, "Especially for men."

"For me too," Madison said, but she didn't elaborate. For as close as she and Alice had become, this wasn't something she wanted to discuss with her. There was only so much she would understand. Alice smiled as if sensing her hesitation and aptly changed the subject.

"Shannon showed me the specs on their new store. Wanted my opinion," Alice said. "It's so large, I had a hard time picturing it all."

"Are they ready to start?"

"We are," Jarod said as he brought over two glasses of iced tea. "There're a couple of things Shannon's not sure about. I think she wanted to run it by you."

"Me?"

"Another opinion," he clarified. He glanced over his shoulder, then back at them. "Lunch seems safe," he said quietly. "Mexican food. Looks like burritos. They're in the oven now."

Madison laughed. "So no need for a burger run?"

"A burger run?" Shannon asked from the doorway. "What, are you guys conspiring?"

Madison met her gaze, returning her easy smile. "Backup plan," she said.

Shannon slid her gaze to her brother with raised eyebrows. "Still scared of my cooking?"

Jarod raised his hands. "What makes you think that was my idea?"

"Because it wouldn't cross Mom's mind to eat anything other than what I offered and Madison is too polite to suggest it." She slapped his shoulder good naturedly. "You're going to love it," she said with a smile. Her gaze again found Madison's. "After lunch, if you can spare a few minutes, I want to show you something," she said.

Madison nodded. "Of course." She glanced at Alice, then back to Shannon. "I kinda wanted to speak with you about something too."

"Okay, sure." She motioned to the door. "Let's eat."

The three of them sat around the small kitchen table as Shannon served them. Each plate held a large flour burrito, cut in half, with a generous portion of black beans on the side.

"Potato and spinach burrito," Shannon said. "Spicy," she warned. She held up a bowl. "Pico de gallo," she said. "I made it fresh this morning."

"I'll have some," Jarod said.

"Me too," Madison said.

"I'll pass," Alice said with a smile. "I can smell the jalapenos from here."

The burrito was crispy, and Madison followed suit, picking it up with her hands as Shannon had done. Firm and crunchy on the outside, the inside was filled with a creamy—spicy—potato mixture. She had to contain a moan as her taste buds exploded.

"This is wonderful," she murmured.

"Thanks."

"Yeah, sis. Good."

Shannon grinned. "Glad you like it."

Conversation was sparse as they all enjoyed their lunch. Jarod told them of his plans to move his family to Brook Hill as soon as school was out, and Alice beamed at the news. Madison was surprised when Shannon hinted she might also stay in Brook Hill for a while. She knew from Alice that Shannon had planned to stay only until the store was up and running.

Madison offered to help clean up the kitchen, but Jarod and Alice waved her away. Instead, she followed Shannon into her small bedroom-office. It was as cluttered as it had been the last time she'd been there.

"Sorry," Shannon apologized. "I'm out of space." She looked around, then cleared some folded laundry from the bed. "Here," she said. "Sit. I want to show you something."

Madison did as instructed, thinking it was only slightly odd that she was sitting on Shannon's bed. Shannon brought her sleek, black notebook over and sat down beside her.

"I need another opinion," Shannon said.

"Okay. But you do know I don't go grocery shopping, right?"

Shannon flicked her gaze at her and smirked. "Yes, I'm sure the world would come to an end if a Lansford set foot inside a grocery store."

Madison laughed, knowing Shannon was teasing. She didn't take offense. "I suppose I will have to learn, though," she said instead. "Once I move, I'll be on my own."

Shannon lowered her voice. "You talked to him?"

"Yes. Last night."

"So…are you okay?"

"Let's just say I haven't dealt with my parents yet. But with Stephen, yes, I'm okay."

"So he wasn't shocked?"

"Yes, he was quite shocked," she admitted. "Not at the circumstances. Our marriage was doomed from the beginning. No, he was shocked that I would verbally bring it to light." She met Shannon's steady gaze. "I told him how miserable I was and that I didn't love him. And he didn't care, Shannon. All he cared about was how his reputation would suffer. You see, he's running for a US Senate seat."

At that, Shannon nearly snorted. "Seriously?" She shook her head. "Let me guess, your parents are behind that?"

"Yes."

Shannon stood up then and closed the door to her bedroom. Madison waited, knowing Shannon was trying to find a diplomatic way to say what she was really thinking. Madison decided to help her out.

"You don't have to sugarcoat it."

"Then tell them all to go fuck themselves," she said. "At what point is it about *you*? Why does everything have to be about *them*?"

Not surprised by Shannon's words, Madison was about to give her standard answer, but she didn't. Instead, she stood too, feeling somewhat empowered by Shannon's protection of her.

"It's not about them any longer. I'm tired, Shannon. I'm tired of living that life. There are so many wasted years. I can't let another one go by." She squared her shoulders and smiled, meeting Shannon's eyes across the small space. "I told Stephen I was moving out of the house. The trouble is, I don't really know how to go about it," she admitted.

"What do you mean?"

At this, Madison was embarrassed. "I've always had everything done for me. How does one purchase a house?"

Shannon's smile turned into a laugh. "You mean, how do *normal* people do it?"

Madison smiled too. "Yes. Tell me."

"Well, you find an area of town you want to live in, you drive around looking for houses that are for sale. Or you check out the local real estate section of the paper. Or you call a Realtor and tell them what you're looking for." Shannon sat down on the bed again and motioned for Madison to resume her seat as well. "There's that new area going up, not far from the store. Really nice houses. The builders out there are leaving the mature trees and building around them."

"Isn't that Lost Creek?"

"Yeah. They call it The Woods at Lost Creek. I've driven through there. It's nice." Shannon turned on her notebook. "What are you looking for? I mean, is this something temporary before you get another huge-ass three-story house that you won't give me a tour of?"

Madison laughed at Shannon's description. "No. Not temporary. But I want something that feels like a home and not... not some—"

"Gross display of wealth? So what? Three bedrooms? Four?"

"Why in the world would I need four bedrooms?"

Shannon shook her head. "Tell you what, how about tomorrow we take a drive through Lost Creek? You can pick some out that you like, and we'll call Realtors and set up appointments to look at them."

"I appreciate that, Shannon, but I'm sure you have things you need to be doing," she said, pointing at the notebook.

"Once I pass the specs over to Jarod, then he's in charge of the contractors and the bidding. I don't come into play again until it's time to stock inventory and hire employees." She shrugged. "So I've got time."

Madison nodded and gave her a quick smile. "Okay, deal. So show me what you wanted me to look at."

Shannon's eyes sparkled as she pulled up the floor plan, and Madison could tell how enthused she was about the project.

"I'm probably overthinking this," Shannon said, "but I want it to be perfect."

"You're not changing your mind on the food court, are you?"

"No, no. I love that. Plus it'll give me a chance to cook. I doubt there are very many vegan or vegetarian chefs in Brook Hill." She handed the notebook to Madison. "Here," she said, pointing to the interior of the store. "I've got two possibilities. This one, where the aisles are pretty standard, symmetrical."

Madison nodded, trying to get a feel for the layout. Shannon reached across her and tapped the screen, then slid across another floor plan.

"This one," she said, "I've tweaked a little on each end."

"I like it. It breaks it up," she said. "But with the aisles slanted, you've created an open space here," she pointed, "and here."

"Yeah. So that could be where we put displays or racks with specialty items. Our bakery is going to be really small, but we could also put some bread bins in that space."

"I like it. If you're asking me to choose, I pick this one," she said.

Shannon nodded. "Yeah. Me too. It's different than what we've done before, but we shouldn't be afraid to change things up." She closed up the notebook and smiled, meeting Madison's eyes. "As they say, change is good."

As their gaze held, Madison felt that old, familiar tug. She realized how close they were sitting and wondered if she should move. Shannon made the decision for her as she stood, putting some distance between them.

"I should get going," Madison said. "No doubt my mother is frantically looking for me."

"Oh yeah?"

"She called right before I came over here. She and my father demanded my presence for lunch."

Shannon raised her eyebrows with a grin. "Seeing as how you're over here, don't tell me you denied their request?"

"I did. Then I promptly turned my phone off," she said. "But I suppose I need to face them."

Shannon's expression turned serious. "If you need some support, I'll—"

"I have to face them on my own. But thanks," she said.

"What about Ashton?"

"I called him the other night. Ashton is…my rock," she said. "Much as you've always been." Madison was surprised by the slight blush on Shannon's face.

"Not always. I haven't exactly been here for you in a while now," Shannon said.

Madison nodded. "Do you know when I needed you the most?" she asked, her voice quiet in the closed room.

"Your wedding," Shannon nearly whispered.

Madison nodded again. "I was…I was a mess. I honestly think that if you'd shown up then, I would have run away with you."

She watched as Shannon visibly swallowed before taking a deep breath. She tried to smile, but it was forced, Madison knew.

"Now you tell me," Shannon lightly.

"I'm sorry."

Shannon shook her head. "What's done is done," she said. "That was so many years ago, there's no sense in going back now, Madison." She moved around to her desk, separating them even further. "We're past all that anyway, right?"

Madison nodded, feeling a sharp pain in her chest. Was she past it? Shannon apparently was. She didn't blame her. There was only so much pain a person could take before severing whatever ties—emotional or otherwise—that remained.

"I should go," she said again, turning to the door. She glanced back over her shoulder, finding Shannon still watching her. "Thanks for lunch."

Shannon raised her head in acknowledgment. "Don't forget our house-hunting date tomorrow."

"Call me when you're free."

Madison closed the door behind her. She wanted to slip out of the house, but she knew it would be terribly rude. So she turned and headed back to the kitchen, intending a quick goodbye to Jarod and Alice.

* * *

Shannon stared at the closed door, wondering why she'd offered to help Madison. She'd known when she'd come back to Brook Hill that their paths would cross. She knew that Madison and her mother had become close. But still, her plan was to keep her distance. That plan had started crumbling the first week. And now, the more they saw each other and the more they talked, their past relationship was being pushed to the forefront. Did they want to examine it? Dissect it? *Talk* about it?

They'd never truly talked about it. Beat around the bush, sure. A few mentioned tidbits here and there. But never a real, honest talk. Not when they were kids, not when they were teens and certainly never as adults. The most they'd ever said about it was the other night at dinner. Even then, they'd only scratched the surface.

Dare they revisit the past by hashing it all out? What good would it do? The pain—for both of them—would be brought to the surface, to be relived again. What purpose would that serve?

No, best they kept to this superficial friendship they'd started, keeping things light and easy, never delving below the surface. Because if they did, if she allowed a real friendship to build with Madison, then the emotional attachment they once had—the one she'd tried so hard to kill—would grow, pulling them together once again. Even now, she could feel it. That need to protect Madison, that need to just be near her, to share space with her and breathe the same air, to hear her voice, to look into her eyes, all things she'd sworn she'd put behind her. She'd buried them but apparently not deep enough.

She took a quick breath, then let it out, trying to expel Madison from her thoughts. With a slight shrug of her shoulders, she sat down at her desk and pulled up the schematics of the store's floor plan. She studied the lines again, unable to resist the urge to tinker with it some more.

CHAPTER TWENTY-FIVE

When Madison finally dared to turn her phone on and check messages, she cringed as she listened to her mother's voice. No less than four messages from her, each one more threatening than the one before. The fifth message was from her father. Short and to the point. They were on their way over.

So when Madison pulled into her driveway she was not surprised to find her father's black Mercedes already there, waiting for her like an ominous cloud. She pulled around it, taking the drive to the back and pushing the remote for the garage. They would already be inside. Thankfully, Stephen's car was gone. She wasn't sure she was up to facing all three of them at once.

She took a deep breath, then paused before opening the door. Shannon's words echoed in her mind and she almost—*almost*—managed a smile.

"Tell them all to go fuck themselves."

She followed the sounds of voices coming from Stephen's office. Mostly her mother's voice. She was in rare form today. Madison stood in the doorway, staring at her mother's back as she continued her tirade. Apparently a divorce would derail *everything* they'd worked for. Her father sat at Stephen's desk, his hands cradling a tumbler, most likely filled with scotch, and nodding at the appropriate times. For the first time she realized how much experience he must have at this. As if sensing her presence, her mother spun around, her piercing gaze rendering Madison incapable of moving.

"Where have you been?" she demanded.

"I told you, I had a lunch date," she said, her voice sounding weak to her own ears.

"And I told you, we wanted to talk to you."

At this, Madison moved into the room. "I assume Stephen called you," she said.

"He most certainly did. Whatever it is you've got in your mind about *divorce*," her mother said, waving her hands dramatically, "is simply out of the question. I will not—"

"It's not your decision. It's mine."

"There is no *decision* here, Madison. I forbid you to ruin your name—*our name*—or Stephen's name. There will be no divorce."

"Mother, I'm not happy. I've never been happy in my marriage. Not ever. And I won't continue to pretend otherwise."

"It's a little late for that now. Your marriage is what you make it, but it is still your marriage. The election is two years away. There will be no further mention of this."

Madison turned slowly to her father, who had yet to say a word. She summoned up the last of her courage as she met his gaze. "May I speak to you? Alone."

Her mother laughed behind her. "I assure you, there is nothing you—"

"Candice," her father said sternly. "Leave us. Now."

Growing up, Madison had had little interaction with her father. Her mother ran the house and managed the staff...and managed Madison as well. She assumed her mother was in charge of all things Lansford. However, the look on her mother's face at those few simple words belied all that. Her father demanded, and her mother immediately took a subordinate role, bowing slightly before slipping from the room, the door closing quietly behind her. Madison was shocked by the transformation.

"Sit," her father said. He held up his glass. "Would you like one?"

"No thanks," she said as she sat down opposite him.

He leaned back in Stephen's chair with a heavy sigh. "Now, what's this about divorce?"

"I'm not happy. I haven't been happy."

"Have you thought about counseling?"

"There is no amount of counseling that could save this marriage," she said honestly. "I don't love him. I was never in love with him."

Her father watched her intently. "Then why did you get married?"

"Why? Did I have a choice?"

He shook his head. "I don't understand."

She stared at him in disbelief. "Were you away from home that much that you couldn't see what she was doing?"

"Madison, I know your mother is…controlling to some extent, but—"

"Controlling?" She laughed bitterly. "That's an understatement." She leaned forward. "Did you know that when I was ten, she told me Stephen and I would start dating when I started high school? Did you know that when we had our first date, she told me we would marry as soon as I finished college?"

She stood. "Did you know I had no choice as to what college I went to? No choice as to what I studied?" She was on a roll and years of pent-up frustration poured out. "No choice as to what *lessons* I took at the country club. Those were all for her. I hated dance. I hated golf. But she wouldn't let me quit. She picked out my wedding date, my wedding dress, my honeymoon. She picked out this house. She *decorated* it. She picked out my son's name."

She took a deep breath, meeting his startled gaze. "Any time I attempted to convey to her *my* choices, *my* likes and dislikes, she brushed them away as if I was invisible. And over time, I gave up. I became invisible. It was easier to let her *control* things, as you say." She sat down again. "But not anymore. I can't waste another year by staying in a marriage I don't want to be in. I won't do it."

He sat his drink down and stood, going to the window and parting the blinds. She doubted anything beyond the window registered to him. He was stalling for time, gathering his thoughts.

"I'm sorry," he said before turning around. "I had no idea." He walked around the desk and sat next to her, meeting her gaze. "I had no idea, Madison. You were involved in so many activities, I thought it was what you wanted."

"No. I think part of it was that she wanted me away from the house, away from Shannon."

"Shannon Fletcher? Alice's daughter?"

"Yes. She was my best friend. My only true friend. But she wasn't good enough for me. Mother wanted me away from her."

He nodded. "Yes, I remember now. She tried to dismiss Alice once." He leaned back in the chair, watching her. "I was away a lot. I didn't see any of that. I guess I should have known on the day of your wedding. You looked so sad. I thought, at the time, that it was just nerves."

"No. It felt like a death sentence."

"And for Stephen?"

"His mother is as much to blame. We're all to blame." She looked away. "Stephen hasn't been happy either. He's too proud— or stubborn—to admit it. We haven't had sex in years," she said bluntly. "I assume he has a mistress."

Her father looked away, embarrassed. "I don't really need to know about your sex life, Madison."

She smiled. "I'm sorry, but I wanted you to know how it was with us."

He took a deep breath. "And Ashton? How will he take this?"

"I've already told him. In fact, he was the one who brought it up months ago. He knew we weren't happy."

He blew out a breath. "Well, obviously your mother is not thrilled by this turn of events. When Stephen called this morning, she was in near hysterics. She has embraced this run for the Senate," he said with a wave of his hand. "I told him I'd support him, but not at your expense, Madison."

"Thank you."

He nodded. "I'll deal with your mother. Now, what is it that you need? I'll assign my best attorney, of course. Stephen will no doubt have someone from his firm handle things for him. What about the house?"

"I don't want it. I want to move out, to a place that I pick out, that I want. I want to start over."

"Okay, of course." He reached inside his suit jacket and produced a card. "You've heard me mention my assistant Mary Ann before, but I know you've never met."

"Yes. She's been with you for years."

He nodded. "Anything you need, you let her know. I'll have my attorney get in touch with Stephen and his attorney. We'll get things going."

It almost seemed too easy, and she wasn't certain she believed him. The look on her face must have told him as much.

"I wasn't there for you growing up, Madison. I want to be here for you now. I'll talk to Stephen today. He won't fight you—me—on this."

"And Mother?"

He smiled briefly. "I can control what she physically does," he said. "But verbally, I'm sure she'll want to have her say. This might be a good opportunity for you to let her know that you're all grown up."

"How sad, considering I'm about to turn thirty-eight."

He nodded. "She never let you grow up, it seems. I regret we didn't have other children. Perhaps then, her focus would have been split and you wouldn't have had to endure the brunt of it."

"Why didn't you have another child?"

He shrugged. "It just never happened." He smiled sadly. "And I was away a lot." He stood and beckoned her to do the same. Never one to show affection, he surprised her by his tight hug. "I'm sorry." He pulled away quickly. "We'll get all of this worked out."

"Thank you."

One last nod and he was out the door, closing it behind him. She stared at it, fully expecting her mother to burst into the room, demanding answers. Instead, all remained quiet until she heard her mother's shrill voice, the words too garbled for her to understand.

The slamming of a door, then all was quiet, signaling to her it was safe to leave Stephen's office. If she'd known her father would have been this supportive, she'd have gone to him years ago. She wasn't certain which surprised her the most. The fact that her father had accepted the situation so quickly and without protest or the fact that her mother's perceived authority—and dominance—was nothing but a farce. So many wasted years of feeling powerless and helpless. So many times she'd felt weak and inept when her mother had effortlessly rebuffed her feeble attempts at rebellion. And it was all just a charade.

She felt as if a weight had been lifted off her shoulders and she smiled, which turned into a laugh.

And it felt so good.

CHAPTER TWENTY-SIX

By the time Shannon handed over the floor plans to Jarod the next day—after she'd tweaked it yet again—it was close to two in the afternoon. Lunch had been vegetables shoved into a pita, hardly enough to make a dent in her appetite. She wondered if Madison would be interested in an early dinner.

Madison had offered to pick her up, but Shannon didn't really think they should go house hunting in a Mercedes. They were less likely to call attention to themselves in her very nondescript white pickup.

As soon as she pulled into Madison's driveway, Madison was out the door and heading her way. Shannon couldn't keep the smile from her face as their eyes met. This was the most casual she'd seen Madison dressed in fifteen years. Khaki pants and loafers and a silky blue blouse that nearly matched the color of her eyes—she was as beautiful as ever.

"Are you sure you don't want to take my car?" Madison asked before getting in.

"Afraid to be seen in my truck, are you?"

"Of course not. I would rather you drive anyway. That way, I can do more looking," she said with a grin.

Shannon arched an eyebrow and Madison rolled her eyes.

"At *houses*," Madison clarified.

"Oh, I see," she said, her voice teasing. "I'm your chauffeur today."

"Yes. So where are you taking me?"

"Let's do Lost Creek. There are lots of nice homes. Some are… well, a bit too uppity for me, but you may like them."

Madison laughed. "Uppity?"

"Fancy."

Madison's smile faded a little. "I want something that feels like home. My parents' place—the mansion—was more museum than home. Where I live now, the only time it felt like a home was when Ashton was there." She looked away. "Even then, it was still so sterile. That never changed."

"What are you looking for?"

Madison turned back to her. "Something *normal*. I just want… normal," she said. "I don't want to be waited on hand and foot. I don't want meals hot and on the table, waiting for the appropriate dinner hour." She paused. "I don't know how to do laundry," she said. "And you already know I can't cook. Those are two things I want to learn how to do."

"You know, I was telling my mother that you were born into the wrong family. That all the things your family name and wealth afforded you were all things you didn't want."

"I didn't know any better, Shannon. Not until you came into my life. That's when I learned that no matter what my name was or how much money I had, happiness can't be bought. All those other things ceased to matter when I was with you."

Shannon kept her eyes fixed on the road, afraid to look at Madison. She was surprised by her honesty. She only wished those words had been said sixteen years ago. At her continued silence, Madison cleared her throat.

"I'm sorry."

Shannon finally looked at her. "Nothing to be sorry about, Madison. We were kids. And we didn't know what the hell we were doing." She looked back to the road. "So, have your parents cornered you yet?"

"Oh, yes. They were waiting for me after lunch yesterday."

"Since you're still going house hunting, I assume you won round one," she said.

"Actually, my father won round one," Madison said. "All these years, I always assumed my mother had the final say. Turns out that wasn't the case at all. My father was mostly oblivious to how things were with me."

"So you're really going through with it then?"

Madison seemed surprised by her question. "The divorce? Yes, Shannon. Did you think I wasn't serious?"

Shannon moved into the right lane and put her turn signal on. "I thought you were serious, I just wasn't sure you'd go through with it."

Instead of being offended by her statement, Madison nodded in understanding. "I know. Honestly, I didn't know if I was brave enough either. But I feel…free." She shrugged. "I don't expect you to understand. For as close as we were, you were still on the outside looking in."

Those words stung. Yes, she had always been on the outside, never quite good enough to be let all the way into Madison's world.

"I know what you're thinking, Shannon, but that's not what I meant."

"No?"

"No. I mean, you saw what was happening—you knew how manipulative my mother was—yet you were still removed from it. It wasn't happening to *you*."

"In a way, it was happening to me," she said. "Because, ultimately, whatever she did affected me as well."

Madison surprised her by reaching across the console and touching her arm. "I'm sorry, Shannon. I'm sorry I wasn't strong enough back then."

Shannon shook her head. "Like I said, we were kids. We need to let it go. It's all in the past. Over with."

She turned into the entrance of The Woods at Lost Creek knowing she didn't really believe her words. It may have all been in the past, but she knew it wasn't over. She still felt the pull, the attraction. That was still there. Sometimes it was there as only a subtle reminder, and sometimes—when their eyes met—it was anything but subtle. She wondered if it was as obvious to Madison as it was to her. She also wondered if Madison was trying to ignore it, as she was.

"The houses that are for sale in which people are still living, we can't go in without an appointment," she explained. "So I thought we could drive around and if you like one, we could call the Realtor and set up a time to view the house."

"Okay."

"But there are some which have just been built so the contractor owns them. No one lives there so we can snoop around a bit, at least on the outside." She turned down another street, remembering a new house she'd seen the other week when she'd driven through here. "How's this one?"

Madison leaned closer to her, peering out Shannon's window.

"Looks big," she said. "But I like the stone around the entryway. And the wooden beams."

"Yeah, but it's not the massive faux-marble beams you have now," she said.

Madison laughed. "What makes you think they're faux-marble? My mother picked it out, remember."

Shannon shook her head. "I don't want to know." She opened her door. "Come on. Let's take a look around."

It was indeed big, but Shannon still wasn't sure what size home Madison was looking for. Madison might think she wanted a smaller home but after the monstrosity she grew up in and now living in a three-story monster, she might be shocked at some of the so-called *smaller* homes.

"I think it's too big," Madison said as she followed Shannon around to the side.

The fence facing the road was wrought iron. Shannon stood on the crossbar and peered over the top.

"Swimming pool," she announced. "Nice landscaping."

"I didn't really consider a pool," Madison said. "Do you think I need one?"

Shannon hopped back down. "Are you still going to the country club? I guess you don't need one then." Shannon went back around to the front with Madison following. "But you know, maybe on a hot summer day, you might have a friend over. Wouldn't it be nice to hop in and cool off?"

Madison smiled. "You?"

Shannon wiggled her eyebrows teasingly. "I'll wear a bikini."

Their eyes held for a long moment before Madison smiled. "I'm thinking a pool sounds really good. In fact, I think it's a must."

Shannon laughed and Madison joined in.

"You want to see the inside?"

"Are you going to break in?"

"Well, I thought we'd try the easy way and call the Realtor," she said as she pulled out her phone.

And a mere fifteen minutes later they were following a very pleasant middle-aged woman inside as she recited all of the attributes of the house. As soon as they were inside though, Shannon knew it wasn't the one Madison would choose. It was dark and dreary and even when the Realtor pulled the drapes back to let in the afternoon sun it did little to brighten the interior. She watched Madison, noting the slight shake of her head at each feature the Realtor showed her. Madison finally turned, meeting her gaze with raised eyebrows.

"Excuse me, but this isn't quite what we're looking for," Shannon said. "Do you have anything a little smaller, a little more…open? Airy? More windows in the back?"

"With a pool," Madison added as she grinned mischievously at Shannon.

The woman nodded. "I think I have something you might be interested in. It's only a three bedroom, but one of the extra bedrooms is a nice mini-master. Square footage though, it's only twenty-five hundred. I'm not sure if you wanted something that small."

Shannon could tell Madison had no clue as to what twenty-five hundred square feet looked like. "My mother's house is twelve hundred," she said. "Your current home, I'd guess was over five thousand, maybe closer to six."

Madison nodded. "Twenty-five hundred sounds like that would be plenty of room. May we see that one?"

"Of course, ladies. It's only three blocks from here."

As they followed the Realtor's car down the street, Madison turned in her seat facing Shannon. Shannon raised her eyebrows, wondering what was on her mind.

"You must think I'm so…I don't know, what's the word? Sheltered?"

"Sheltered? I suppose that could apply to you since you've always had things done for you," she said.

"I feel inadequate," Madison said. "Or maybe incompetent fits better."

"Look, you're not incompetent," she said. "This is simply something you've never had to do before. You've never been exposed to this sort of thing. That's the price you pay for being one of the privileged ones," she said with a smile, hoping Madison didn't take offense to that.

"I just…thank you for taking the time to do this with me. I'd be lost without you."

Again, the look that passed between them belied any notion that their past was still firmly in the past.

"I'd do anything for you, Madison. You know that."

"Why is that? I've hurt you so badly. Why would you still do anything for me?"

Shannon looked back at the road, thankful the Realtor had stopped. She pulled behind her on the street, not bothering to look at the house she'd guided them to. Taking a deep breath, she turned and met Madison's gaze. "I think you know the answer, don't you?"

Madison stared into her eyes, nodding slowly. "Yes."

Shannon nodded too. "Come on. Let's see if you like this one."

The Realtor was heading to the front door, but Madison stopped her.

"I'd like to go in through the garage," she said.

"Oh. But—"

"The owner of the home would enter through the garage," Madison said. "I'd like to start there."

"Very well. I'll meet you back there. I don't have a remote for the garage doors so I'll need to go in from the front."

Shannon bumped her shoulder. "You're learning."

"I like the stonework on this one too. Are they all three-car garages?" Madison asked.

"I'd assume out here they all are," she said as the door opened.

The Realtor was waiting with a beaming smile as she held open the back door. "This way, ladies."

It was an extra-wide hallway, Shannon noted as she followed Madison into the house.

"The utility room is here," the Realtor said, opening a door on the left. "Not as large as the other house, but enough to include built-in cabinets and a folding table. This space here is for an extra refrigerator or freezer," she explained.

Madison looked at Shannon with raised eyebrows.

"Beer fridge," she murmured with a grin.

"The spare bedrooms are both on this side of the house," the Realtor continued. "There is a half-bath here," she said, quickly opening a door. "The mini-master I was telling you about is here. It's larger than a standard spare bedroom and has a direct door opening into a very large spare bath. Of course, there's a direct opening from the hallway as well so that guests in your third bedroom have access to the bath."

Shannon waited in the hallway as the Realtor took Madison in for a quick tour of the mini-master and bath. She opened up another door, finding a small spare bedroom that appeared standard size.

"Oh yes, and that's the other bedroom."

Shannon stepped out of the way as Madison peeked inside.

"Back this way," she said, leading them back down the hallway before turning into another hallway to the right, "is the kitchen and living areas. The appliances are already installed but can be changed if you don't like stainless steel."

"Oh, wow," Madison said. "I love it."

The kitchen was large and an island separated it from a sitting area. Beyond the sitting area was a wall of windows looking out on the patio and pool.

"This is your informal sitting room," the Realtor explained. "French doors going out to the main patio and also a side door here, to a smaller covered patio. And the pool, of course."

Madison turned, meeting her eyes, and Shannon could sense

her excitement. "I love it," Madison whispered to her as they followed the Realtor deeper into the house.

"The great room," she said. "Your formal sitting area. Gas fireplace. Dining room is back here. And there is a small office," she said, opening a door immediately off of the entryway.

"The master suite?" Shannon asked.

"Yes, separated from the rest of the house," she said, taking them down a short hallway opposite the great room. "Here is another half-bath," she said, opening a door. "Two linen closets here in the hall." The hallway made an L-shape and she opened another door, leading them into a brightly lit bedroom.

"Nice large room," she told them. "As you noticed, there were no drapes or blinds facing the back. There are no neighbors behind you. In the bedroom, of course, we have drapes for privacy." She pulled them aside, revealing large windows looking out onto the wooded backyard.

"Is that a greenbelt?" Shannon asked.

"Yes. The creek is actually down the hill. That's why there is a wrought iron fence along the back, so you'll have a view of the woods. Privacy fences are on both sides, of course." She opened yet another door. "Back here is the master bath. Huge walk-in shower, Jacuzzi tub," she said, pointing. "And," she said dramatically as she opened another door, "what every woman dreams of: a walk-in walk-around closet."

"It's as big as my bedroom," Shannon murmured.

"Built-in drawers and shelves here in the middle and wall-to-wall closet space."

Madison walked into the closet, circling the center drawers and coming around the other side. "Nice."

"Nice? It's crazy."

Madison shrugged.

"Oh, I see. It's because I have no idea what your current closet looks like," she said. "This might be small to you."

Madison gave her a half-smile, then glanced at the Realtor. "May we go outside?"

"Of course. Let me show you the pool and patio."

Shannon stood back, letting Madison take it all in, watching her as she walked slowly along the edge of the pool to where the grass merged with the wooded area in the back. She stood there staring out into the woods. Shannon wondered if she was listening to the quiet or if she heard the tiny sounds of leaves rustling and birds chirping.

Madison turned, finding her eyes. "I love it."

Shannon nodded.

Madison then walked directly toward the Realtor. "I'll take it."

The Realtor—and Shannon—stared at her.

"Madison, we should look at—" Shannon began.

"No. I love it," she said. "Do you have a card?"

"Of course," the Realtor said, quickly fumbling in her purse to find one.

"I'll have my people contact you. Thanks for showing it on such short notice," Madison said as she took her card.

"It's my pleasure. Let me know if you need a second showing." She held her hand out. "I'm sorry. I don't even know your name."

"Madison Cole," she said.

"Nice to meet you." She paused. "Madison...*Cole*? Aren't you—"

"Yes. Thank you. As I said, I'll be in touch."

As they walked back to the truck, Shannon murmured, "Your *people*?"

Madison smiled. "My father has given me the use of his personal assistant. I know you're supposed to make an offer and they counter and all that. So I'll leave that up to someone who knows how."

Shannon started the engine and pulled out into the street. "And I suppose the news that Madison Cole is looking to purchase a home will have tongues wagging?"

"Doesn't matter," Madison said. "Everyone will know soon enough." She reached across the console and squeezed her arm. "Thank you for taking me today. I really, really like that house. It felt...well, it felt like I could make it into a home."

"I like it too," she said. "So do you need to be somewhere? Or can I steal you for an hour or so?"

"Steal me?"

"I'm starving. How about an early dinner?"

Madison nodded quickly. "Of course. I'd love to."

* * *

The Mexican restaurant was close to empty at this early hour. Madison followed Shannon inside and they took a table near the windows. The tablecloth was stained but appeared clean. She leaned back as a waiter brought a basket of tortilla chips and two bowls of salsa.

"Something to drink?"

"Iced tea for me," Shannon said.

"I'll have the same."

When they were alone, Shannon leaned closer. "I take it you've never been here before?"

"What gives you that idea?"

"Because you're staring at this stain," Shannon said, rubbing the spot on the tablecloth nearest Madison. "And you're wondering if it's safe to eat here."

Madison laughed. "Okay. Busted."

"The food is great. Jarod brought me here last week."

"And what can you eat here? I don't imagine tofu is on the menu," she said.

"No, but they have spinach and mushroom enchiladas smothered in a cheesy sour cream sauce that are delicious," Shannon said. "Not vegan, but they fit my *mostly* vegan diet."

Madison watched as Shannon took a chip and loaded it with salsa before taking a bite. She did the same, although she was a bit more conservative with the salsa.

"So, how do you feel?" Shannon asked. "Excited? Scared?"

"Mostly excited. It'll be nice to be on my own," she said. "Ashton comes back at the end of May. I hope I can be in there by then."

"Maybe. Since it's owned by the builder, the closing shouldn't take the normal sixty days." Shannon grabbed another chip. "Does Ashton have summer break or something?"

Madison shook her head. "I forgot to tell you. He's decided medical school is not for him."

"Really?"

Madison leaned away from the table as the waiter brought their tea. "Thank you."

"Ready to order?" he asked.

"Oh, I haven't even looked at the menu yet," she said.

"No problem. Take your time. I'll give you a few more minutes."

Madison opened up the well-used menu, scanning the items. "Ashton was really pushed into medical school." She looked up. "If you can believe that," she said sarcastically.

"So what does he want to do?"

"Astrophysics. Or astronautical engineering. One or both, I can't remember which," she said.

"Okay, that's like rocket science, right?"

Madison laughed. "I suppose, since he said he wanted to build a spaceship."

"So has it been tough, having a whiz kid?"

Madison nodded. "In some ways, yes. I feel like he missed out on being a kid. There were so many things I wanted for him that I never had. But then, I didn't want to emulate my mother and make him do things to satisfy me. I wanted him to be himself." She took a sip of tea. "That's why his switch from medical school to astrophysics is totally his choice. He's going to start at MIT this summer."

"Wow. Well, good for him."

"He'll only be here a couple of weeks, but it would be nice to have the house somewhat set up." She looked up from the menu. "Will it offend you if I have chicken enchiladas?"

"Of course not. Get what you want."

After they'd placed their orders, they nibbled on chips, but their conversation lagged. Madison finally broke the silence, motioning between them.

"A few months ago, would you have thought we'd be sitting here together having dinner?"

Shannon shook her head. "A few months ago I was explaining to my friends why I stayed away from Brook Hill."

"I'm sorry for that."

Shannon brushed away her apology. "I was at dinner with my two best friends. I realized I had never told them about you... about us, about when we were kids. I'd convinced myself for years now that I no longer even remembered everything, that I didn't remember the details, that I didn't remember what it was like to be with you."

Madison didn't say anything. She just watched as Shannon absently broke her chip into tiny pieces, crumbling them on her napkin.

"I was shocked as I was telling them our story, shocked because it was so obvious I hadn't forgotten a thing. Everything was still fresh in my memory, and I was stunned because I had tried so hard not to even think about it, about you. Because…well, just because."

Shannon looked at her, their eyes meeting, holding. "Everything was still there. Everything. We were kids and I remember sitting in the big kitchen, waiting at the bottom of the stairs for the door to open, waiting for you to be there, to beckon me to come up, where you would let me into your world."

Shannon visibly swallowed and Madison did the same. "Just for a little while. I think telling them about that made it sink home. I was never really ever in your world, Madison. It was stolen moments here and there, especially when we got older." Shannon sipped from her tea before continuing. "I think telling them our story, it finally hit me. We never really *had* anything and for so long I had held onto the hope that maybe one day we would. But it was all in vain. When I think about it, we really had so little time together. I lived there for ten, eleven years with you and out of all that time, what did we have?"

Madison looked down, picking up another chip, something to occupy her hands. "What do you want me to say?" she asked quietly.

Shannon shrugged. "I guess it took me telling them our story to realize how futile things were, had always been. It felt good to talk about it. It put things in perspective. It helped me get past it."

"Are you past it?"

Shannon again met her eyes. "Yes."

That word would have been a dagger to her heart, if not for the fact that she knew Shannon was lying. But she would go along with it. Maybe it would be easier for both of them if they pretended there was nothing there. So she nodded.

"Me too."

CHAPTER TWENTY-SEVEN

Madison stood in her new kitchen, her gaze lingering on the sparkling water in the pool beyond the patio. The late afternoon sun filtered through the trees, dancing across the ripples. Even though she was trying to get out of the shadow of her parents and their name, she was thankful for the power her father had. In less than four weeks, the house was now hers.

She wished Shannon was here to share this moment, but she had been away for the last week, tending to business at one of their stores. While she and Shannon hadn't spent even one second alone with each other since their dinner, they'd seen each other often. Madison visited Alice frequently, and she'd even taken Alice to the new store to view the construction. But now that she'd closed on the house, now that she could officially move in, she wished Shannon was here.

"Oh, well," she murmured out loud. Ashton was coming home tomorrow. She would drag him out shopping with her and Alice. Alice had volunteered to look at furniture with her. She refused to hire a decorator. She wanted to make the house a home, not a showcase.

Her own mother had spoken to her exactly three times since she'd told them about the divorce. All three conversations had escalated into harsh words and anger between them, and each time Madison had effectively ended the call by hanging up on her mother. Childish, yes, but she simply couldn't endure her mother's attempts to make her feel remorseful about her choice. She wanted to get on with her life, and if that meant shunning her mother, she would do it.

When she heard a car door slam, she turned and headed back out to the garage, which she'd left open. She assumed the Realtor had forgotten something. She was shocked to find her mother standing there.

"So this is what you've stooped to? This...this house is barely large enough to be considered servants' quarters."

Madison stared in disbelief, then laughed outright when she realized her mother was being serious. "Really? Did you just *really* say that?"

"You're leaving your elegant—beautiful—home, which is in one of the most prestigious neighborhoods in Brook Hill, for this?"

"First of all, yes, it is elegant. But I wouldn't call it beautiful and it certainly is not a home. This," she said, waving behind her, "is going to be a home. And as far as prestigious," she smiled, "don't you mean *pretentious*?"

"I see you haven't come to your senses yet," she said with her usual air of superiority.

"Yes, I have. That's why I left my marriage." She turned to go back into the house. "Now, did you come by for a tour? Or just to belittle me?"

"I am your mother. I thought I should at least see where you will be living." Her mother squared her shoulders. "It's an embarrassment to the family, of course, but that seems to be your intention."

Madison bit her lip, refusing to give in to the guilt her mother was so good at dishing out. "I'll give you a quick tour if you'd like. I don't, however, need—or want—any suggestions from you. This will be *my* home. Not yours."

"I know what you are insinuating, Madison. Your father says I have interfered in your life, which we both know is nonsense. I have only—"

"Oh, please," she said, realizing she had no more fear of her mother. "You've controlled everything in my life. It's your fault I'm getting divorced," she said, pleased to see her mother gasp.

"How dare you!" her mother hissed. "Do not lay that blame on me."

"It's your fault I'm getting divorced because it's your fault I got married in the first place. You pushed Stephen and me together. You and his mother." She walked inside, feeling her mother following. "I suppose it was some plan you devised one afternoon over cocktails at the country club."

"I don't appreciate you speaking to me this way."

"I suppose not. But I'm through cowering before you, Mother. You have controlled and manipulated my life for the last time. It took me all of these years to realize that beneath it all, you're really just a bully." She pointed down the hallway. "Spare bedrooms and bath are down there. This way is the kitchen," she said, going down the hallway.

"I don't know what's gotten into you, Madison, but you're hardly acting like yourself. You speak to me as if—"

"As if I'm tired of you making all my decisions for me," Madison said. "I'm a grown woman. I can make my own decisions." She stopped in the kitchen. "This is my favorite part of the house. I love the kitchen and the bar and the informal sitting room. And I love all the windows and the pool." She turned to her mother. "It's open and airy and fresh."

Her mother looked around the kitchen slowly. "And who will cook for you?"

"I'm learning to cook," she said. "Alice Fletcher has been teaching me."

Her mother glanced at her sharply. "Alice? You still see her?"

"Of course."

"And her cancer?"

"It's in remission." She paused, wondering how much to tell her mother. "Shannon and her brother, Jarod, are back in Brook Hill. They're opening up a store."

"A store?"

"A natural foods store. They own three others," she said, feeling proud for Shannon.

"Really? Well, at least she didn't follow in her mother's footsteps."

Madison bit her lip, wanting to defend Alice but knowing her mother was only baiting her. "Would you like to see the pool?"

"I'm not sure why you bothered with a pool. You have your choice of three at the country club," she said.

"Yeah, but some of her lowlife friends aren't allowed in the country club."

They both turned, Madison nearly laughing at Shannon's words. "I thought you were still out of town."

Shannon sat a pizza box and a six-pack of beer on the counter. "Mrs. Lansford, you're looking well," she said, holding out her hand.

Her mother stared at Shannon's hand and for a moment, Madison was afraid she would refuse to acknowledge it. She finally touched it briefly.

"Shannon Fletcher, it's been a long time," her mother said. "In fact, I hardly recognized you."

Madison knew at one time, Shannon was as terrified of her mother as she herself had been. Today, however, Shannon simply oozed confidence. She gave her mother a lazy smile as she picked up the beer. "I'll take that as a compliment." She slid her eyes to Madison. "It's all yours, huh?"

"Yes." She glanced at the pizza box. "Dinner?"

"I thought we could christen the place, if you don't already have plans," she said as she put the beer in the fridge. "My mom said you closed on it today."

"Thanks, I'd love pizza. When did you get back?"

"A few hours ago."

Madison realized they had been ignoring her mother. She turned back to her now. "I'll show you the rest of the house, if you want," she offered.

"I think I've seen enough." She looked pointedly at Shannon. "And how long have you been back in Brook Hill?"

"Oh, I don't know. Going on three months, I guess."

"I see." Her eyes narrowed. "Madison, you will escort me out, please."

She glanced at Shannon. "Be right back."

Her mother was silent until they reached the garage. "And I suppose we have Shannon Fletcher to thank for putting all these crazy ideas in your head?"

"Mother," Madison warned.

"She always brought you down, Madison. Always. And now she's back and you—"

"Stop it," Madison said firmly. "I will not have this discussion with you. Shannon is my friend. She's always been my friend. My choice to divorce Stephen has nothing to do with Shannon. Now please, I'd like for you to leave. Once I get furniture and everything, I'll have you and Father over. Ashton comes home tomorrow, by the way."

"Yes, Stephen told me. Some nonsense about him quitting medical school. Your father and I will not stand—"

"It's his choice, not yours," she said with finality. "Goodbye, Mother." She punched the button to close the garage door, leaving her mother staring at her in disbelief. She shook her head, wondering why she'd been so scared of her all these years.

She found Shannon standing by the pool, and she paused in the kitchen, watching her through the windows. While they were both so far removed from where they'd been as teens, even young adults, Shannon was still as attractive to her as she'd always been. When they were growing up, Madison was always the prim and proper one, her clothes always immaculate and of the latest fashions. Shannon was quite the opposite—rarely seen in anything other than jeans or shorts, the epitome of casual and everything Madison wished she could be. The constraints her mother had on her were firm, though, and only in Madison's dreams had she been able to break free of those controls.

Yet here they were again. Shannon was back in her life... somewhat. Their attempt at friendship was just that—an effort to rebuild something they'd lost years ago. But underneath it all, there was that attraction, that pull that had always been there, even though Shannon denied that it lingered still. If there was one person on this earth that Madison could read like a book, it was Shannon.

Madison moved finally, noting the pizza box was missing. She glanced around, seeing the oven lights on, no doubt keeping it warm. She opened the fridge, which was completely bare except for the beer that Shannon had brought. A six-pack that now held five. She took one for herself and joined Shannon out on the patio.

Shannon took the bottle from her at Madison's failed attempt to open it. She produced an opener from her pocket and popped the top off.

"Not a screw top," Shannon explained as she handed her the beer. "But I do believe this is the first time I've ever seen you drink a beer."

"You'd be right." Madison took a swallow, then had to prevent herself from spitting it out. "God, that's *awful*," she said with a grimace.

Shannon laughed. "Beer is an acquired taste, much like fine wine."

"Maybe I should stick to fine wine then," she said, daring to take another sip. It tasted no better the second time.

"So how are things with your mother?" Shannon asked.

"My mother doesn't quite know what to make of the new me," she said. "I would venture to say she doesn't like me very much."

"But you're speaking."

"We're speaking. We're not really talking," she clarified. "My mother doesn't want to talk or should I say listen? She wants to dictate to me how things should be."

"As she's always done."

"Yes. Which is why she doesn't care for the new me," Madison said. "Ashton comes back tomorrow."

Shannon nodded. "Yeah, that's what Mom said."

"So she tells you everything?"

Shannon raised her eyebrows. "Doesn't she tell you everything?"

Madison nodded slightly. "She did mention that once you got back, you weren't going to stay long. Are you running away from Brook Hill again?"

Shannon met her eyes, albeit briefly. "Not yet, no. We've got a managers' training scheduled. It's something we do once a year.

Both Jarod and I usually attend, but with the new store going in, he's going to stay here."

"How long will you be gone?"

"I leave on Monday. It's a two-day event, but I'll head to my house and check on things. Charlotte and Tracy are planning a dinner party for that Friday night. I'll probably drive back on Sunday." At Madison's raised eyebrows, Shannon clarified. "The friends I was telling you about."

"And are they also friends with, what was her name? Ally?"

Shannon nodded. "Yes, she'll be there."

Madison tried very hard to keep her expression even, although she avoided Shannon's curious gaze. Instead, she turned to the pool.

"I don't know if I'm more interested in furnishing the inside or getting patio furniture and a table for out here," she said. "I rarely used our backyard. It was designed for entertaining and it was as sterile as the inside was," she admitted.

"Did you entertain much?"

Madison sighed. "Yes. Stephen took over his father's law firm several years ago. Thanks to my father, his clients are pretty much the Who's Who of Brook Hill."

"And you won't miss that?"

"God, no."

Shannon walked farther along the sidewalk, away from the pool. An extension of the sidewalk was off the side, and Madison watched as Shannon inspected it.

"Great place for a gas grill," she said. "You know, for those times you want to throw a steak on."

Madison smiled at her. "Is that something a vegetarian should be suggesting?"

"No. Don't tell anyone," she teased, but the smile didn't last long. She glanced at the house. "Pizza?"

Madison nodded, noting the distance that had suddenly grown between them. She didn't know what to say to diminish it.

CHAPTER TWENTY-EIGHT

Shannon stood in her driveway, noticing the lawn had been recently mowed. She made a mental note to thank Greg, the neighbor's high school son. She'd lived here four years and whenever she was away, he always took care of her yard. She eyed the garage, but instead, pulled out her keys and went to the front door, her overnight bag slung on one shoulder.

The staleness of the house hit her immediately and she opened windows, letting in some fresh air. It was warm enough outside for the AC, but having the house closed up like it was, it was still cool inside. She moved about at will, landing in the kitchen. She opened the fridge, glad she'd thought to clean out all perishables when she'd left three months earlier. Two beer bottles and a can of Coke were her choices of drink. Well, there were the water bottles, but she grabbed a beer instead.

She walked through the house aimlessly, her glance landing on familiar items. She went down the hallway, pausing to look into her bedroom. The bed was in Brook Hill, of course, leaving a void in the room. She went to the spare room and pushed the door opened. It was as she'd left it, and she tossed her bag on the bed. When she'd moved to her mother's, she hadn't considered sleeping arrangements here. She only wanted to be comfortable and taking her bed with her was a must.

Shannon went back through the house and stood in the living room, wondering why she was feeling so uneasy. This restlessness had followed her all week and she couldn't shake it. Truth was, she wanted to be back in Brook Hill, as strange as that sounded. Oh, it would be good to see Charlotte and Tracy again, but she wasn't up for a party. Actually, she wasn't up to seeing Ally.

She finally went back into the kitchen and out through the back door, finding a chair in the shade. She sunk down and stretched her legs out, balancing the beer bottle on her stomach, looking at the familiar surroundings, yet feeling so out of place. Maybe since being back in Brook Hill she had realized how little this resembled a home and how it was very much just a house she lived in when she wasn't bouncing around from store to store. But she didn't want to dwell on that. That would only make her miss what she didn't have.

Which, in turn, brought Madison to mind. She admitted that, yes, she missed her. Even though there was a tension between them whenever they were alone, they were still friendly with each other. That part was easy. But constantly trying to tell herself that she wasn't still attracted to Madison was exhausting.

She thought back to their impromptu pizza party, the two of them sitting on the floor in Madison's kitchen. She smiled as she remembered Madison's face as she bravely finished off the beer she didn't like. But her smile faded as she also remembered the look in Madison's eyes when she'd mentioned the party...and Ally.

But hell, she didn't know what Madison wanted from her. She was still married, for God's sake. She was still...married to a man.

Shannon got up abruptly, ending that train of thought. She went inside to take a shower. She knew neither Charlotte nor Tracy would be upset if she arrived early. She only hoped they'd be as understanding if she left early as well.

* * *

"Well, she returns," Charlotte said, hugging Shannon warmly. "Good to see you again."

"You too. I hope you don't mind," she said. "I'm a bit early."

"I was hoping you'd come early. Tracy is busy in the kitchen. We'll have a few minutes to talk."

Shannon nodded. "Let me pop in and say hello."

"I'll meet you on the patio."

Shannon peeked in the kitchen, finding Tracy bent over, putting something in the oven. "Smells good," she said.

Tracy popped up, her face breaking into a smile. "Shannon, you're early," she said as she moved closer for a hug. "We've missed you."

"Thanks. I missed you guys too."

"You've been gone three months and you've called us twice. Does that mean you've found someone to occupy your time?"

Shannon shook her head. "Just been busy," she said vaguely.

"So you don't mind that Ally is coming tonight?"

"No, of course not. It'll be good to see her. We actually spoke on the phone earlier this week."

"Good. Because I didn't want to make things uncomfortable for you, in case, you know," Tracy said with a teasing smile.

"If you are insinuating that Madison is back in my life, then no. Not like that anyway."

"But you've seen her?"

"Yes. I've actually had dinner with her a couple of times."

Tracy smiled broadly. "That's great. Because—"

"I told you, it's not a fairytale," Shannon warned.

"Oh, I know. But your story broke my heart. I hope—"

"Let's stick to the present," she said quickly. "I'm supposed to join Charlotte on the patio. Pretense of visiting, but I'm sure she wants to shrink my head," Shannon said with a smile.

"Yes, those damn psychologists," Tracy laughed. "Always want to see what's going on in your head." She pointed to the kitchen bar. "There's wine," she said. "Or beer. Whatever you want."

"I'll wait," Shannon said.

Charlotte was sitting alone on the patio, the ceiling fan blowing cool air around. She pulled out a chair next to her.

"You look tired," Charlotte observed.

"Long week," she said, but Charlotte continued to study her.

"So, on our few phone calls, you've been very noncommittal as to what it's like being back in Brook Hill."

Shannon sighed. "Well, Dr. Rimes, it's actually been better than I expected."

"In what way?"

Shannon looked away, wondering why she was allowing Charlotte to question her as if she was one of her patients. Maybe because she wanted—needed—to talk.

"I've seen Madison," she said. "Quite often, actually."

"Because of your mother?"

"Initially, yes." She glanced at her quickly. "We've had dinner a couple of times. And she bought a new house."

Charlotte simply raised her eyebrows.

"She's left Stephen. She's filed for divorce."

Charlotte leaned back. "Wow. I didn't see that coming. From everything you've told us, she was very robotic in her life, her marriage. What changed?"

"Are you thinking I had something to do with it?"

"Did you?"

Shannon shook her head. "No. In fact, she made it clear that it wasn't about me. I think, it's just that she's older now, more confident in herself. Plus her son is gone, is moving on with his life, and I think she realized how unhappy she really was. That decision was made before I showed up."

"So the timing of it is just a coincidence?"

"Coincidence or not, she needed to get out of her marriage. I'm happy she did. She's a completely different person now. She's more like her old self. The few times I've seen her in the last fifteen, sixteen years, she's been…yeah, robotic. Going through the motions."

"And have you two resolved anything?"

"Resolved? What do you mean?"

Charlotte shook her head, going on to another question. "Have you talked about your past yet?"

"Not really. It's been brought up, of course. But we haven't dissected it, if that's what you mean."

Charlotte leaned closer, her voice low. "Do you still have feelings for her?"

It was a question Shannon had asked herself, but she hadn't dared to answer it. Yes, she still cared for Madison, that much was obvious. But those feelings from years ago, those insane feelings where nothing else mattered but Madison, surely those feelings were gone. She'd told Madison she was past all that. Problem was, only a small part of her heart truly believed that. While she and Madison hadn't been alone much, when they were, there was always some tension between them. Sexual? Perhaps. Even though she had made a concerted effort to leave their past relationship in the past, there were times when she looked at Madison that their past didn't seem all that long ago. She swore she could still remember the taste of her skin, the sound of her sighs, the musky scent of her arousal.

She turned to Charlotte, not shying away from her discerning gaze. "I'll probably always have feelings for her," she admitted. "Truth is, we're kinda walking on eggshells around each other."

"For fear of what?"

Shannon shrugged. "Fear of the past."

"Afraid that it'll happen again?"

Shannon took a deep breath. "Yes." She paused. "And afraid that it won't."

Charlotte reached over and patted her knee but, surprisingly, said nothing else. A few minutes later Tracy came out with a wine bottle and three glasses.

"I thought we could have a glass before the others get here," she said. She eyed them suspiciously. "Charlotte, please tell me you haven't been questioning her to death."

Shannon laughed. "Only as much as I let her." She took a glass from Tracy. "Thanks."

"So, how long will you stay?"

"I'm leaving in the morning," she said.

"Oh," Tracy said, her voice sounding disappointed. "We were hoping you'd stay the weekend."

"I need to get back," Shannon said.

"Not too many months ago you were dreading going to Brook Hill. Now you're rushing to get back there," Charlotte said, stating the obvious.

"Jarod and his family are coming on Sunday," she said. "They close on their house Monday, so he'll be back and forth moving them. I need to be there for the contractors," she explained. It wasn't imperative that she be there, of course, but they didn't need to know that. She was surprised, however, that she was actually making up an excuse to be there.

"So we'll only get to see you tonight?" Tracy asked.

"Yeah. But I'm sure I'll be back before too long," she said, knowing that probably wasn't the case.

The doorbell rang, interrupting any further questions. Shannon was thankful the party was starting. The sooner it started, the sooner she could get out of there. That thought, however, surprised her. These were her two closest friends, after all. With a sigh, she followed them inside, preparing to make mindless conversation with people she only knew in passing. Ally, it appeared, was running late.

Shannon busied herself in the kitchen, helping Tracy with appetizers and making sure wineglasses didn't empty. Charlotte was watching her, but she avoided being cornered by her. After she'd spent an hour wearing a plastic smile and pretending to be interested in the conversation around her, Ally magically appeared at her side. Shannon wasn't looking forward to their reunion. She had only spoken to Ally twice in the last three months and hadn't seen her since the week before she left for Brook Hill. Remembering that she'd been naked at the time only deepened her apprehension.

"Do I at least get a hug?"

Shannon opened her arms, feeling Ally's supple body press against hers, albeit briefly. It was long enough, however, that Shannon didn't miss the obvious innuendo as Ally's hand lightly brushed her breast as she pulled away.

"You look as...enticing as ever," Ally whispered in her ear.

"As do you," she replied, letting her eyes rove over Ally's body, landing on the tantalizing cleavage her low-cut blouse afforded. Tantalizing—yet not even tempting—but Shannon raised her eyes, her smile almost apologetic. "I'm afraid it's a short night for me," she said. "I'm leaving very early in the morning."

"I don't mind a short night, Shannon. I've missed you."

Shannon leaned closer. "Oh, come now, Dr. Hatcher, surely you haven't had a hard time finding someone to share your toys with."

Ally laughed delightfully. "Of course not. But I would prefer you. I think you enjoy playing hard to get," she said.

"Me? I'm the one who forgets dinner dates, remember? That's not playing hard to get. I believe your words were 'inconsiderate' and…what was the other? 'Selfish?'"

Ally's smile faltered only a little. "Self-absorbed."

Shannon nodded. "That's right. Self-absorbed." Shannon leaned back against the counter, putting a little space between them. "So how have you been? Busy?"

"Always. And you? Is the store coming along?"

"Yeah, right on schedule." She was about to launch into an animated discussion of the store—when the freezers and coolers would be delivered, when they'd start hiring, when the inventory would start rolling in—but she remembered Ally's normally bored expression whenever she spoke of their stores. Thankfully, Tracy announced that dinner was ready and Shannon wordlessly followed Ally into the dining room.

CHAPTER TWENTY-NINE

Madison laughed as all but one candle blew out in her attempt to get all thirty-eight. "Oh, no, that's bad luck," she said.

Ashton swooped in and got the last one, grinning as if it was his own birthday.

"Double chocolate fudge?" Madison turned to Alice with raised eyebrows.

"I know, I know. It's Ashton's favorite. But when you and Shannon were kids, I do believe this is the one she had me bake for you nearly every year."

Madison's smile faltered a bit at the mention of Shannon. She had hoped that this year, Shannon would remember her birthday or at least acknowledge it, but she hadn't heard from her all week. Alice thought Shannon was coming back home tomorrow. And now, like other years, she felt a sadness overtake her. Blue. She felt blue. She tried to push it away, but Alice's eyes softened and she reached out a hand to squeeze hers.

"I want this corner," Ashton said, oblivious to his mother's mood.

Madison squeezed Alice's hand back, then took up the knife. "Here you go," she said as she carefully cut him a large piece. She and Alice took much smaller pieces and it was as delicious as always.

Ashton finished his piece in three large bites, then he took the laptop she rarely saw him without over to the sofa.

"I think he sleeps with that thing," she whispered.

"He seems very excited," Alice said. "Much more than when he headed off to medical school."

"Yes. I think this will be good for him."

"And what about you? He's only here another week. Will you be okay in your new house alone?"

"I'll be fine. I love it so far. Of course, you know how little furniture I have. That will keep me busy and I have enjoyed shopping. Especially for clothes. I now own several pairs of jeans and shorts." She leaned closer. "It's been *so* nice not having Mother with me."

Alice laughed quietly. "Well, please don't tell her I helped pick out your bedroom suite."

"It doesn't matter. She'll find fault with it regardless."

They were quiet for a moment, and Madison felt Alice's watchful eyes on her. She looked up, feeling a bit melancholy again.

"Has Shannon not called you?"

Madison shook her head. "I don't know why I was expecting her to. It's not like she's called in the last sixteen, eighteen years." She reached for her coffee cup, then put it back, knowing the coffee was cold. "Even though Shannon and I have gotten closer again… it almost feels like we're pulling away from each other."

Alice nodded. "Yes. That's what people do when they're afraid of getting too close."

Madison wanted to share some things with Alice, but she wasn't sure how appropriate it was considering Shannon was her daughter. Then again, besides Shannon, Alice was her closest friend, despite their age difference. She glanced over her shoulder, making sure Ashton was still absorbed in his computer.

"Those old feelings…they're still there," she said quietly. "It scares me. I imagine it frightens Shannon too."

Alice leaned closer, her voice equally as low. "So you have no wish to revisit that again?"

Madison smiled. "Revisit?"

Alice actually blushed. "I was trying to put it delicately."

Madison's smile faded and she twisted her fork in her fingers, finally putting it down beside what was left of her cake. "Right now, I've got so much change happening in my life, adding that to the list might push me over the edge," she admitted. "I need to focus on me. I need to get *me* back first."

* * *

The drive home was made in near silence and she glanced at Ashton, who stared straight ahead, his face expressionless.

"What's wrong?"

He looked at her and shook his head. "Nothing."

"You're awful quiet," she said.

He shrugged. "Just thinking."

"About?" she prodded.

He turned to look at her again, blinking several times. "When you were talking to Miss Alice, you were talking about all the change in your life," he said.

She gripped the steering wheel a bit tighter. So he *was* listening after all. She nodded slowly. "Yes."

"Mom…were you and Shannon…more than friends?" he asked, his voice sounding small and childlike in the quiet car.

At one time, this question would have sent her into a tailspin. Now, she wanted to tell him the truth, to get it all out. It would be a relief not to have to hide that from him. But did he really want to know the answer? Is that something a son wants to know about his mother? He seemed to sense her hesitation.

"It's okay, Mom. You can tell me."

"You really are all grown up, aren't you?"

"Was she your first love?"

Madison smiled at his choice of words. "Yes. Yes, she was." She glanced at him quickly. "I know that must shock you."

"Does Dad know?"

"No."

She turned into her new driveway and punched the button for the garage door. Before pulling inside, she glanced at him, meeting his intelligent eyes, which were full of questions.

"Is that why you're divorcing Dad?"

"No, honey. Your dad and I, well, we were pushed to marry much like you were pushed to go to med school." She drove into the garage and parked. "Remember earlier in the spring when you told me I didn't look happy?"

"Yes."

"I tried. All these years, I really tried to make it work with your dad. But I never loved him the way you need to if a marriage is going to survive. And every year that passed, the unhappier I got. Do you understand?"

"Yes. I know, Mom. I could tell." He twisted his hands together. "But Dad is really upset about this. He said he doesn't know how he's going to make it without you."

Madison bit her lip, trying to find a diplomatic way to say that Stephen was using Ashton for his own purposes. She decided she couldn't.

"That's laughable," she said. "Agnes takes care of him. Not me." She got out and slammed the door. "I'm sorry, but he's really only worried about what his colleagues and clients will say. He's not going to *miss* me being in is life, Ashton."

"I'm sorry, Mom."

She went to him and pulled him into a tight hug. "You don't have to apologize, honey." She released him. "Now, you only have another week here. If you want to spend some time with your dad, I'll understand."

He nodded. "I'll spend a couple of days there. I don't know his schedule yet."

"Okay. How about tomorrow we have a play day. We'll have our own pool party."

"Deal."

She brushed the hair away from his eyes. "I hope I haven't disappointed you," she said.

"You could never disappoint me, Mom."

Later, with Ashton again engrossed in his computer, she filled a glass with wine and took it out to the pool. She'd purchased some furniture—a table with an etched glass top and four chairs, a couple of chaise lounges, and a wicker loveseat with thick cushions. She chose the loveseat, stretching her legs out while she watched the pool lights flickering beneath the water. It was a quiet evening with only the occasional sound of a car driving by. Her neighbors on each side of her were older, without children. She hadn't seen much of them and she wondered if they enjoyed their backyards or if they preferred to stay inside. While she was growing up, the only time her parents ever used the backyard and patio was for entertaining. Even the gazebo—only she and Shannon used it. She couldn't remember a single time when her parents—one or the other—simply went outside to sit. And once she was married, she rarely went outside either, even though their patio was quite elaborate.

Maybe that was the problem. It was elaborate, but it wasn't inviting. Not like Alice's small patio, with her flower pots sitting around. That's what she wanted this to be like. Nothing fancy, just attractive and welcoming, a place where she could sit and contemplate the day.

Like now. Her birthday. Thirty-eight years old. God, where had the years gone? They had slipped away without her really noticing them. She had gone through the motions, day after day, week after week, until sixteen years of marriage had trickled away like sand through an hourglass. But here she sat, in her new home, the first one of her choosing. Her new life was just beginning.

When her phone rang, disturbing the silence, she very nearly turned it off without looking. She'd been avoiding her mother all day. The voice message that she'd left early that morning was enough to put a damper on her day. She had no desire to actually speak to her. She glanced at the phone and felt her pulse increase. It wasn't her mother.

"Hi," she said.

"Hey. I wanted to wish you happy birthday."

She closed her eyes for a moment. "You remembered."

"I always remembered, Madison," Shannon said softly in her ear. "Did you have a good day?"

"Yes. Ashton and I went out for lunch. Then your mother had us over for dinner. And she had a decadent double chocolate fudge cake," she said with smile. "Just like old times," she added.

"I'm sorry I missed it."

"You sound tired," she said.

"It's been a long week. I'm ready to come home."

Madison was surprised Shannon was referring to Brook Hill as home. Pleasantly surprised. Then she heard voices in the background, and she tilted her head, listening to laughter.

"Party?"

"Yeah. Dinner party," Shannon said.

"That's right. Your friends," she said. And Ally, the woman you've been sleeping with, she added silently. She closed her eyes at that thought. "Well, I don't want to keep you. You should get back." She cleared her throat quickly. "Thank you for calling. It means a lot."

She disconnected before Shannon could reply. She held the phone to her chest, feeling blue all over again.

CHAPTER THIRTY

Shannon headed east to Brook Hill, enjoying the view of the sunrise as it crested the tall oak trees on the horizon. She didn't bother making an excuse as to why she'd left so early. There was no excuse. She simply wanted to be home. The fact that she associated Brook Hill with home no longer surprised her. But it was Madison she wanted to see. For some reason, this last week away had been endless, culminating with a dinner party she didn't want to be at.

And then there was Ally. A beautiful woman with flowing auburn hair, funny, charming and intelligent...and Shannon couldn't even feel the tiniest bit of attraction. Had it ever been there? It must have been. She'd found herself in Ally's bed often enough. But that was the extent of their relationship. As she'd told Madison once, she wouldn't really call it dating. Was that why—when Ally had cornered her in the bathroom at the party—she was repulsed by her attempt at seduction? She didn't want her kisses. She didn't want Ally's hands on her breasts. A knock on the bathroom door had pulled them apart, and she had as much as fled from the party, pausing barely long enough to tell Charlotte and Tracy goodbye.

Inconsiderate?

Perhaps. But at the time, it seemed the best course of action. She did, however, refrain from driving back to Brook Hill right then and there. She'd grabbed a few hours of sleep, waking well before dawn. After a shower and coffee, she felt somewhat refreshed as she started out on the five-hour drive. Refreshed and, yeah, she'd been inconsiderate and thoughtless last night. She glanced at her phone, knowing she owed Charlotte and Tracy—and Ally—an apology. Only she didn't think they would appreciate it at six in the morning.

Traffic was light and she made good time, hitting the outskirts of Brook Hill before lunch. She drove directly to her mother's house, happy to be back. She found her mother at the breakfast table, putting together a puzzle.

"New hobby?" she asked after she'd leaned down for a quick hug.

"Ashton left it for me," her mother said. "Did you have a good trip?"

Shannon held the fridge open, peering inside. "Yeah. Long week," she said. "Have you eaten?"

"I had a late breakfast. Do you want me to fix you something?"

"That's okay. I've got some frozen burritos here in the freezer. I'll nuke one real quick." She took a water bottle and twisted the cap. She paused as she eyed the birthday cake sitting on the counter. She was aware of her mother watching her.

"Did you call Madison yesterday?"

"It was her birthday. Yes."

"Good. I'm glad you remembered."

"Although I think we always celebrated it the day after, didn't we?" She lifted the lid and scooped a finger full of icing from the edge. "Mmm," she said as she licked her finger.

"She seemed a little down yesterday," her mother said. "I worry about her."

"Yeah? Well, I thought I might swing by her place later," she said as nonchalantly as she could. "Has she gotten furniture yet?"

"Some. Her bedroom and Ashton's. Not much else, I don't believe." She shook her head, then smiled. "Lord only knows what she's going to do about her kitchen. She won't have a clue."

Shannon laughed. "Yeah, I know. Maybe I'll give her a hand with it." She unwrapped a burrito and put it in the microwave. "Has Jarod called? Do you know what time they're coming tomorrow?"

"I talked to him Thursday. He said they'd be here early afternoon. He wanted you to go by the house and make sure the power got turned on."

"Okay, sure," she said. She took the burrito out and pushed on it, feeling a cold spot. She put it back in for another minute. "You're looking forward to them moving here, aren't you?"

"Yes. It'll be nice to see the grandkids more than a couple of times a year," she said. "It's been good having you both here. I know your life has been disrupted because of me."

"Oh, Mom. That's not true. Honestly, it's been nice being back. It feels comfortable here. I think putting a store here was a good idea," she said.

"I hope so."

* * *

Shannon felt a little nervous—and perhaps a little silly—as she walked up to Madison's front door. She'd stolen a candle off of the birthday cake at her mother's and had stopped at a bakery, picking out a small, but oh-so-delicious-looking chocolate cheesecake that was dripping in white chocolate sauce.

She waited several minutes before ringing the doorbell a second time. She finally saw movement inside and stepped back, hiding her cake behind her.

Madison's eyes lit up and she smiled, bringing a smile to Shannon's face as well.

"Hi," Madison said.

Shannon nodded, then produced her prize, watching as Madison's lips parted in surprise.

"Happy birthday," she said quietly.

Madison covered her mouth with her hand, and Shannon was surprised to see tears in her eyes. She turned away from her and Shannon followed her inside.

"Madison? What's wrong?"

She hurried after her, through the great room which, she noticed, still had no furniture and into the kitchen. She found Madison leaning against the bar away from her, and Shannon set the cake down, slowly turning Madison around, still finding tears in her eyes.

"What's wrong?" she asked again.

"You…you remembered," Madison whispered. "You always brought me a cake the day after my birthday." Their eyes held. "Our own party."

Shannon reached out, brushing a tear from Madison's cheek. "Yes. And this made you cry?"

"I missed you."

Shannon took a deep breath, then pulled Madison to her, folding her in her arms. "I missed you too."

Their hug was tight, almost desperate, but they pulled apart guiltily when the French doors opened. Ashton, still wet from the pool, was watching them.

"Mom?"

Madison stepped farther away from her, motioning him inside. "Ashton, honey, you remember Shannon, don't you?"

He was much taller than she remembered, but of course he was five years older too. She felt as if she was being inspected head to toe.

"I remember," he said, but his glance went back to his mother. "Why are you crying?"

"Nothing, just…old memories," Madison said, smiling.

He looked back at Shannon accusingly, and she thought they owed him an explanation.

"See, when we were kids, I wasn't allowed to attend any of your mother's birthday parties. So every year, I'd get my mother—Alice—to make a small cake, and your mother and I would have our own little party. Always the day after," she said. She pointed to the cheesecake on the counter.

He tilted his head, still studying her. "Why weren't you allowed to go to her parties?"

Shannon looked at Madison and shrugged. "You want to answer that one?"

"Your grandmother wouldn't let me invite her," Madison said simply. "I didn't realize how wet you are. Outside," she said, turning him around. Madison held her hand out to Shannon. "Come see the patio."

Whiz kid or not, Ashton was still just a kid as he ran toward the pool and splashed in. It was only then that Shannon realized Madison was wearing a beach cover-up, not an oversized T-shirt. Which meant she was wearing a swimsuit. She also realized she was staring as her gaze traveled over Madison.

"Yes, I'm wearing a swimsuit," Madison said with a grin. "We decided to have a play day and take a break from shopping."

"And I see where your priorities are," she said. "Your patio is furnished but not your house."

Ashton hung on the side of the pool watching them. "Why wouldn't she let you invite her?"

"Are we still on that?" Madison asked.

"Because I was the maid's daughter," Shannon supplied. "We weren't supposed to be friends."

"Oh."

"Can you stay?" Madison asked.

Shannon shook her head. "I've got some things I need to do. Jarod's coming back tomorrow, bringing his family. Have you met Joan?"

"No, I haven't. Alice tells me she's the perfect daughter-in-law, though."

"Yeah, she's great. And the kids are tolerable," she said with a laugh.

Madison laughed too. "Maybe I'll need to invite them over to swim this summer."

"Yeah, I'm sure they'd like that." She looked down at Ashton. "Good to see you again. Good luck at MIT."

He smiled. "Thanks."

"I'll walk you out," Madison offered.

Back in the kitchen, Madison walked over to the cake. "I'm sorry about earlier. It was so sweet of you," she said. "I was touched."

"It's okay."

"Would you like a piece?"

"No. You and the Whiz Kid can enjoy it. I should get going."

They stood staring at each other and it took all of Shannon's willpower not to pull Madison into her arms again. She was aware, however, of a very curious young man watching them from the pool. Madison finally looked away, releasing her.

CHAPTER THIRTY-ONE

Madison knew it probably wasn't the best idea she'd ever had—inviting Shannon over for an afternoon swim and dinner. She put the neatly folded towels on each chaise lounge, wondering if she should call and cancel.

In the last two weeks they'd seen each other three times, twice at Alice's for lunch and once for dinner when she'd met Jarod's family. She had been surprised they'd included her in the family dinner. She didn't know if it was Alice's doing or Shannon's. She had enjoyed herself nonetheless, but she and Shannon hadn't had a single moment alone.

She remembered Shannon's hesitation when she'd invited her to come over. Yes, they would be completely alone, something that hadn't occurred in nearly two months, not since the afternoon they'd gone house hunting. Whether it was wise or not remained to be seen, but she missed her.

God, I hope she wears a bikini.

She shook her head and smiled at her thought. No, it would definitely be better if Shannon did *not* wear a bikini. In fact, the more she thought about it, the idea of them swimming was looking worse and worse. Ashton was no longer there to act as an unwitting chaperone; it would just be the two of them.

"We're adults, for God's sake," she muttered. Besides, Ashton had quizzed her extensively after Shannon's last visit. She had assured him that there was *nothing* going on with Shannon. They were friends. Nothing more. For all of Ashton's brave words regarding her happiness, she could tell he was upset that she and Stephen were divorcing. She suspected the only thing worse would be to find out his mother was having an affair with another woman. Which would not happen. She and Shannon had each said there would be no affair.

Then why was she so nervous? Well, she had no more time to contemplate it. She heard Shannon drive up, heard her truck door slam. She hurried back into the house, taking one last look around, making sure everything was in its place before answering the door.

"You got furniture!" Shannon exclaimed as she inspected the great room.

"Yes, finally. None of which I have used yet. I spend all my time in the other room," she said, leading Shannon back toward the kitchen.

"So you are enjoying your house?"

"Very much. It's been fun decorating it the way I want. Of course I've not had my parents over yet. I can only imagine what my mother will say."

"It's a great house, Madison. If you like it, then that's all that matters."

"I do love it." She laughed. "In fact, I could probably live with just my bedroom and this," she said, waving at the open kitchen and informal sitting room.

"Glad you got the pool, huh?"

"Oh, yes. I've enjoyed the patio immensely." She pointed at the bag Shannon held. "Did you bring your own dinner?"

"Wine. I wasn't sure what you were having," Shannon said. "But I see you're stocked," she said, motioning to Madison's wine rack.

"I got it last week. I didn't really need one that held thirty bottles, but I wanted one with a wineglass rack too," she said.

"What *are* we having, by the way?"

"You don't trust my cooking?"

Shannon looked at her skeptically. "Do you not remember your attempt at spaghetti?"

Madison laughed and took the wine from her. "Well, like I said, you're very hard to cook for. So I stuck with Italian but ordered some dishes from Sapori D'Italia," she said. "We'll just have to warm them later."

"Good idea."

They were quiet for a moment, and Madison tried not to stare, envisioning what Shannon was wearing beneath her clothes.

"Feel like a swim?" she finally asked.

"Sure."

Madison raised her eyebrows. "Bikini?"

Shannon laughed. "Gonna hold me to that one, are you?"

"Of course. That's the only reason I got the pool," she said with a wink, shocked that she was actually flirting with Shannon. Talk about playing with fire.

But fire was exactly what she felt as Shannon stripped off her clothes, revealing a tiny black bikini. Shannon had been twenty-one years old the last time she'd seen her…naked. The years had been kind to her. As a thirty-eight-year-old woman, she was as attractive to her as ever. She finally let her breath out after Shannon dove into the pool, disappearing beneath the surface.

"Oh…*my*," she whispered.

"Your turn."

Shannon hung on the side of the pool, her dark hair slicked back from her face. Madison nodded, feeling Shannon's eyes on her as she took off her cover-up. Even though her suit was a one-piece, she still felt exposed. She paused, looking down at Shannon. Their eyes met, held, and she was surprised to see an old, familiar look in Shannon's. Now, like all those years ago, it caused her pulse to race.

She walked over to the edge of the pool, pausing only a second before diving in. The cool water helped temper the sudden heat in her body, and she surfaced on the other side, away from Shannon.

Shannon looked at her, one eyebrow arched. "Do we *really* think this is a good idea?"

"It's most likely a terrible idea," Madison agreed. "But you owed me a bikini," she said with a laugh.

By mutual—and silent—agreement, they let the subject of swimwear drop. They enjoyed almost an hour in the pool, their conversation hitting many topics but never once delving into their past or, more importantly, their present.

Shannon had brought a change of clothes, so while she went into the spare bathroom to change, Madison put their dinner in the oven to warm. She was heading to her own bedroom when Shannon came back in.

"Open a bottle of wine, would you?" Madison asked.

"Any preference?"

"You choose," she called over her shoulder.

She stopped for a second, taking time for a quick glance around her bedroom. She loved it. She kept the drapes pulled open until bedtime; the setting sun was casting soft shadows inside now. For some reason, she found peace in this house. She didn't know if it was the fact that she was alone and on her own, free to do as she chose, or if it was that she finally had escaped the confines of a totally controlled life. She felt relaxed, calm and peaceful. It was almost as if her life was going in slow motion and she was afforded the time to enjoy—savor—every moment. For her, that was so different from the life she had been living, simply getting through each day, wishing for it to be over with and then doing it all over again the next day.

She put on a pair of her new jeans, wondering if Shannon would notice. Even in high school, she only owned a few pairs of jeans, but they were designer jeans, the only kind her mother would allow her to wear. Now she wanted something more casual, like what Shannon wore. She admitted she felt a little self-conscious when she was shopping, at first going to the places her mother always dragged her to. But the clothes that were there were just what she already had in her closet at Stephen's, clothes she planned to donate. She wanted nothing to remind her of those lost years. So she went to one of the department stores in the local mall, knowing her mother would have been embarrassed to no end had someone recognized her there. She escaped without notice but had had so much fun that she'd been back three times. Her new closet was filling with new clothes, mostly casual and mostly fun. Her mother would be horrified.

Shannon was standing at the French doors, looking outside as dusk settled over the backyard. The pool lights were on, turning the water a pretty blue. Shannon turned when she approached, her glance taking in Madison's attire.

"Wow…you look nice," Shannon said.

"Thank you. I don't know if I told you, but I didn't take a single article of clothing from the old house. I wanted a completely fresh start."

"A little more casual?"

"Yes. I want my whole life to be more casual, not just my clothes," she said.

Shannon had already filled two wineglasses. Madison picked one up and handed it to her, then took the other for herself. She lightly touched Shannon's glass and smiled.

"Thank you for coming over today. I've enjoyed spending time with you."

Shannon nodded. "I've had a good time too."

"You don't mind eating at the bar, do you? I haven't bothered getting a formal dining table yet," she explained.

"I don't mind at all. As you know, formal dining is not really my thing."

"I know. And honestly, I've had enough to last a lifetime," she said, knowing it was true. Her mother had been a stickler for it, of course, but even Stephen insisted on a proper evening meal in the formal dining room. Agnes was only too happy to oblige him. She and Ashton had hated it and on nights when he was away, they would eat at the table in the kitchen, something Agnes frowned upon.

"You've changed, Madison."

"Have I?" She went to the oven and peeked inside. "Maybe outwardly. You of all people should know I never really wanted any of that."

"No, you didn't want it. You just couldn't say no to any of it."

Madison wanted to be angry, but she knew it was the truth. "I didn't know how to say no."

"Does it feel good to say it now?"

Madison nodded. "It feels…freeing. Of course my relationship with my mother is in tatters," she said. "She still thinks if she badgers me enough, I'll come to my senses, as she says."

"And Stephen?"

Madison was surprised Shannon had brought up Stephen. She rarely mentioned his name. "He's dragging it out. I've stopped taking his calls. He's either angry at me, or he's upset and hurt, or he's trying to make me feel guilty for breaking up our perfect little family." She shook her head. "All of which is ridiculous."

"So he's not ready to sign?"

"No. And as much as my father has helped me, I'm trying to let the attorneys handle it. But I won't wait much longer before getting my father involved. I'm ready for it to be over with." She sighed. "But I really didn't invite you over here to discuss all that. Let's eat."

As she took the four dishes out of the oven, Madison was at a loss as to how to serve it. She had dishes and place settings, but she didn't really have serving dishes. Shannon must have sensed her hesitation.

"How about we leave them on the stove and eat buffet-style," she suggested.

"Is that okay?" Madison asked.

"Casual dining, remember," Shannon said. "And it smells delicious."

"I wasn't sure what all to get. There's vegetarian lasagna, a spinach and mushroom fettuccini Alfredo dish, and this," she said, lifting the lid, "is broccoli and mushrooms in a pesto sauce over angel hair pasta."

"Oh, that looks good. I love pesto."

Madison pointed to the last dish. "That one you won't want, but it's something I love. Linguini with clam sauce."

Shannon smiled. "Yeah, I'll let you have that one all to yourself."

They filled their plates. Madison knew she'd never be able to eat that much but it looked so delicious, she wanted to try it all. Shannon brought the wine bottle over and refilled their glasses before sitting down. Once again they touched glasses.

"Everything looks wonderful, Madison. Thank you."

The only sound in the room was their quiet moans as they took their first bites. Shannon's "mmm" was all she needed to hear to know she was pleased.

"This is fabulous," Shannon mumbled as she chewed on the fettuccini.

"It's my favorite Italian place, although I haven't had any of these dishes before, except the clam sauce," she admitted.

"Do you go out to eat much? I assumed you had a...well, a cook or somebody," Shannon said.

"Agnes," Madison said. "And she caters to Stephen's every whim. Dinner was rarely out but lunch, I would meet Mother, or Stephanie sometimes. There was a group of us that would meet once a month."

"Country club friends?" Shannon guessed.

"I wouldn't exactly call them friends," she said as she sampled the lasagna. "But I haven't seen them since, well, since I left Stephen. Stephanie has called me once, not to see how I'm doing but to let me know I had made a *huge* mistake that I would regret very soon."

"And do you?"

"God, no. It's the best thing I've ever done." She took a sip of her wine, watching as Shannon twirled angel hair pasta on her fork. "Why do you think we never talked about us?" she asked suddenly.

"Us?"

"I mean, in high school, all that we did, why do you think we never talked about it?"

Shannon took a sip of her wine too. "Maybe we were afraid of it. You know, I told you I was telling my friends about us." She paused. "Charlotte is a psychologist, so I'm not sure if she was genuinely curious or if she was practicing her craft," Shannon said with a short laugh. "Anyway, when I was telling them my side of the story, they asked what you thought about it or what you said about it all. I told them we didn't talk about it. They were floored that with all that was happening between us at that young age, we never talked about it." Shannon shrugged slightly. "She asked me that same question. Why? Why didn't we talk? And I really didn't have an answer. I guess I thought, what was there to talk about, you know? We both knew what was happening and we both knew how it would end."

Madison nodded. Yes, they had known.

"We knew you would get married," Shannon continued. "But if you look at it from the outside, it is odd that we never spoke of it." Shannon's eyes held hers. "What was there to talk about? It just…"

"It just *was*," Madison supplied.

"Yeah. It just was. What would we have talked about? We knew what was going on." Shannon shrugged again. "But we were kids." She sighed. "Crazy stuff." She shook her head with a smile. "I can't believe we did all that and we never once—"

"Got caught?"

Again, their eyes held. "Yeah. Got caught."

As was often the case, the underlying tension between them flared up. It seemed to grow each time they saw each other. Madison felt it. The look in Shannon's eyes said that she felt it too. They continued to eat in silence, both surprisingly finishing most of the food on their plates. Shannon finally put her napkin down and picked up her glass, finishing the last of her wine.

"Dinner was great, Madison, but I should probably get going."

Madison nodded. Yes, it was probably best that she flee. She wouldn't try to stop her.

"I'll help you clean up, of course," Shannon continued.

"No need. I can do it. I'm still practicing my kitchen skills, remember."

"Sure?"

"Yes. It was good to spend time with you." They carried their plates to the sink. "Thanks for coming," she said.

Shannon hesitated, taking a step away from her, then she stopped, coming closer again. It was the most natural thing in the world for Madison to slip into her arms. While she was certain Shannon meant for the hug to be quick and impersonal, as soon as they touched, as soon as their bodies made contact, it changed. Madison closed her eyes as Shannon's arms tightened around her and Madison allowed her own hands to slip over Shannon's shoulders. She relaxed into the hug, burying her face against Shannon's neck, breathing in her unique scent. Before she could stop herself, her lips moved, brushing against her skin lightly. She heard a quiet sigh and stepped even closer, her body melting when she felt Shannon's mouth against her throat, finding her most sensitive spot, a spot Shannon used to know so well. Her pulse raced, her breath caught—she couldn't believe she was in Shannon's arms.

"We shouldn't do this," Shannon murmured, her lips inching closer to Madison's mouth.

"Yes, I know," Madison agreed, her breath mingling with Shannon's.

Their lips were so close...but they paused, their breathing ragged as their eyes met. Madison knew it would only take one kiss to break their resolve. Shannon was the one to stop, to gently untangle their arms. She took a deep breath, blowing it out slowly.

"I'm sorry," Shannon said. "But I won't have an affair with you."

Madison took a step away, separating them. "I know. I don't want an affair either." Madison tucked her hair behind her ears, trying to settle her pulse. "No one...no one's ever affected me the way that you do," she admitted.

Shannon gave her a gentle smile. "Well, you've only had two of us to use as a reference," she said.

Madison pulled her eyes away, embarrassed. She tried to turn away, but Shannon stopped her.

"Madison?"

Madison looked down at the floor. "One time...one time when I came home, and you and I talked, I knew—when you said you'd been dating—that you'd had other lovers. So when I went back to school, well, I slept with someone." She raised her head, facing Shannon. "A girl from one of my classes." She shook her head. "It was a disaster. I wanted it to be you. I called out your name," she said. "And when it wasn't you, I started crying. The girl freaked out and fled," she said with a short laugh. "She never spoke to me again."

Shannon came closer, her eyes holding Madison's captive. She cupped her cheek, her thumb rubbing lightly against her lower lip.

"Are you gay, Madison?" Shannon whispered.

Madison leaned into her touch. "That's always been your question…and your doubt." She sighed, pulling away from Shannon. "I don't know, Shannon. That's something I could never come to terms with. A question I didn't want to answer."

Shannon nodded and shoved her hands into her pockets, as if she was afraid she might touch Madison. Once again, Shannon searched her eyes.

"And now?"

Madison swallowed. "Now? Now I'm still as attracted to you as I was back then. And it frightens me just as much."

CHAPTER THIRTY-TWO

Shannon stood at the kitchen counter, watching through the window as her mother and Madison chatted outside. It was a warm and humid day with rain in the forecast, but Sunday brunch—eaten outside on the patio—had become their norm lately. But seeing as it was already past noon, brunch would be a late lunch today.

She turned away from the view and went back to slicing the mushrooms. Since their afternoon swim party and subsequent dinner, she and Madison had seen each other often, but never alone. They'd gone to lunch a couple of times, arriving and leaving separately. Jarod had included Madison when he'd had a pizza party for Crissy's birthday. Last Saturday, Madison had invited her and her mother over for hamburgers. She wanted Shannon to teach her how to use the new gas grill she'd purchased for her patio. And this week, Madison had been to the store twice—once to watch as the freezers were installed and then again when they were bringing in the kitchen for the food court.

Neither of them ever suggested they have dinner alone and Madison did not invite Shannon back over to swim. Because the tension was there. Always. Shannon paused, staring at nothing as she remembered watching Madison in the store, looking so comfortable in her shorts and sandals, her legs tan, providing evidence that she was spending many afternoons by her pool. When Madison had turned, finding Shannon watching her, the look in her eyes made Shannon want to drag her into a back room and kiss her senseless.

And that was the problem. Yes, Madison was still married. And no, she didn't want an affair with her. But *God*, sometimes the pull was so strong, she just wanted to hold Madison, kiss her, touch her, be with her…get naked with her. And the look in Madison's eyes said she wanted the same things.

But they weren't teens anymore, they weren't the young women they'd been when their raging hormones had overridden any good sense they might have had. They were adults, both so far removed from who they'd been back then. They'd changed—both of them. Yet sometimes, when she looked at Madison, nothing had changed at all.

But here they were, trying to form a new friendship, trying to eliminate the chasm that was between them and learn to trust again. Which would be all well and good, if only she didn't still have this want—*need*—to know Madison in a much more intimate manner.

"Daydreaming?"

Shannon turned, finding Madison watching her. She still held the knife, but she'd barely made a dent in the mushrooms. She smiled sheepishly.

"Yeah, daydreaming."

Madison came closer, stopping only a few feet away. Again, the look in her eyes was nearly too much to resist. Shannon's gaze dropped to her lips, and *God*, she wanted a taste.

"About?"

The question was barely a whisper, letting her know that Madison knew exactly what she'd been daydreaming about. Shannon decided it would be too dangerous to play this game, however she couldn't resist a little tease.

"Well, if my mother wasn't here, I'd show you," she said with a smile. She handed Madison the knife. "Finish this, would you? I need to start the sauce."

"What am I doing exactly?"

"Just slice them and add them to the pan with the onions."

* * *

As much as Madison loved Alice, this was one of those times she wished she and Shannon were alone. Those times were becoming more and more frequent. Of course, she and Shannon had no business being alone, not with the direction her thoughts had been taking lately.

"Will Ashton be here long?" Alice asked.

"No, no. Just the weekend. I'll only get to see him Friday night," she said. "He's going with his father to his cousin's wedding Saturday evening. He wants me to come up and visit him soon though. We were so rushed when I took him to Boston, I didn't really get a chance to see anything. Ashton has a whole list of places he wants me to see."

"So the Whiz Kid likes it up there?" Shannon asked as she took their plates inside.

"Loves it. He seems thrilled every time I talk to him."

As soon as Shannon was out of earshot, Alice leaned closer. "How long are you two going to keep this up?" she asked quietly.

"What do you mean?"

"Tiptoeing around each other like you do."

Madison feigned ignorance. "Is that what we're doing?"

"Isn't it?"

"Maybe we're taking baby steps," she conceded. She stood. "We should help Shannon clean up."

"Yes, we should." Alice took all three of their tea glasses. "I'll admit, I'm getting used to her vegetarian cooking." She laughed. "Please don't tell her that."

Shannon was on her way out as they were coming in. "You didn't have to do that. I can get it," she offered.

"You cooked. We should clean up," Madison said with a playful bump of her arm. "Relax."

Knocking brought all three of their gazes to the front door.

"Wonder who that could be," Alice said. "Jarod wouldn't knock."

Shannon shrugged and went to open it. Three women stood there. Madison watched Shannon's expression turn from shocked surprise to slight embarrassment.

"What the hell are you doing here?" Shannon asked with a laugh.

"We wanted to surprise you."

"Well…it's…certainly a surprise," Shannon said as she accepted a hug from each of them. She stepped back. "Come in." Shannon looked around, meeting Madison's eyes only briefly before looking away again. "This is my mother," she said, pointing to Alice. "And this is a…a friend of mine, Madison Cole." Shannon turned to a strikingly tall blonde. "This is Dr. Charlotte Rimes and her partner, Tracy Truman. And this," she said, turning to a beautiful woman with shiny auburn hair, "is Dr. Ally Hatcher."

Doctor? She's been dating a doctor?

Madison kept her expression even, and she stepped forward, shaking each of their hands. "Nice to meet you all," she said politely. She glanced at Alice, who finally moved forward as well.

"Always nice to meet Shannon's friends," she said. "Welcome to my home."

"I hope we're not interrupting anything," Ally said, "but we did want to surprise you."

"You just drove down for the day?" Shannon asked.

"No, no. We got rooms. We thought maybe you could show us the town."

Madison took this as her cue to leave. She turned to Alice. "I should get going," she said quietly.

She and Alice slipped into the kitchen as Shannon and her friends chatted. Her chest felt tight and she kept glancing at the woman—Ally—who obviously was very comfortable with Shannon. Her arm was linked possessively through Shannon's. She turned to Alice and was surprised to find herself enveloped in a tight hug.

"Don't run away from this," Alice whispered in her ear. "Don't run from Shannon."

Madison pulled away. "It's so hard."

"Yes. Love is hard. If it wasn't, it wouldn't be so special." Madison looked at her helplessly and Alice hugged her again. "It'll all work out."

Madison nodded skeptically. "Maybe." She picked up her purse. She wanted to just dart from the house, but she wouldn't be rude. "Nice to meet you all, but I need to get going. Enjoy your stay in Brook Hill," she said as she smiled at them, neatly avoiding looking at Shannon. She was out the door in a flash, but she heard Shannon's voice behind her.

"Madison."

She turned, finding Shannon standing at the door.

"You don't have to leave," Shannon said.

Madison met her eyes, holding them for a long moment as the first drops of rain began to fall. "Yes. Yes, I do."

CHAPTER THIRTY-THREE

Shannon followed behind Charlotte's car, the windshield wipers swooshing intermittently as the light rain continued. She glanced over at Ally, who was watching her with a smile that Shannon knew all too well. That smile—and the hand that brushed back and forth across her thigh—indicated only one thing.

"I've missed you," Ally said. "I thought if we came here, you wouldn't be able to run away this time."

Shannon raised her eyebrows. "So this was your idea?" She had thought perhaps Charlotte had planned this.

"Oh, we had too much wine the other night. It seemed like a good idea at the time," Ally said with a laugh.

"So where are you staying?"

"Tracy found a nice hotel over on Broadway." Ally's fingers pressed down against her thigh. "There doesn't seem to be much nightlife in this town, though."

Shannon shook her head. "No, there's not much."

"Guess we'll have to find some other way to kill time then," Ally said with a seductive smile.

Shannon wanted to feel something. She really did. But Ally's touch meant nothing to her, and she wasn't going to pretend otherwise. She slowed, turning down a side street and finally pulling to a stop.

"We should talk," she said.

"Talk?" Ally's hand slid higher along her thigh. "Shannon, I assure you, I didn't drive five hours to *talk*."

"I'm sorry if you came here with the expectation that we'd sleep together," she said. "I've tried to be honest with you from the start."

"Yes, I know. Just sex. And I was honest with you too. I'm not looking for a relationship, Shannon. If I was, it wouldn't be with you."

"Yes, you've been brutally honest about that," Shannon said dryly.

Ally smiled. "But the sex? We did that pretty well, if I remember."

Shannon stared out the window, watching the rain as it came down harder now. She was tired. Tired of the games, tired of pretending. Tired of it being *just sex*.

"I'm sorry," Shannon said again. "I've…I've changed. And I don't want to sleep with you."

Ally stared at her, the seductive smile fading from her face. "She's very beautiful. Are you still in love with her?"

Shannon raised her eyebrows, surprised by her assumption.

"Charlotte told me about you and Madison. About your past." Ally finally withdrew her hand from Shannon's thigh. "So? Are you?"

Shannon let out a deep breath, unable to run from the truth. "Yes. Yes, I am."

Ally gave a short laugh. "Wow. I didn't think you'd actually admit it. In love with a married woman? To put it bluntly, that must suck."

Shannon pulled back into traffic. She had no intention of discussing her feelings for Madison with Ally. She again turned onto Broadway, heading to their hotel. Charlotte and Tracy were waiting in the lobby for them.

"Get lost?" Charlotte said with a smile. "Or happy to see each other?"

"Hardly," Ally said dryly. "We'll be lucky if we can talk her into having dinner with us."

"Well, we have plenty of time before dinner," Tracy said. "Let's go to the bar. We can sit and visit," she suggested, her gaze alternating between Ally and Shannon.

Shannon nodded. "Sure."

"I need to run up to my room," Ally said. "I want to change shoes. I stepped in a puddle."

Shannon didn't miss the look Charlotte gave Tracy so she wasn't surprised to hear Tracy offer to go with her.

"Let's get a table," Charlotte suggested.

Early afternoon on a Sunday, the bar was nearly empty. Charlotte chose a table the farthest away from two men watching a baseball game.

"I'll guess by your demeanor that you're not thrilled to see us."

Shannon rested her elbows on the table, her chin leaning on her folded hands. "A little head's-up would have been nice," she said.

"Well, then it wouldn't have been a surprise."

"And whose idea was this?"

"Ally's initially. But I will admit, I was curious as to what your reaction would be."

Shannon leaned closer. "I'm not one of your patients, Charlotte. If we're friends, then treat me like a friend, not an experiment."

Charlotte seemed shocked by her words. "Of course you're our friend, Shannon. I'm sorry if you feel like I've got you on my couch." She paused. "So you're angry that we're here?"

"Angry? I don't know if anger is what I'm feeling. A little pissed, yeah," she said.

"Because we interrupted your time with Madison?"

"Jesus, Charlotte, you just can't help it, can you?" she said, softening her words with a smile. "Okay. You want me to be one of your patients, let's do it." She leaned back. "Yes. I'm upset that you interrupted my time with Madison. I'm upset at what Madison is thinking right now. I've told her about Ally. She's probably assuming that I'm going to stay here tonight."

"And you're not?"

"No, I'm not."

Charlotte looked surprised. "So you and Madison…are what?"

"We're friends. We've talked some…you know, about the past, about us. We're trying to get our friendship back. That's all. She's got a lot going on. She left Stephen and she moved out. She and my mom are close, so she's around a lot."

"So she's really going through with the divorce?"

"It appears that way."

"How do you feel about that?"

"I'm happy for her. She's had a miserable life so—"

"You're happy for her? Are you also upset by it?"

"Upset?"

"Upset that she married him and wasted these years. Years that you could have possibly had."

Shannon shook her head. "I don't think of it like that. Back then, she couldn't have *not* married him. Because that was who she was. But she's changed. We've both changed."

"But you still have feelings for her?"

Shannon smiled. "Is it cliché to say I'll always have feelings for her?"

"The attraction is still there?"

"Yes."

"For both of you?"

Shannon didn't have to hesitate long, remembering the look in Madison's eyes whenever Shannon caught her staring. She nodded. "Yes, for both of us."

"She's very pretty. I'm not certain what I was expecting, but she's…quite beautiful." Charlotte glanced at the entryway. "They're back," she said quietly.

After the bartender had taken their orders and after they'd been served, the conversation was sporadic at best. Tracy did her best to keep things flowing, but Shannon simply wasn't in the mood to placate her.

"So what do you do for fun here in Brook Hill?"

"What do I do or what do most people do?" Shannon asked.

"Have you made friends here?" Ally asked, a hint of mockery in her voice.

Shannon flicked her eyes at her, not in the mood to play games. "Not really. Madison and I have reconnected, obviously. I spend most of my time at the new store or with my mother. Or with Jarod and his family." She decided not to spare them details of the store this time. "The interior is coming along faster than we expected. I've already started working on our inventory. And, of course, I've had to make trips to our other stores as well, so I've been busy," she said. "We're shooting for a November opening."

"How long do you plan to stay here after it opens?" Tracy asked.

"I don't know yet. We haven't decided if we're going to hire a manager or not. Since Jarod has relocated here permanently, he could manage it. That's still up in the air," she said.

"That seems logical, since he'll be living here," Charlotte said.

"Yes, but if he's responsible for the store here, from top to bottom like a manager would be, then that leaves me to handle the other three stores."

"But they all have on-site managers, right?"

Shannon nodded. "We still like to put in an appearance at least once a week. I'll be on the road a lot if that's going to fall to me."

"Sounds like you're leaning toward hiring a manager," Charlotte said.

Shannon nodded. "There's also my mother to consider."

"So tell us about Madison," Ally said, changing the subject abruptly.

"I thought Charlotte had already told you about her," she said, glancing sharply at Charlotte.

"She told me you used to be lovers. And that she's married." She took a sip of her drink, locking eyes with Shannon. "Are you having an affair with her?"

"Are you asking me that as a friend...or because you want to sleep with me?"

Ally smirked. "I think you've already made it clear you aren't going to sleep with me."

Shannon was aware of Charlotte and Tracy's rapt attention, and she wondered why they all seemed so curious about her relationship with Madison. She slid her glass to the middle of the table.

"You know what? I've had a really busy week and a long day. I'm tired." She stood. "Call me tomorrow when you're up and about. I'll show you around, take you by the new store. There's a great little Mexican food place, we'll have lunch."

She turned to leave and she knew Charlotte was following her. She paused at the door when she felt a light touch on her arm.

"Are you okay?"

"Yeah. I…I need to go. I'm sorry."

Charlotte squeezed her arm. "Do you need to talk?"

Shannon shook her head. "No, I'm fine. I'll see you tomorrow." She paused. "Apologize to Tracy for me, would you?"

"Only Tracy?"

"Yeah. Only Tracy."

As soon as she stepped outside, the rain turned into a downpour. She ran to her truck, dodging puddles, but she was still soaked when she got inside. She reached in the backseat, found the hand towel she always kept there and dried her face and hair. She sat there for a few minutes knowing she'd been incredibly rude to her friends, especially since they'd driven five hours to see her.

"It's not like I invited them," she murmured. Well, it still wasn't an excuse and she'd have to make it up to them tomorrow. But right now, she wanted…she just wanted to see Madison. Probably not a good idea, but she drove in that direction anyway.

Thunder rumbled overhead when she got to Lost Creek, but the downpour had slackened to a steady rain. She pulled into Madison's driveway, hesitating, wondering if she should just leave. But she kept seeing that look in Madison's eyes as she was leaving—a wounded look fringed with sadness that made Shannon's heart ache.

Without another thought, she ran out into the rain, leaning her head against Madison's front door for a few seconds. She rang the doorbell, then pounded on the door.

"Madison," she called. "Madison." She knocked again. "Madison."

The door finally opened, and Madison stood there, surprise… and something else showing on her face.

Shannon was at a loss for words. Forgetting that she was soaking wet, she walked inside, pulling Madison into a tight hug.

Madison's arms pulled her closer and Shannon felt that old familiar ache—wanting Madison so much but knowing she couldn't truly have her.

Was that still the case?

Who moved first, she didn't know, but with Madison's mouth barely an inch away, she couldn't resist. The fire ignited when their lips met, and she held Madison against the wall, their bodies so close they were nearly one. She should have stopped, she should have pulled away, but Madison's arms held her tight, her mouth opened, her tongue meeting Shannon's as the kiss deepened.

Shannon's knees felt weak, but her body was on fire. Her hands slid up Madison's body, cupping her breasts, feeling her nipples harden. Madison tore her mouth away, gasping for breath as she pressed against Shannon.

"God...*Shannon*," she whispered before her mouth found Shannon's again.

Shannon was about to kick the door shut with her foot, she was about to pull Madison's blouse over her head...and she was about to lead her into the bedroom and make love to her. But a loud clap of thunder brought her back to her senses, and she stepped away from Madison. Their chests were heaving, both breathing hard, both aroused. Yet they stood there in shocked silence, their eyes locked together, questions flying between them—questions neither were ready to answer. She dropped her gaze to Madison's lips—red, wet, almost bruised from her kisses. They were parted slightly as Madison drew in quick breaths. It was the hardest thing she'd ever done, but she stepped farther away from her.

Without a word, she turned, heading back out into the rain, the drops cooling her, tempering her arousal. She didn't look back. If she did, she was certain she would go back to Madison again, this time closing the door to the world.

Instead, she got in her truck and drove away.

CHAPTER THIRTY-FOUR

Madison stared at the papers in her hand, then shoved them back into the envelope, slowly sliding her gaze back to her mother. "He asked *you* to bring the divorce papers? Is that even legal?"

"I had lunch with Stephen yesterday. He can't believe that you're actually going through with this. He thought—we all did—that you'd have come to your senses by now."

"Mother, are we going to have this conversation every time you come over here? Every single time?" she asked. "Because nothing has changed. I'm still signing the papers."

"So when you divorce him, then what? Are you going to start dating? Are you going to scour the bowels of Brook Hill and try to find someone to date? You're almost forty, Madison. What are you going to do?"

Madison rolled her eyes dramatically. "Barely thirty-eight. And is that what you're most worried about—who I'm going to date? Whether they're of the right social standing?"

"This isn't to be taken lightly, Madison. There are *gold diggers* in Brook Hill, in case you didn't know. That is why Stephen is perfect for you. There was never any question of money, of his family's standing. And you want to throw it all away," she said, her voice getting louder. "What is wrong with you?"

Madison was sick to death of this argument, and she knew of only one way to put an end to it. She faced her mother, meeting her angry gaze.

"Do you want to know what's wrong? Do you *really*? You want to know why I'm divorcing Stephen?"

Her mother stared back at her, and she thought she saw a hint of fear in her eyes. Not fear of Madison but of what she was about to say. Madison's pulse was beating nervously, but she squared her shoulders as she took a deep breath.

"I'm gay. Gay. That's why I'm divorcing him." *God, it felt good to say that.*

Her mother actually gasped and held a hand to her chest. "Gay?" she whispered. "You're not gay. Lansfords are not *gay*."

Madison flashed a quick smile. "Yes, apparently they are. One of them at least."

"You have lost your mind," her mother said slowly, enunciating each word precisely. "You can't be gay. You have a son."

Madison laughed. "Oh my God, I'm the first lesbian to get married and have a child," she said sarcastically. "Call the newspaper!"

"There is no need to mock me," her mother said. "This is serious."

Madison's smile faded. "Yes, I know."

Her mother started pacing then, and Madison waited for her next outburst.

"Who have you told this ridiculous story to? Can you imagine if this got out?"

Madison rolled her eyes again.

"You think this is funny? Is this the excuse you're going to use? You have no legitimate reason for divorce so you're going to use this one?"

"Legitimate reason? I'm in a loveless marriage, one you forced me into," she said.

Her mother's eyes bored into her own. "You have a child," she said pointedly. "There must have been some intimacy."

"Yes. Because I tried *not* to be gay," she said, shocked that she was actually having this conversation with her mother. "Stephen and I haven't been...intimate in years."

Her mother seemed to be at a loss for words. But it was only temporary, as her pacing began again in earnest. Madison prepared herself for the next battle.

"I suppose you're going to tell me that Shannon Fletcher has nothing to do with this?"

Madison should have known she'd bring Shannon's name up. It was a very old argument between them. She feigned ignorance.

"What do you mean?"

"Oh, come now, Madison. Shannon shows up back in town and you suddenly decide to leave Stephen? Shannon...who has never married. Do you think I'm stupid?"

"Shannon had nothing to do with my decision to leave my marriage, as I've already told you," she said, believing it was the truth. "I've wanted to leave him for years, but I never had any support. Shannon coming back and her willingness to be a friend gave me the encouragement I needed."

"So you admit she encouraged you?"

"That's not what I mean, Mother. If you want to point fingers at someone, point them at Ashton. He was the first to bring it up, the first to notice how unhappy I was. The first to suggest I make a change."

Her mother smiled ruefully. "Now you're blaming your son? Why are you trying to spare Shannon the blame?" Her mother's eyes narrowed. "I warned you about her, Madison. I told you she would bring you down. You wouldn't listen to me. You kept letting her back in your life. Now look what she's done."

For a moment, Madison felt like she was back in high school, fifteen years old, and her mother was once again lecturing her about having Shannon as a friend. Back then, she would stand by mutely as her mother listed off all the reasons Shannon Fletcher was "not good enough" for Madison to waste her time on. She would nod as if she agreed—part of her had still wanted to appease her mother— and she even went so far as to avoid Shannon for a day or two. But it never lasted. The pull between them was too strong.

Like now. She still hadn't reconciled what had happened the other night. She had been consumed with jealousy, watching Ally with Shannon. Her imagination had taken over and she'd convinced herself that Shannon was with her in her hotel room—touching her, kissing her, making love to her. She had almost made herself sick as images of them kept flashing through her mind. Then the loud banging on her door, Shannon's voice calling to her. Her heart had been hammering in her chest as Shannon stood there, soaking wet from the rain, yet her eyes were filled with the kind of heat Madison used to know so well. There was no denying Shannon. Not then. Not now.

She squared her shoulders again, her chin raised defiantly as she stared at her mother. "Shannon has been my only true friend in my entire life. If you want to place blame, then look in the mirror. If not for you, I would never have married Stephen in the first place. Then you wouldn't have to suffer this *embarrassment* of a divorce."

Her mother also squared her shoulders. "There will be no divorce," she said forcefully. "I refuse to let you sign these papers," she said as she snatched them up. "I will not be made the laughingstock of Brook Hill—nor will Stephen be—by you deciding suddenly that you're *gay*. I won't have it."

A few months ago, Madison would have simply cowered to her wishes, ignoring her own happiness in order to assuage her mother, just like she'd done her entire life. She supposed this was her mother's attempt to get her control back. But it wasn't going to work this time.

Madison's smile was as threatening as her mother's glare. "You don't own me," she said quietly. "You don't speak for me. You don't *control* me. You no longer have the power to forbid me to do *anything*." She pointed to the door. "Now put the papers down and leave."

Her mother's lips pursed together as her hand tightened possessively on the envelope. Madison held her gaze, refusing to back down. Her mother finally tossed the envelope back on the table but not without getting in one last parting shot.

"I think you need psychiatric help."

As soon as the door closed, Madison let out her breath and sank down in a chair. Her hands were shaking slightly as her nervousness came back in full force. *Did I really just tell my mother that I'm gay?*

"Yes."

She shook her head slowly. Yes, she had. And her mother was more concerned with public perception than the fact that her daughter had been in a loveless marriage for the last sixteen years. She leaned back, letting a smile come to her face. She had actually stood up to her mother, actually told her she was gay. And it felt so damn good.

Her glance slid to the table where the envelope lay. She didn't need to read it. Her father's attorney had already gone over it with her. Since she didn't want the house or any of its contents, Stephen was paying her for half. Everything else had been evenly split. All she had to do was sign. Sign her name and she was free.

And she did just that.

CHAPTER THIRTY-FIVE

Shannon walked slowly through the empty store, touching bare shelves as she went. They were almost through with the inside—a couple more weeks at best. She and Jarod would have their official walkthrough with the contractor then, but she found herself here nearly every night, checking their work.

The food court turned out exactly as she'd envisioned and the angled shelves on each side of the store added a different dimension to the standard grocery store aisles. Her gaze traveled from side to side; she was again overwhelmed by the space. They would need a *lot* of inventory to fill it. Panic set in for a moment. Maybe it was too big. What if it didn't go over? What if no one in Brook Hill was interested in natural foods?

"I love it."

Shannon turned, startled by the voice. Madison was the last person she expected there.

"It's big."

"Not too big."

Shannon walked on, heading to the back where the coolers were. She felt Madison following her.

"How did you know I was here?" she finally asked.

"I saw your truck out front. And you probably should lock the doors if you're here alone," Madison said with a smile.

"Yeah. Never know who might walk in off the street," she teased. Her smile faded as their eyes met. "About the other night," she said. "I should apologize."

"And what exactly would you apologize for?"

Shannon looked away. "I didn't invite them here. And Ally and I...there's nothing between us, Madison."

"You don't have to explain to me."

Shannon met her eyes again. "Don't I?"

Madison was the first to look away. "She seemed...very possessive of you," she said. "She made it clear you were more than friends."

"That's just it. We're not really even friends," she said. "Charlotte told her about you, about us—our past. I think her curiosity was piqued more than anything."

"And she wanted to let me know that you two also had a past," Madison stated.

Shannon turned to her. "Ally likes to play games. I don't."

Madison walked closer, her hand reaching out to Shannon's, their fingers entwining. "Good. Because I'm too old to play games."

Shannon tugged her closer, their eyes holding. "What do you want from me?"

Madison tilted her head. "I think the question is...what do you want from me?"

Shannon squeezed Madison's fingers, pulling her ever so closer. "I want what I've always wanted. But what I could never have," she said, dipping her head down, brushing Madison's cheek with her lips. "I want all of you," she whispered. She slid her hand up Madison's body, pausing under her breast. "Not just your body," she said, letting her hand finish its trek, seeing Madison's eyes darken as she raked her thumb across her nipple. "Your body, your soul...your heart."

"You've always had my heart, Shannon," Madison murmured as her lips moved to Shannon's mouth.

Shannon let the kiss deepen, her tongue tracing Madison's lower lip before slipping past, meeting Madison's tongue in a hungry battle. She pressed her against the cooler door, her thigh nudging Madison's legs apart. Madison clung to her, tiny sounds of pleasure eliciting a reciprocal moan from Shannon.

Shannon pulled back slowly, smiling against Madison's lips. "Why does this always happen?"

Madison leaned away from her, their gazes locking together. "Because we're in love with each other."

Shannon nodded. "Yes. Always."

Madison ducked her head then, but not before Shannon saw tears in her eyes. She pulled her into a hug, holding her tightly.

"I'm so sorry," Madison whispered as she buried her face against Shannon's neck. "So many wasted years."

"No, don't cry," Shannon said softly. "Right here, right now... nothing is wasted." She squeezed her tighter, then released her, tipping up her chin with her hand. "We were just kids back then. What were we supposed to do? Run away? Like you said then, we knew your parents would never allow that."

"I should have told them."

"About us?" Shannon shook her head. "No. Your mother would have probably had me thrown in jail," she said with a smile. "And my mother would have been out on the street." She paused. "Things would be different. I wouldn't have my stores. You wouldn't have the Whiz Kid," she added. "Maybe things were supposed to happen this way."

Madison's hand brushed across Shannon's face and into her hair. "I want to be with you," she whispered. "I want to make love with you."

As always, Shannon's heart raced, but she shook her head. "I told you, I won't have an..."

"I...I signed the papers," Madison said. "And I told my mother."

Shannon frowned. "You signed the divorce papers?"

"Yes."

She let out a deep breath. "I was so afraid you wouldn't go through with it," she admitted. Then she raised her eyebrows. "You told your mother what?"

"I told her...that I was gay."

Shannon's heart nearly stopped beating and she stared at her in disbelief. Madison smiled at her.

"Are you shocked?"

"God, yes," she said. "You never could admit that to *me*."

"I couldn't admit it to *myself*," Madison corrected her. "The other night when you came by, it was all so crystal clear. I hated that you were with Ally and what you might be doing. And when you showed up, the look in your eyes…it was all so clear. That's the look I want to see for the rest of my life."

"God…*Madison*." Shannon reached for her, pulling her close again, feeling Madison's arms snake around her waist. "I want this to be real."

"It is real. This time it's real."

Shannon kissed her slowly but pulled back when she felt Madison's hands move up her body. For everything she wanted with Madison, the store was no place to start it.

"And your mother? She freaked out?"

Madison nodded, stepping away from Shannon. "To say the least. Her last words to me were 'I think you need psychiatric help.'"

Shannon smiled. "I can't believe you told her. God, I wish I could have been there."

"You were there in spirit. Don't think she didn't blame you."

"If I only had that power," she murmured as she pulled Madison close again, unable to resist her.

"Come home with me," Madison whispered into her ear. "It's been so long, Shannon. I want to make love with you. Tonight."

Shannon kissed her hard. "Yes. God, yes."

She took her hand, leading her quickly through the store. She was about to lock up when her phone rang. It was Jarod. She had every intention of ignoring it, but Madison nodded at her.

"It's okay. Answer it."

She nodded. "Hey, what's up?" she asked.

"It's Mom. We're on the way to the hospital."

Shannon froze. "What happened?"

"I don't know. We found her on the floor. She was groggy, unresponsive."

Shannon grabbed Madison's hand and squeezed. "I was just there, not even an hour ago," she said.

"Hell, I don't know, Shannon. Maybe she had a stroke or something."

"Okay. I'm on my way." She glanced at Madison, seeing the fear in her eyes.

"Alice?"

"Yeah. Jarod found her on the floor. He thinks she may have had a stroke or something."

Madison squeezed her hand tightly. "Let's go."

CHAPTER THIRTY-SIX

Madison stared across the waiting room at Joan, Jarod's wife. Crissy and Kenny sat beside her, all three with solemn looks on their faces. Madison sat still, refusing to believe the worst. Over the years, Alice had become so much more than a friend to her. Madison was closer to Alice than she was to her own mother.

She closed her eyes for a second, wishing she had the right to be with Shannon. Shannon had looked so scared. Madison had wanted to comfort her, but, well, she didn't know how much—if anything—Jarod and Joan knew of their past relationship. She wondered if they thought it odd that she was even here in the first place.

"You know Alice thinks of you as a daughter, don't you?"

Madison was startled by Joan's voice. She smiled slightly. "I appreciate that. I've known Alice my whole life. Over the years, she's been more of a mother to me than my own."

Joan opened her purse and took out some bills, handing them to Kenny and Crissy. "Why don't you go get us something to drink?" She looked at Madison with raised eyebrows, but Madison shook her head. As soon as the kids were gone, Joan got up, joining Madison on her side of the waiting room. "May I sit with you?"

"Of course."

Joan folded her hands together, letting out a deep sigh. "Jarod has been so excited to be back here, with his mom and with Shannon. He feels like he missed out on so much while he was in the military. He wanted some time with them. As a family."

"Alice is a very strong woman," Madison reminded her.

"She's just been through so much." Joan surprised her by reaching out and taking her hand. "I know you and I aren't exactly friends, but over the years, Alice has spoken of you often. I hope I'm not out of line by saying this, but her greatest wish has always been for you and Shannon to find each other again."

Madison was shocked by her words. "And here I thought you and Jarod had no idea of our past," she said, feeling a bit embarrassed to know that they did.

"Yes. We've tried to include you in our family." She squeezed her hand then released it. "Shannon thinks she hides things so well, but when she looks at you, well, you'd have to be a fool not to see how she feels."

"Do the kids know?"

"They know their Aunt Shannon is gay, yes. I don't know whether they've linked you two together yet." She smiled. "Or am I being presumptuous?"

This time Madison blushed freely. "No," she said. Thankfully the kids came back, ending the conversation. They sat down beside their mother after handing her a Coke. Madison leaned her head back against the wall, waiting for Shannon to return.

She didn't have to wait long before Shannon and Jarod walked back into the waiting room. Her eyes flew to Shannon's, pleased to see some of the anguish gone. She stood when Joan did, waiting for the news.

"We don't know much," Jarod said, "but they've ruled out a stroke."

"That's good news, right?" Joan asked.

"I guess," Shannon said. "They're going to keep her. Do some more tests tomorrow. She doesn't remember what happened. She said she was watching TV, then the next thing she knew, Jarod was there, helping her up."

"How is she now?" Madison asked. "Is she focused? Alert?"

"Yeah, she seems fine," Shannon said. "She wants to see you." Shannon glanced at Joan. "And then she wants to see you and the grandkids," she added. "Room 2118."

Madison was thankful Alice had asked to see her, and she smiled quickly at Joan. "I won't be long. I know you and the kids are anxious to see her."

Madison squeezed Shannon's hand as she walked past her and into the hallway. She turned right, following the signs for the range of rooms. The door was cracked open, but she knocked softly.

"Alice?"

"Come in, Madison."

Alice was sitting upright, looking no worse for wear. She smiled and patted the bed, beckoning Madison to join her.

"You gave everyone a fright," Madison said.

"Apparently. They've been fussing over me. I just had a little mishap," she said as she took Madison's hand.

Madison sat on the edge of the bed beside her, smiling as Alice engulfed her hand with hers. "You fainted. More than a mishap," she said. "But they were afraid you had a stroke."

Alice shook her head. "I doubt when I leave this world it will be because of a stroke," she said.

It was then Madison saw it—how tired Alice looked, how drawn her face was. She met her eyes and held them. "Is the cancer back?" she whispered.

Alice squeezed her hands almost painfully hard. "Yes."

Madison's shoulders sagged as she squeezed back. "How long have you known?"

"A couple of weeks. It's been exhausting trying to hide it from Shannon and Jarod, trying to put on a happy face whenever they're around," she said. "I think I was just mentally done in by it all, with worry, with trying to keep it to myself."

Madison bent down and hugged her. "You could have told me," she said.

"You've got enough going on in your life. I didn't want to burden you."

"Oh, Alice, you've been there for me so many times. You would never be a burden."

Alice looked away. "I don't know that I'm strong enough to go through all of this again. The treatments take so much out of you; I don't know how much I have left."

"You're strong. You're a fighter. You've beaten it twice," Madison reminded her.

"Yes, but maybe the third time is not the charm," she said with a sigh. "But enough of that. They'll all know soon enough so I'm sure we'll talk it out to death." She sighed again. "It's you I want to talk about. You and Shannon," Alice said.

Madison nodded. "We're...we're good," she said.

"Don't let Shannon be alone tonight. Take her with you. To your home. When I go to sleep tonight, I want to know that my girls are together."

Madison felt a tear trickle down her cheek, and she nodded. "I'll take care of her," she whispered.

"Good. And she'll take care of you. That's how it should be." Alice leaned back against the pillows. "I'm suddenly very tired. You best send in Joan and my grandkids."

Madison stood, then bent down and kissed her cheek. "You're not planning on leaving us tonight, are you?"

Alice smiled weakly. "Not just yet. Like you said, I'm a fighter."

"Okay. Then I'll see you tomorrow." She turned to go, then stopped. "I love you."

She was surprised to see tears in Alice's eyes. "I love you too."

Madison left quickly, afraid her own tears would spill. Those were three words she'd never said to her own mother. And three words her mother had never uttered to her.

She stopped at the waiting room door, knowing the burden was now hers. Should she tell Shannon? Could she keep it from her? No, Shannon deserved to know. She took a deep breath, letting it out slowly, finally pushing open the door. She smiled, hoping it reached her eyes as she glanced at Joan.

"She's asking for you."

CHAPTER THIRTY-SEVEN

"Hell of a way to end the day," Shannon said as she drove them back to the store and Madison's car.

Madison reached across the console and rested her hand on Shannon's thigh. "Alice gave me some instructions," she said.

"Oh yeah?"

"You're to come home with me."

Shannon laughed. "She said that, huh?"

"Among other things, yes." Madison bit her lip, knowing now wasn't the time to tell her. "We haven't eaten dinner. How about we pick up something and take it home?"

"You sure?"

"Yes. We should talk," she said vaguely. Shannon stared at her for a long moment, and Madison saw questions in her eyes. She offered a quick smile. "I want to sleep with you tonight," she said. "We don't have to make love. I just want to be with you."

Shannon covered her hand with one of her own, pressing it down hard into her thigh. "I haven't forgotten our conversation from earlier," she said.

Madison nodded, relaxing her hand, letting Shannon's warmth seep into her.

After Shannon assured her veggie burgers were on the menu at a local fast-food restaurant, they decided on burgers and fries and large Cokes, something Madison rarely had. She went ahead to her house as Shannon went to pick up their dinner. It was a pleasant evening, not too warm. She went out to the patio and turned on the ceiling fan, deciding they would eat outside by the pool. She only wished the conversation was going to be lighter, but she wouldn't keep Alice's cancer news from Shannon.

Ten minutes later Shannon came in carrying two bags. Madison took one from her, smelling the addicting aroma of fast-food fries. She snatched one out of the bag, chewing with a smile.

"This is so good," she said. "Wonder why I don't get them more often?"

"Because they're not good for you," Shannon said as she too stole one from the bag. She glanced to the patio, which was lit up. "You want to eat outside?"

"Do you mind?"

"Of course not. The pool looks inviting," she said, wiggling her eyebrows.

Madison smiled, wishing they could forget everything and… and get naked already. She could imagine Shannon's glistening skin with the water cascading off of it.

"What naughty thoughts are going through your mind?"

At that, Madison laughed. "Skinny-dipping."

Shannon's gaze held hers. "Then why don't we?" she suggested.

"Tempting…but we should talk," she said, leading Shannon outside.

Madison was afraid her appetite would leave her, but one bite into the burger brought it back in full force. "This is delicious," she murmured with a nearly full mouth.

"Again, not good for you," Shannon said as she bit into her veggie burger. "Not bad," she said before dipping a french fry in ketchup. "Now, what is it you want to talk about?"

Madison wiped her mouth with her napkin, then took a sip of her drink. No sense putting it off. "It's Alice," she said.

Shannon put her burger down, eyebrows raised. "Something she told you?"

Madison nodded.

Shannon stared at her, slowly shaking her head. "The cancer is back?" she guessed.

"I'm sorry," Madison said quietly. "She said she's known for a couple of weeks, but she didn't want to tell you."

"Shit," Shannon whispered as she leaned back, running her hands through her hair.

"I hadn't noticed before how tired she looked," Madison said. "Lying there in the hospital bed, she looked almost frail. She didn't exactly tell me," she said. "I asked her."

Shannon nodded. "Yes, now that you mention it, she has looked tired lately." She let out a heavy breath. "So when is she planning on breaking this to us?"

"I would imagine tomorrow. I don't think she was ready to deal with it tonight." She reached across the table and took Shannon's hand. "I'm sorry, Shannon. But your mother is a strong woman. We've just got to be there for her and make sure she doesn't give up."

"She's been through so much already," Shannon said. "Now that Jarod and I are here, well, I'd hoped we could have some time with her."

"Shannon, this isn't a death sentence. She's beaten it twice before," Madison reminded her.

"Yeah, I know. But she was younger then. She's over seventy now. Is she still strong enough?"

"If her spirit is willing, then yes." Madison looked at her burger, then folded the paper around it. "I suppose I should have waited until after we ate," she said.

Shannon grabbed a fry and nibbled it slowly. "Did she want you to tell me?"

"No, but I wasn't going to keep it from you."

"Thank you. I would hate to be blindsided by it tomorrow. I suppose I should let Jarod know," Shannon said as she pulled her phone out of her pocket.

"Why don't you wait until the morning?" Madison suggested. "There's not anything he can do tonight."

Shannon hesitated, then put her phone back. "You're right." She smiled slightly. "Is this why she told you I was to come home with you?"

"Her words were, 'When I go to sleep tonight, I want to know that my girls are together.'" She was surprised to see a misting of tears in Shannon's eyes.

"She thinks of you as family, you know."

Madison nodded. "Yes. The feeling is mutual. When we were growing up, I often wished she was my mother," Madison admitted. "She was always so warm and caring, something my mother never was."

"Affectionate," Shannon said. "She was always affectionate with me. Even now."

Madison stared at the pool, the water moving ever so slightly, causing the lights to twinkle below the surface. "Do you know my mother has never hugged me?" She felt Shannon's eyes on her and she turned to her. "Not even when I was a kid. I have no recollection of her ever hugging me."

"Your father?"

Madison shook her head. "No. In fact, now—going through the divorce—is the closest I've been to him. For the first time, we actually talk." She let their fingers entwine when Shannon's hand covered hers. Madison met her eyes. "You taught me how to be affectionate." She watched as Shannon swallowed, apparently gathering her thoughts.

"I…I was insanely in love with you," Shannon said. "Almost to the point of desperation. Back then, I was consumed by it…by you." Shannon's thumb slowly caressed her hand, mesmerizing her. "I could never make love with anyone…there was never a time I didn't think of you, wish it was you I was touching. I wanted it to be you. I always wanted it to be you."

Shannon had tears in her eyes. Madison got up and went to her, pulling her up as well. Shannon had always been the strong one. She wondered how much the news about her mother was affecting her emotions now. She cupped her face, looking into her eyes.

"I'm so sorry."

Shannon shook her head. "No. Let's don't say we're sorry. It's over with. In the past. Let's don't ever say we're sorry again."

Madison brushed at the corner of her eye, wiping a tear away.

"I want...I want to think about the future now," Shannon continued. "I really want my future to be with you." She took Madison's hand and kissed her palm. "Is it too soon? These last five or six months, I feel like we've gotten to know each other in a different way. Not like when we were young and we just wanted to be together. I feel like I've gotten to know the real you and you've gotten to know me," she said. "I know we're different people now than when we were young, but the one thing that's the same...is that I'm still insanely in love with you."

Madison brushed a tear from her own eye. "I've hurt you so much." She put a finger across Shannon's mouth when she would have spoken. "I promise you, I will never hurt you that way again. Because I'm in love with you too. I want to be with you. We didn't have a life then, but we can have one now. A life, out in the open, not hiding. You want that too, don't you?"

Shannon leaned closer and brushed her lips with her own. "I want everything with you."

Madison stepped into her arms, pulling Shannon into another kiss, letting it deepen, knowing they didn't have to hurry, knowing there were no longer any restraints on them. She felt Shannon lift her blouse, exposing her skin to the night air before Shannon's warm hands slid around her.

"I want to make love to you," Shannon murmured as her lips left Madison's mouth and moved to her neck, suckling the sensitive spot that only Shannon knew.

"Yes," she whispered, arching her neck and giving Shannon full access. She moaned when Shannon's hands slid along her skin, cupping her breasts.

"I've dreamed of you so many times," Shannon whispered into her ear.

Madison closed her eyes as Shannon's thumbs circled her nipples. "We don't have to dream anymore, sweetheart." She took a deep breath, then stilled Shannon's hands. "Let's go to bed."

* * *

Madison stood still, belying the nervousness she felt as Shannon slowly removed her clothing. It had been so long and she wasn't a young woman any longer. Her nerves got the best of her and she stopped Shannon as she was about to undo her bra.

"I'm not twenty-one any longer," she said quietly.

Shannon stared into her eyes, then leaned closer and kissed her softly. "You're beautiful, Madison. I love the woman you've become." Shannon removed her bra then, her eyes drawn to her breasts. She was pleased to see Shannon's eyes darken. "You're every bit as beautiful as I remembered."

Those words chased her nervousness away, and she reached for Shannon's shirt, tugging it over her head. Hands fumbled together as they undressed, laughing quietly when Shannon's bra got tangled in her shirt.

The sheets were cool as she lay down, her gaze raking over Shannon's body as she stood before her. Shannon had always been a little taller than she was, a little thinner. Seeing her now—naked— after all these years of only dreaming of her, she realized how truly magnificent Shannon really was. She reached for her hand, pulling her down to the bed. For a second, she had to remind herself that she wasn't dreaming. Shannon was here, in her bed. They were about to make love. The years melted away as Shannon's kisses became more demanding and Madison yielded to her, welcoming Shannon's weight on top of her.

All other coherent thoughts were lost when Shannon's mouth brushed across her breast, her tongue flicking her nipple, turning it rock hard. She moaned quietly as Shannon teased her, lips and tongue. Shannon finally closed over her nipple fully, gently suckling, and Madison moaned again, holding Shannon to her for fear she'd stop. It had been so terribly long since they'd been together, yet she remembered it like it was yesterday. Shannon's skin was as smooth and soft as it had always been, and she ran her hands across her back now, pulling her even closer to her body.

Shannon nudged her legs apart, and Madison opened to her, shocked by the wetness she felt between them. It had been so long since she'd been sexually aroused that she hardly recognized it. Her hips involuntarily arched into Shannon.

"I've missed you so much," Shannon murmured as her lips trailed kisses along her neck to her mouth.

Her kiss was slow, but oh so thorough, and Madison savored it, letting Shannon do as she wished, her body simply melting beneath her...all from only a kiss. It wasn't the hot, fierce kisses they had shared when they were younger, kisses meant to hurry— before they got caught. There was no one to catch them this time, no need to hurry.

But when Shannon dipped her head to her breast again, when her hand moved between them, *hurry* was the only thing Madison was thinking.

"It's been so long, Shannon," she whispered. "*Hurry*."

Shannon lifted her head, her smile soft and lazy, her eyes clouded with desire. "Hurry? No, sweetheart. I intend to take my time," she murmured as her fingers slipped effortlessly into her wetness, brushing across her clit, causing her hips to jerk.

"We can go slow the second time," Madison countered as she held her gaze. "And the third and the fourth. But right now, I want your mouth on me."

Shannon's lips were gentle on her own. "Is that what you want?" she murmured.

"God, yes," Madison whispered.

She heard Shannon's breath catch at her words, saw her eyes darken even more. She barely heard Shannon's whispered "then that's what I want" as she moved down her body. Oh, it had been so long. She moaned as Shannon spread her thighs even further. Her eyes slammed shut when she felt Shannon's warm breath on her, felt the first touch of her tongue.

"Shannon...*yes*," she breathed, opening herself fully as Shannon's mouth settled over her, tongue and lips devouring her. She was gasping for breath, one hand clutching the sheet, the other Shannon's shoulder as her hips moved wildly against Shannon's face. No one but Shannon had ever done this to her. Memories came rushing back, memories of two young girls making excuses to kiss, to touch and, finally, to make love. Two girls, learning from each other and falling more and more in love. Now, like then, Shannon knew exactly how—and where—to touch her, bringing her just to the edge, letting it build and build until Madison exploded. But now, unlike then, she didn't have to temper her response, she didn't have to fear getting caught. She arched her hips again, feeling Shannon hold her down as she sucked her clit into her hot mouth. Like all those years ago, her world exploded in blinding colors, and she cried out, the sound coming from deep in her soul as Shannon drew out her orgasm, her tongue only stopping when Madison collapsed limply on the bed.

She felt Shannon leave tiny kisses on her thighs, her belly, her breast, her face, felt her warm skin again covering her own. Her eyes fluttered open, and she managed a smile when Shannon kissed her mouth.

"Okay?"

"God, yes," she murmured, reaching for Shannon and pulling her close. "I love you."

Shannon brushed the hair away from her face, her eyes looking into her own. "I love you, Madison. I've always loved you."

Madison nodded. "Yes. Always." She rolled them over, resting on top of Shannon now. "It feels so incredibly good to be with you," she said. "We have the night to ourselves," she whispered as she kissed her. "No interruptions. No curfews. We have a lot of time to make up for."

"You can take all the time you want, sweetheart."

Madison grinned as she moved lower, capturing Shannon's nipple with her mouth, memories again rushing in—the softness of her, her scent, her taste. Yes, all the time in the world. And she intended on using every minute of it.

CHAPTER THIRTY-EIGHT

Shannon had already broken the news to Jarod, and they waited now, waited for the doctor to finish. Joan and the kids had stayed at home, but Madison had wanted to come, so she'd followed in her car. She sat beside Shannon, twisting her hands together nervously. Shannon reached over and stilled them, smiling slightly.

"Sorry," Madison said quietly.

Shannon leaned closer. "Are you more worried about what the doctor is going to say or whether she's going to guess what we were doing last night?" She laughed quietly as a bright blush covered Madison's face.

"Considering neither of us look like we've slept, there won't be much guessing involved."

Shannon's gaze landed on Madison's mouth, her lips still slightly swollen from their night—and morning—together. She looked up, their eyes holding, and she suddenly wished they were anywhere but a hospital waiting room. She wished they were back in the shower where Madison had pinned her against the wall and brought her to orgasm so fast it was a blur. Madison smiled and nodded, acknowledging the direction of her thoughts.

"Fletcher?"

They all turned and the nurse waved them over. "You can see her now. The doctor will be right back in to visit with you."

"Thank you," she said, allowing Jarod and Madison to go ahead of her.

Her mother, thankfully, looked well rested. Shannon bent down quickly and kissed her cheek, noting that her mother already had taken a hold of Madison's hand.

"I'm feeling much better," she said. "I don't want anyone fussing over me."

"Mom, we know about the cancer," Jarod said.

Her mother flicked her eyes at Madison and smiled. "I never thought you'd keep it to yourself," she said. She eyed Shannon and Madison, her gaze going between them. "Would it be inappropriate of me to say that you're both glowing this morning?"

Shannon blushed head to toe. "Really, Mom? Really? *Now*?"

Jarod laughed. "So that's why you look like you got no sleep."

Shannon looked at Madison helplessly, but Madison simply laughed and squeezed her mother's hand. "I took your advice," she said.

"Can we please discuss your health?" Shannon said, still blushing.

Her mother's smile faded. "There is nothing to discuss. I already know my options."

"Where...where is it?"

"My breast again. I'm going through with the surgery this time." Her mother looked away from them. "I should have done it before, I guess, but losing one's breasts...well, I wasn't prepared back then."

"Okay, if you do a total mastectomy, will you still have to do chemo or radiation?" she asked.

"The doctor said they would see how invasive the cancer is. That will determine whether I'll need additional treatment." Her mother laid back against the pillow. "The thought of going through chemo again...well, I don't know if I can handle it."

"But—"

"No. I'm tired of thinking about it. We'll take it one step at a time." She took a deep breath. "Now, let's talk about something else." She turned to Madison. "Isn't Ashton coming home this weekend?"

Madison nodded. "Yes, I'll get to see him tomorrow evening."

Shannon had forgotten that Ashton was coming home. "That's right. He's staying with you tomorrow night," she said. Now that she and Madison had, well, *reconnected*, she didn't want to spend even one night apart. Madison seemed to read her mind.

"He's leaving Saturday afternoon to go with Stephen."

Her mother laughed. "Isn't love grand when you just want to be together constantly?"

"Mom, *please*," Shannon groaned, blushing yet again.

Madison bent down and kissed her mother's cheek, a smile still playing on her mouth. "I'll tell you all about it later," Madison said, just loud enough for Shannon to hear. Her mother laughed delightfully. Madison stood, her gaze meeting Shannon's. "I should get going. The doctor will be in here soon. I haven't even begun to get ready for Ashton."

Shannon nodded. "I'll call you later."

Madison squeezed her arm affectionately as she passed, and Shannon watched her go, feeling her mother's and Jarod's gaze on her. She turned to them with a sheepish smile.

CHAPTER THIRTY-NINE

Madison hugged Ashton tightly, swearing he'd grown another four inches since she'd seen him.

"You're taller than I am," she said.

"Yeah. How about that?"

She held him at arm's length. "God, you're all grown up. When did that happen?"

"I'm almost sixteen," he reminded her. It was his turn to study her, and she very nearly blushed at his scrutiny. "You look different."

"Different?" Could he really know what she'd been doing the last two nights? Surely not.

"So it's official? The divorce?"

"Yes. I suppose your father told you?"

He nodded. "We talk more now than when I lived here."

She didn't say anything as she led him into the kitchen. While Stephen was a good enough father, he was absent a lot in Ashton's young life. Something she could relate to as her own father had rarely been around when she was growing up.

She had the small table set for their dinner, but she hadn't dared to attempt to cook anything. She decided to get his favorite.

"Bruno's pizza okay?"

"Oh, yeah. I haven't found anything up there that I like as well."

She eyed the neat black iPad that he set down beside him. It was rare if she saw him without either it or his laptop. She was sometimes still amazed by his intelligence, wondering once again how she and Stephen could have produced a "whiz kid," as Shannon called him.

She took the pizza out of the oven where it had been warming and put the box on the table. He pulled out a piece and had it in his mouth even before she sat down.

"Thanks, Mom," he mumbled as he chewed.

"Sure. So tell me about school."

He rolled his eyes. "We talk almost every day. You know everything."

That was true, but she needed some filler before she broached the subject of Shannon. Apparently, Ashton was not only book smart. His gaze settled on her almost uncomfortably.

"Tell me what you've been up to," he said instead. "When we talk, it's always about me. Dad says he never sees you and you won't take his calls."

While his tone was only slightly accusing, it did make her wonder what all Stephen had been telling him. She wasn't going to hide things from him.

"I stopped taking his calls because he didn't want to discuss the divorce, he wanted to discuss reconciling. When I wasn't receptive to that, he resorted to anger or he tried to make me feel guilty, mostly because of you. So yes, I stopped taking his calls."

"Grandmother too?"

She shook her head. "Your grandmother and I had a… conversation that didn't go her way. She stormed out of here and hasn't spoken to me since." She put her pizza down. "And please tell me your grandmother has not been calling you."

Ashton, too, put his pizza down. "She did call me. She said you were having a crisis or something."

Madison stared at him in disbelief. "You're sixteen. Surely they're not trying to drag you into these games they're playing," she said bluntly.

"Mom, I don't really understand everything that's going on. I know you weren't happy. And I told you I would be okay with a divorce. And I am. But they're acting like you're having a midlife crisis and that you're not making sound decisions."

"And you're supposed to intervene? You're my son, Ashton. My very, very intelligent son and I love you, but I'm not having a crisis." She took a deep breath, letting it out slowly. "I don't know what all your grandmother has told you, but I do have something to tell you." He looked almost frightened, and she took his hand, holding it tightly.

"Is it about Shannon?"

She nodded. "Yes. It is about Shannon." God, how did she say this without just blurting it out? She swallowed down her nervousness. She needed to tell him. "Everything I was supposed to feel with your father...I feel with her." She paused. "Do you understand?"

He tilted his head slightly. "So...you're gay?"

She held his eyes. "Yes."

His expression was unchanged for a long moment, then he smiled. "Okay."

She raised her eyebrows. "Okay? That's it?"

He shrugged. "What do you want me to say?"

"Well, I don't know, but shouldn't we discuss this? Don't you have questions?"

He picked up his pizza again. "I've had a week to digest this, Mom."

"Oh my God. She actually *told* you? Did she tell Stephen too?"

"Remember this summer when you told me about you and Shannon and when you were younger? That she was your first love? I guess maybe I kinda knew then. When she came over for your birthday, when I saw you hugging." He shrugged almost apologetically. "I never once saw you hug Dad like that."

"Oh, honey, I'm sorry."

"So when she called me and said you had 'lost your mind' and that I needed to try to reason with you before it got out, I knew that...well, that you and Shannon had..."

Madison smiled at his attempt to explain. "If it makes any difference, I'm madly in love with her," she said easily, not wanting to hide anything from him.

"Something you never were with Dad?"

She shook her head. "No. Never."

"But then why did you—"

"Get married? I told you, your grandmothers had our marriage arranged by the time we were twelve. When someone tells you something long enough, you eventually believe it. And I believed what she said, that Stephen was perfect for me and we'd make a most excellent couple."

"But Shannon was the one—"

"That I was in love with? Yes." She reached out and touched his face. "I won't lie. I've regretted it many times. But I wouldn't have you. And I love you very much."

He smiled sweetly at her. "I love you too." He studied her. "Did you think I was going to freak out?"

"Freak out like your grandmother did? No. But I didn't know how accepting you would be," she said honestly. "And I need you to be accepting."

He continued eating his pizza. "In my generation, well, it's everywhere. TV, movies, music. Kids are more open about it. It's not that big of a deal." He shrugged. "I have two professors who are gay. No big deal." Then he did what he'd been doing all of his young life—jumping from the boy he was to the adult within. "I want you to be happy, Mom. You can't please everyone—Grandmother least of all. If Shannon is who you want to be with and if she's the person who makes you happy, then all of us who love you should support you." Then he grinned, his boy-like features returning. "How's that?"

She returned his smile. "Have you been practicing that?"

He nodded. "Yeah. Can you tell?"

She leaned over and kissed his cheek. "Not at all," she lied.

He reached for his third piece of pizza. "So, is she coming over?"

"Tonight? No." She paused. "Why? Did you want to see her?"

He glanced at her quickly, then away, and she saw embarrassment on his face. "Are you like...you know...sleeping together?"

She felt a blush cover her face, nearly matching his. "I don't think we need to delve that far into it, do you?"

He laughed. "That means yes."

She shoved a piece of pizza in her mouth to avoid answering. While she was happy he was accepting, she had no intention—*whatsoever*—of discussing her sex life with him.

CHAPTER FORTY

Shannon was hovering, and she knew it, but apparently she got her stubborn streak from her mother.

"I told you, I feel fine," her mother said for the fourth time.

"The doctor said to take it easy," she reminded her.

"And you take that to mean I should be in bed resting?"

"Yes."

"Madison and Ashton are coming over, and I'd rather visit with them in here than in my bedroom," her mother said as she settled on the sofa. "After lunch, I promise I'll go lie down."

While Shannon didn't want to treat her like an invalid, she had been there when the doctor told her to rest. They still had no explanation for her fainting spell. But she had no more time to argue. A couple of light knocks on the front door told her that Madison…and Ashton…were already there. And she didn't mind admitting she was a little nervous. Madison had said she planned to tell Ashton about them, not wanting to hide it from him…from anyone. Shannon could face Madison's mother, her father, even Stephen. But her son? She knew what she was really afraid of was that if he didn't support it, didn't accept it, then Madison would run from it again, shunning what she felt in her heart for the sake of someone else.

Her mother must have sensed her hesitation. "Ashton loves his mother very much," she said. "He'll only want her to be happy."

"Oh? So now you can read my mind?" she said as she headed to the door.

"I could always read your mind," her mother said with a laugh.

She took a quick breath, then opened the door, her gaze landing first on Madison before sliding to Ashton. She was surprised to find a hint of amusement there. Was her nervousness that obvious?

"Hey, come in," she said, stepping out of the way. "Glad you could come by." She motioned with her head. "She's in the living room on the sofa."

As soon as Ashton was out of earshot, Shannon turned to Madison. "How did it go?" she asked quietly.

Madison touched her arm, letting her fingers linger. "It went fine." She leaned closer. "I missed you last night," she whispered.

Shannon was sure her relief was visible. "So we're not in trouble?"

"We're not in trouble." Then Madison raised her eyebrows. "What were you afraid of?"

Shannon looked away, hearing her mother and Ashton talking but not listening to their words. She met Madison's gaze, holding it. "I was afraid he...he wouldn't accept it, and then you...you would tell me..."

"Oh, sweetheart," Madison murmured, pulling her into a tight, intimate hug. "I love you, Shannon. I wouldn't let anyone—not even Ashton—keep us apart again."

Madison kissed her and Shannon felt all her worries melt away, making her feel foolish for them in the first place.

"Geez, you two, can you not wait?"

They pulled apart guiltily, both blushing as Ashton stood watching them.

Shannon opened her mouth to apologize, but Madison stopped her with a quick laugh. "Then quit sneaking up on us," she said, going to him and linking her arm with his. "How is Alice?"

Shannon followed them inside, meeting her mother's laughing eyes. She blushed again.

"He's gotten so tall," her mother said.

"I know. He's taller than me," Madison said. "How are you feeling?"

"I feel fine, even though this one," she said, pointing at Shannon, "insists I should be in bed." She patted the spot beside her. "Come sit with me," her mother invited and Madison nodded, sitting down next to her.

Shannon knew immediately that her mother and Ashton had been scheming about something. Ashton glanced at her.

"Is there something I can help you with in the kitchen?"

Shannon couldn't believe she was afraid of this sixteen-year-old kid, but she was. "Sure," she said as she walked into the kitchen. "I'm…uh…making a tofu and vegetable stir-fry," she said, pointing to all the veggies already cut up. "And we're going to have it over pasta."

He wasn't looking at the vegetables. "My mom says you love her."

Shannon bit her lower lip. "Yes. I do."

"She says she loves you too."

Shannon nodded. "Yes."

Ashton stared at her for a long moment, long enough for Shannon to shift nervously from foot to foot. "She and my dad… they were never affectionate with each other. Never."

Shannon didn't know what to say so she just nodded.

"You promise you won't hurt her?"

"I will never hurt her."

* * *

Madison squeezed Alice's hand. "Do you think Shannon needs rescuing?"

"I think Ashton needed to know if her intentions were good," Alice said. "What about you?"

"Me? What do you mean?"

"You told him about you two, he said. Are you okay with everything?"

"It wasn't a shock to him since my mother had already told him I'd lost my mind," she said with a quiet laugh. "But, yes, I'm okay."

"I can't believe you told your mother. I imagine that sent her into a spin."

"We haven't spoken since," she admitted. "I keep waiting for my father to call or come by, but he's been conspicuously silent."

"Well, I would think it's not quite as big a shock to him. I would suspect—when you were younger—that he, like me, knew there was more to your relationship with Shannon than just being friends."

Madison shook her head. "I don't know. He wasn't around all that much." She shrugged. "What about you? How are you really feeling?"

"Tired. Very little energy."

"Have you decided when you're going to have the surgery?"

"We're going to schedule it as soon as possible. The doctor said I could wait until after the holidays, but I want to get it over with. Shannon and Jarod, they've got the store. I know they wanted to have it opened by November. I don't want to be a burden to them."

"Alice, they would never—"

"I know, I know. But the sooner I have the surgery, the sooner I can recover. I don't want Shannon to feel responsible for me. I would rather she be with you."

Madison leaned closer and hugged her. "We'll work something out," she said. Yes, she wanted Shannon to be with her, every day, every night. But not at the expense of Alice being alone.

"You guys ready for some lunch?" Shannon called from the kitchen.

"Wonder what she's whipped up this time?" Alice teased.

CHAPTER FORTY-ONE

Shannon skidded to a stop in Madison's driveway, feeling every bit like the hormonal teenager she once was. She'd left her mother napping while Joan and the kids kept watch. She had a couple of hours to spare before she'd need to relieve them. Tomorrow—Sunday—she was planning a family dinner and would take a cue from Madison and order a variety of dishes from Sapori D'Italia. But now—right now—she just wanted to be with Madison.

She knocked on her door and rang the doorbell both. Madison was expecting her and she opened it only a few seconds later. They stood staring at each other and the look in Madison's eyes caused her pulse to race. Yeah, just like when they were teenagers. And like then, Madison drew her inside, closing the door to the world.

"You're alone, right?" she asked, knowing that she was.

Madison slipped into her arms, her kiss slow and gentle, teasing Shannon's lips before pulling away. "You said we had two hours. I don't want to spend them talking," Madison said with a smile as she led her toward her bedroom.

Shannon pulled her shirt off along the way, reaching for Madison's as soon they entered the bedroom. She nearly groaned when she found no bra and she fumbled with her own, dropping it on the floor beside her shirt before pulling Madison to her, their breasts mashing together.

"God, I missed you," she murmured against Madison's lips. "Last night was endless."

Madison's hands moved between them, unbuttoning her jeans and lowering the zipper, just enough to get her hand inside. "And I missed you," Madison said, her fingers, her hand, slipping past her panties and touching her skin.

Madison's tongue was insistent and Shannon let her lead, her own tongue being bathed by Madison's. She moaned when Madison's fingers slipped through her damp curls, touching her clit, rubbing against it lightly.

"I'm going to fall down," she whispered.

"Open your legs," Madison said, ignoring her warning.

Shannon did her bidding, trying desperately not to lose her balance. She hardly had time to think before Madison's fingers were filling her. She held on to her, breathing hard as Madison moved her fingers inside of her.

"Lower your jeans," Madison requested, her eyes like blue fire as she stared into Shannon's.

Shannon pushed them down her thighs to her knees, moaning loudly as Madison began thrusting against her, inside of her. Shannon's hips moved with her, matching each stroke. She tried to kiss Madison, their tongues dancing together, but she was gasping for air and she leaned heavily against her, both their skins damp with perspiration, both panting as they drew breath.

"You're so wet," Madison whispered. "Can you feel me inside you?"

"God, yes," Shannon hissed, her hips trying keep pace. "Don't stop."

"Never."

Her legs were shaking, threatening to give way as they thrust together. Madison's free hand was around her back, holding her close, and Shannon knew it was the only reason she was still upright. Each stroke brought her closer, and when she felt Madison's thumb rake across her clit, she threw her head back, the pressure building and building. She wanted to hold on, to go even higher, but her resolve shattered as her orgasm knocked the breath from her.

Madison held her tightly and Shannon clung to her, gasping for air. She squeezed her legs together, keeping Madison's fingers inside of her a little longer.

"If you let me go I'm going to fall," she murmured, her eyes still closed.

"I'll never let you go."

* * *

"You're insatiable," Shannon accused as they sat side by side on the patio.

"Me?" Madison laughed. "I think the shower was your suggestion."

Shannon rolled her head, meeting her gaze. "I don't want to leave."

"And I don't want you to leave." They'd spent the better part of two hours making love and they were both still languid, their eyes dreamy. Now wasn't the time for a serious discussion. But she broached the subject anyway. "I have room here, you know."

Shannon raised her eyebrows.

"For you and Alice," she said. When Shannon didn't say anything, she continued. "The mini-master would be perfect for her. And after her surgery, while you and Jarod are getting your store up and running, I could be here for her."

"I can't ask you to do that, Madison."

"You're not asking. I'm offering." She sat up. "Alice is like a mother to me," she said. "I want to help." She took Shannon's hand, letting their fingers entwine. "I want us to be together, Shannon. Not simply stealing a few hours here and there, like we did today. That feels too much like...well, like we're still having to sneak off to be together."

Shannon hesitated. "You don't think it's too soon?"

"It's sixteen years too late."

Shannon studied her for a moment, her gaze slipping away to the pool. "What do you think she'll say?"

"I think she would be thrilled," she said. "And it'll give her some purpose. Alice is a caregiver. She needs to feel like she's taking care of someone. She can teach me to cook, we can plant flowers together." Madison smiled at her. "I know you. You're going to be busy with the store, and then you'll feel guilty for leaving her alone."

Shannon nodded. "You know, when we first started this project, it was because we were thinking it was time to move her into an assisted living facility."

Madison's eyes widened. "Are you serious? Alice does not need to be in one of those places. I won't let you," she said, shocked that Shannon and Jarod had even discussed such a thing.

"I know. I guess we jumped the gun a bit. Neither of us were around her that much, and it seemed like she was getting older, she just looked tired all the time. There was so much she couldn't do anymore," Shannon said. "When we started this project, neither of us anticipated moving here permanently. That's obviously changed since Jarod's got his whole family here now."

Madison had a moment of panic as she searched Shannon's eyes. "And you?" she dared to ask.

Shannon's expression softened. "I love you, Madison. There's no place in this world I'd rather be than here with you."

Madison let out a relieved breath. "I was afraid...well, for a moment there, I thought you were going to say you weren't going to stay. I mean, I know you have a home, friends," she said.

"My home is a house," Shannon said. "And my friends...well, after their little surprise visit last month, let's say our relationship is a bit strained. Ally has become a good friend to them and I don't really fit into their group anymore."

"Because of me?"

"I'm not sure I really ever fit in," Shannon said. "They're all doctors and attorneys and such. When Tracy and Charlotte and I were alone together, we got along great. There were no pretentions. But dinner parties with eight or ten or twelve, no, that wasn't in my comfort zone."

"So...so you'll stay then? Here? With me?"

"If my mother is living here, we're going to have to alter those plans for skinny-dipping next summer," Shannon said with a smile.

"Oh, I think we can still manage to sneak away for that." She tugged Shannon closer, kissing her gently, letting her lips linger. She pulled back when her desire flared. She knew Shannon had to leave.

"If you're sure about this, how about we mention it to Mom at our family dinner tomorrow?"

Madison loved being included in the "family." Everything she ever learned about family, she learned from Alice, not her own mother. Her relationship with Ashton was based on how she'd seen Alice and Shannon interact, on how Alice treated Ashton. If not for that, she would have most likely imitated her mother's parenting style. She could only imagine the train wreck that would have been.

When she didn't answer, Shannon nudged her. "Is that okay?"

She nodded. "It's perfect."

CHAPTER FORTY-TWO

Shannon put the last dish in the oven, pushing them tightly together to get it to fit. Too much food for seven people, but she hadn't been able to decide what to order. She got the clam sauce that Madison loved. She got spaghetti and meatballs for the kids. Lasagna, of course. Vegetables in a pesto sauce over angel hair pasta for her. Fettuccini Alfredo. Two half loaves of garlic bread dripping in butter and cheese. She closed the oven door, her mouth already watering.

"Smells good, sis." Jarod eyed the two bottles on the counter. "Wine?"

"Sure. Why not?"

He picked up one bottle, turning it around in his hand. "Are we celebrating something?"

"Maybe."

He put the bottle back down. "You look good," he said. "Happy."

She smiled. "Thanks. I am."

"So does Madison. It's obvious what you feel for each other," he said. "I'm glad you two worked it out."

She raised an eyebrow skeptically. "How did you know there was anything to work out?"

"Did you think it was a big secret as to why you avoided coming to Brook Hill?" His voice lowered. "By the way, the kids know about you two so there's no need to pretend you're just friends," he said with a grin.

"Well, glad to know my personal life is all out in the open," she said, trying not to feel embarrassed. After all, Joan and the kids had been there yesterday when she'd snuck off for a couple of hours.

He leaned against the counter, his arms crossed casually. "So you wanted to talk about Mom?"

Shannon glanced into the other room where Madison and Joan sat chatting and their mother was playing a board game with the kids. Maybe she would get Jarod's opinion instead of simply springing it on everyone.

"Madison wants me and Mom to move in with her," she said. "You've been to her house. It's sort of a mother-in-law plan anyway. That way, she'll be there to look after Mom, especially after her surgery. We both know these next six weeks you and I will be swamped getting the store up and running." She looked at him questioningly. "What do you think?"

"Are you sure? I mean, you and Madison just got started here. Having a third person around might—"

"Yeah, I'd rather have her all to myself and chase her naked through the living room if I wanted," she said with a grin. "But that's not an option right now. Mom can't live with you. You've got a house full."

"We talked about moving her to an assisted living apartment or something," he said.

"I know, but I don't think it's time for that. Once she's recovered from surgery, she may be just fine." She glanced into the other room. "Besides, Madison already told me that wasn't an option."

Jarod nodded. "I know Madison cares for her a lot."

"She's closer to her than her own mother, yeah."

"So I take it you haven't mentioned this to Mom yet?"

"No. I thought we could discuss it today. As a family."

"Well, you know what she's going to say."

"Yeah, that she'd be in the way and she doesn't want to be a burden and that she's perfectly capable of living alone," she said.

"And you know if she hadn't had that fainting spell, I think she'd be okay living alone. We're both here. We could check on her daily."

"But she did have that fainting spell," Shannon reminded him. "And after her surgery, she's going to need help. It's already October. With me getting the inventory in and us both doing the hiring and the training, what are we going to do?" She shrugged. "We could hire someone, but why? Madison has offered her home to us. She's offered to take care of her."

"I hate putting that burden on her."

"That's just it. Madison doesn't think of it as a burden." Shannon raised her eyebrows as Joan joined them in the small kitchen.

"What are you two whispering about in here?" she asked as she linked arms with Jarod. "Can I help with something?"

"Just warming everything up," Shannon said. "The kids getting hungry?"

"Oh, they're enjoying playing with your mom. She doesn't look as tired today."

"Shannon's got a proposal," Jarod said quietly. "Or rather Madison does."

Joan smiled. "And I think it's a good one."

"She told you?" Shannon asked.

"Yes. It'll allow the two of you to be together and, as I'm sure you know, Madison genuinely cares for Alice."

"So everyone's on board? Well, I guess we just need to convince Mom then."

"I'll set the table," Joan offered. "We can discuss it over dinner."

* * *

Through the small talk and idle conversation, Madison could tell Shannon was having a hard time trying to find an opening to propose their plan to Alice. Shannon was still convinced that Alice would balk at it. She, however, didn't think so. Oh, Alice would most likely offer some feeble excuses as to why it wasn't a good idea, but in the end, she would agree to it. Or at least she hoped she would.

With the meal almost over—Kenny having snatched the last piece of garlic bread—Shannon finally broached the subject.

"Mom, we've been talking about your living arrangements after the surgery," she said.

Her mother stared at her across the table. "Oh? We *have*?"

Madison hid her smile as she recognized the amusement in Alice's voice. Shannon apparently did not.

"Well, me and Jarod," she said. "And Madison and Joan," she added with a quick glance her way.

"And what did *we* decide?"

Shannon looked at her helplessly, and Madison shook her head. Was Shannon actually afraid of what her mother would say? Well, there was no sense in beating around the bush.

"Alice, I want you to come live with me," she said. "You and Shannon both."

She wasn't surprised by the warm acceptance she saw in Alice's eyes. She suspected that part of Alice's anxiety was fear that Shannon and Jarod would suggest the dreaded *assisted living* arrangement that they'd talked about earlier.

"I appreciate that, Madison, but wouldn't I get in the way? You and Shannon—"

"Are grown women, not teenagers," she said. "Besides, our bedrooms will be separated by half of the house. You won't hear a thing."

Shannon covered her face and groaned. "*Really*? Do we have to talk about that?"

They all laughed as Shannon blushed a bright red.

"After your surgery, you're going to need help, Mom," Jarod said. "Shannon and I, well, we've got the store. We all think that this is the best option."

Alice turned, her eyes questioning. "Are you sure, Madison? I don't want to be a burden, and I don't want to jeopardize your and Shannon's relationship."

"I'm sure. You're as much my family as anyone else." She smiled. "In fact, I would never extend this offer to my own mother."

Alice smiled too, then glanced quickly at Shannon. "And you're okay with this?"

Shannon nodded. "I'm okay with this."

Alice glanced around the table, looking at each of them, finally nodded. "Then I guess I'm okay with it too."

Shannon let out a relieved sigh as she nodded at Madison. "Great. Now I can enjoy this very chocolate, very decadent dessert I ordered." She stood. "Who saved room?"

The kids were the first to raise their hands and Jarod and Joan joined in.

"Anything chocolate, I can find the room," Joan said with a grin.

"I'll help," Madison said, following Shannon into the kitchen.

They were both smiling at each other and Madison moved closer, not really caring if anyone could see them. Right now, she needed this closeness with Shannon.

"So? We're good?"

Shannon pulled her closer. "We're good," she murmured, her lips moving from her ear across her face to her mouth.

They kissed slowly as Madison's hands moved across Shannon's shoulders and around her neck.

"I love you," Madison whispered.

Shannon pulled back enough to look into her eyes and Madison saw a host of emotions there. Gratitude, love and affection, and, yes...desire. And now, finally, they were free to express those things to each other...and to others. There would be no more hiding.

"I love you. Now, always," Shannon whispered back.

One more kiss and she pulled out of her arms. She turned, finding Alice standing at the edge of the kitchen, watching them. She was about to apologize for such a public display of affection when Alice smiled at them.

"Your love for each other just radiates off of you," she said. "It always has, even when you were both denying it." Alice looked from Shannon back to her and smiled. "And I don't mind you stealing kisses in my kitchen."

Madison hugged her quickly. "We're so used to...hiding our feelings," she said.

"You'll tell your mother?" she asked.

Madison nodded. "Yes." She glanced at Shannon. "Yes, we're going to tell my mother."

Shannon opened the fridge, taking out a huge chocolate pie. "We?"

Madison laughed. "Yes, *we*."

"Are you still afraid of her?" Alice asked.

Shannon raised her eyebrows. "What makes you think I'm afraid of her?"

"Oh, Shannon, you were always terrified of Madison's mother." She laughed quietly. "Of course, now I know why. You were afraid she'd catch you in Madison's room."

Shannon's face turned a lovely red, and Madison wondered if she would always blush when her mother teased her.

"How about dessert?" Shannon said, giving a subtle wink to Madison.

CHAPTER FORTY-THREE

Shannon held her hand over the gas grill, determining that it was hot enough. She had an assortment of veggie burgers and frankfurters, and she brushed each with olive oil to prevent them from sticking.

She turned as a huge splash in the pool elicited laughter all around. It was one of those glorious early summer days—blue, cloudless skies, little to no breeze and the temperature just perfect to be enjoying the patio and pool.

She glanced across the backyard, taking pride in the fact that—unlike all the neighbors—she and Madison maintained their own lawn. She had been a little surprised at Madison's exuberance, especially when it came to mowing, but Madison found it was something she enjoyed. Shannon couldn't, however, take credit for the flowers. That was all Madison's and her mother's doing.

She looked at them now, with Jarod and Joan, lounging by the pool as Kenny and Crissy and two of their friends splashed like the kids they were. Her mother had a contented smile on her face as she listened to the conversation between Joan and Madison.

Shannon had to admit that moving her mother here was the best decision they could have ever made. Her mother had thrived after her surgery and seemed years younger.

Shannon went back to the task of flipping the burgers and frankfurters, smiling as she listened to the laughter of the kids. She'd been back in Brook Hill over a year now and she found it hard to imagine living anywhere else. She and Jarod were as close as they'd ever been, and there were rarely any disagreements over their business practices. All four of their stores were prosperous and they couldn't be more pleased.

Her relationship with Charlotte and Tracy, on the other hand, was nearly dissolved. As time passed, they spoke less and less. Ally had a steady girlfriend now, and the last time they talked, the four of them were planning a cruise together. She would like to say that she missed their friendship, but she really didn't. As she'd told Madison, she never really quite fit in with them. She'd pretended to be the person they wanted her to be and it had been easy to fit that mold. But being back in Brook Hill, she realized how empty it all was…how empty she was.

"Hey. You daydreaming again?"

She smiled as Madison stood close to her, their shoulders brushing. "Yeah. Daydreaming."

Madison tilted her head. "Are you happy? You're getting to cook."

Shannon laughed. "Not sure you can really call this cooking," she said as she flipped the burgers one more time. "Are you happy?"

Madison leaned closer. "I'm so very happy," she said. "I love having your family over."

"Our family," she corrected. "All we need is Ashton to make it complete." She closed the lid on the grill and turned the fire off. "And you'll get to see him in about three weeks."

"And he'll be here for a whole month," Madison said, smiling. "I'm anxious for you and him to spend some time together."

"Me too." She took Madison's hand and tugged her inside, pausing to glance over her shoulder, finding Jarod watching them. He smiled and shook his head. She grinned back at him.

Once inside, she pulled Madison into her arms. "God, I love you," she whispered, kissing her lightly, slowly.

Madison's arms tightened around her. "I love you. Always."

Their eyes held and Shannon saw everything she needed in life, right there in Madison's eyes. It was a look she'd first seen when...

"I was ten," she whispered.

Madison frowned at her words but Shannon simply smiled and kissed her once again.

"Nothing...just...I love you."

Bella Books, Inc.

Women. Books. Even Better Together.

P.O. Box 10543
Tallahassee, FL 32302

Phone: 800-729-4992
www.bellabooks.com